MW01533184

Cyberevolution: VI

Total Recall

By

Kaitlyn O'Connor

Futuristic Romance

New Concepts   Georgia

Be sure to check out our website for the very best in fiction at fantastic prices!

When you visit our webpage, you can:
* Read excerpts of currently available books
* View cover art of upcoming books and current releases
* Find out more about the talented artists who capture the magic of the writer's imagination on the covers
* Order books from our backlist
* Find out the latest NCP and author news--including any upcoming book signings by your favorite NCP author
* Read author bios and reviews of our books
* Get NCP submission guidelines
* And so much more!

We offer a 20% discount on all new Trade Paperback releases ordered from our website!

Be sure to visit our webpage to find the best deals in e-books and paperbacks! To find out about our new releases as soon as they are available, please be sure to sign up for our newsletter (http://www.newconceptspublishing.com/newsletter.htm) or join our reader group (http://groups.yahoo.com/group/new_concepts_pub/join)!

The newsletter is available by double opt in only and our customer information is *never* shared!

Visit our webpage at:
www.newconceptspublishing.com

Total Recall is an original publication of NCP. This work
has never before appeared in book form. This work is a
novel. Any similarity to actual persons or events is purely
coincidental.

New Concepts Publishing, LLC.
5202 Humphreys Rd.
Lake Park, GA 31636

© Aug. 2009 Kaitlyn O'Connor
Cover art (c) copyright 2009 Alex DeShanks

All rights reserved, which includes the right to reproduce
this book or portions thereof in any form whatsoever except
as provided by the U.S. Copyright Law.

If you purchased this book without a cover you should be
aware this book is stolen property.

NCP books are available at special quantity discounts for
bulk purchases for sales promotions, premiums, fund
raising, or educational use. For details, write, email, or
phone New Concepts Publishing, LLC., 5202 Humphreys
Rd., Lake Park, GA 31636; Ph. 229-257-0367, Fax 229-
219-1097; orders@newconceptspublishing.com.

First NCP Trade Paperback Printing: September 2009

DEDICATION

In loving memory of my sister, Maureen. We had some great times
together.

Chapter One

Chloe had been studying the game board intensely for a while before the sound of the alert buzzer finally penetrated her absorption. Frowning, she lifted her head and turned to stare at the ship's console. It was the message alert annoying the shit out of her, she realized with more than a touch of irritation.

Struggling to tune the noise out, she returned her attention to the game and finally made her move. For a few moments she hovered over her decision and finally set the piece down and stood up. "Don't touch anything until I get back!" she said. "One of you cheated last time!"

Jared and Kane exchanged a long look.

"We were not programmed to cheat," Jared responded.

"You're sure Pops didn't tinker with your programming?" Chloe threw back at him. "Because that move looked a lot like something he would've done."

"Pops cheated?" Kane asked blankly.

Chloe turned and grinned at the two cyborgs as she reached the console and punched the button to silence the alert buzzer. "Don't tell me! He told you it was a new rule, right?"

Jared and Kane shared a glance.

"It was not?" Kane asked.

Chloe chuckled. "I knew it was you, Kane!"

His olive complexion darkened with a mixture of discomfort and anger—well, simulated, she reminded herself. She shook her head at herself. What did it matter, really? If they seemed real enough that she had to keep reminding herself that they weren't, then why do it?

Because she worried, that was why.

It had been different when her father was alive. Working as deep space salvagers, they spent a lot of time in space, just the two of them after her father's last two crewmembers quit. As her father often said, they kept each other sane. The loneliness of spending weeks or months in space without seeing another soul could fuck up a person's head if they didn't have someone to interact with.

She didn't know what she would've done if they hadn't picked up the two cyborgs, Jared and Kane, on Xeno-12. They'd been seriously fucked up at the time, horribly! Her father had been more inclined to leave them than to gather them up with the other salvage but, as it turned out, the cyborgs were the only thing they'd picked up that were worth anything. Most of what they'd collected had been so degraded by the frigid temperatures they'd had to sell it for scrap and they'd been damned lucky to get anything for it.

Jared and Kane—well, they'd 'recovered' amazingly enough—so well it was impossible to tell, looking at them now, that they'd been so damaged that they'd looked downright nightmarish. Even before they'd fully recovered, they'd proven they could pull their own weight as crewmembers. They *were* cyborgs, designed as soldiers, which meant they weren't much for conversation but then again the two crewmembers they'd replaced hadn't been either.

Truthfully, they were way better company than the two jerk-offs they'd replaced, worth their weight in platinum, especially after her father had died. She'd had reason to be grateful she'd talked her father out of selling them for scrap!

Shaking her thoughts before she could get caught up in her grief over her father, she turned her attention to the computer and pulled up the incoming message that had set off the alert. She'd been expecting junk mail since she didn't know anybody who would actually send her a personal message. She skimmed through the message the computer pulled up skeptically and with very little interest. The alert at the top caught her attention, however.

TOTAL RECALL! Attention all owners of cyborgs manufactured by Robotics, Inc. in the S-series. Due to a suspected defect in programming that could cause serious injury or death, Robotics, Inc. has issued a total recall of all units in this series. Consumers will be compensated and/or the unit replaced with a model of comparable value once the unit has been returned and processed. If you own a cyborg of the S-series, please return it to your nearest dealer at your earliest convenience, or if there is no dealer conveniently located near you, the nearest military facility, police station, or ranger outpost for collection. This recall includes all cyborgs shipped as soldiers, sexdroids, and med techs ....

"Woah! Hey guys! You've been recalled!" Chloe said with a chuckle. "Says right here that you're defective."

Jared and Kane, she saw when she glanced at them, were staring at her blankly. They exchanged a long look and she chuckled again.

"I'll just file this in the trash. I think if either of you were defective I'd know it by now."

Punching the delete button, she hurried back to the game they'd been playing, studying the board suspiciously until she'd determined that all the pieces were just as they had been when she'd gotten up. Satisfied, she looked up at Jared. "Your move."

He stared at her for so long that she realized he'd actually been disturbed by the message—well, confused, maybe. It was hard to say exactly how their minds processed. They had AI besides their programming. Of course, the cyborgs sold as soldiers as these two had been weren't expected to interact socially on a very refined level. They didn't need to as soldiers, and she supposed, since that was all they were exposed to initially, that their 'personality' was pretty well established before she and her father had picked them up. They were 'born' soldiers and she doubted their AI was sophisticated enough for them to 'adjust' now to anything else.

Well, they worked just fine with the salvage operation, but that wasn't actually all that different than what they'd done before—except for the fighting, which wasn't something they had to worry about too much. Occasionally, they ran into pirates or rival salvagers and things could get hairy, but that was rare. They *had* encountered a nasty rival salvage operator since they'd taken the two cyborgs in, which had required the cyborgs' battle skills and was probably the only reason she was still alive. That was certainly the reason her father wasn't, but battle wasn't something they commonly had to worry about.

"Hey! Don't worry about it! I know you aren't defective. *I'm* not worried about it and it isn't like me and Pops bought you two, you know? They aren't going to have any records of a transaction. Of course, I guess we'll have to watch it when we get into port to sell the salvage, but we don't even have the hold half full. It'll be months before we hit another port and by that time this will all have blown over. And, if it hasn't—well, I'll just tell them you're crewmembers. No sweat. If I didn't know for a fact that the two of you were cyborgs, I'd never believe it. You can pass as human without any problems."

Jared glanced at Kane again, but then focused on the board. Chloe could see he was still tense, though. Searching her mind for something to redirect their minds, she suddenly thought about Damon.

It wasn't a particularly happy thought. She'd worked damned hard to put Damon out of her mind, but since he'd popped up, she figured, maybe, it would be a good thing to talk about. It would distract them and maybe it would help her to get it off her chest. It wasn't something she'd been able to talk about with her father and she didn't have anybody else.

"Say, did I ever tell you guys about my first?" she asked. She noticed when she glanced at them that she had their attention and she snorted faintly with a mixture of embarrassment and self-deprecation.

"Ok, so this is embarrassing—don't laugh! I was like—oh—twelve,

I guess, maybe thirteen when mom was killed and they notified Pops so he could come and collect me from the juvenile holding facility. Anyway, I never quite got around to—doing it—you know."

She saw when she glanced at them that they were staring at her blankly in confusion. "Sex," she clarified wryly. "I'd done a little messing around, but nothing much. Honestly, it was so awkward I wasn't really comfortable with it. Anyway, I didn't and I sure as hell wasn't interested in any of the other crewmembers on board the ship. Take my word for it! Total creeps and nasty! So one day Pops gets drunk as a coot and asks me about it. Mind you, I was twenty at the time, and he finally gets around to talking sex education!" She shook her head. "Good old Pops! I'd pretty much figured it all out by then, of course. I just hadn't had any experience. So I'm thinking Pops has forgotten all about it by the time we hit another port, but, hell no! The first thing he does after we've processed the salvage and collected our money is insist that the two of us need to head down to a brothel and get our pipes cleaned!"

She shrugged. "I wasn't really that comfortable about Pops suggesting it, but I wasn't against the idea. He'd pretty much convinced me when we had the talk before that I couldn't go wrong by going to a sexdroid the first time since they're just—well! Anyway, so we get to the brothel and there's this absolutely *divine* cyborg sexdroid named Damon! And he didn't just look yummy. He had all the right moves!

"I was stiff as a poker," she added, laughing. "But he knew exactly what to do and not only did it not hurt—at all—but it was …. Well, it was just wonderful! It wasn't at all like it was when I was a kid with the other kids. No slobbering or groping. He kissed dreamy and … everything else. I enjoyed myself so much I didn't want to leave," she said, chuckling, "I tried my best to talk the owner into selling him to me, but the dip-shit wouldn't go for it.

"Pops laughed his ass off that I'd gotten so … attached to him, but I sure as hell hated to leave him. Said I took to sex like a duck to water … whatever that is."

She hadn't expected it to depress her to tell them the story. She'd thought it was funny—sort of—and it would lighten the mood. There was no getting around the fact that it *had* depressed her, though.

"I was fully programmed to perform as a sexdroid," Jared said after a fairly lengthy pause.

Kane frowned at him when he said nothing else and finally turned to her. "I was also."

Chloe looked at both cyborgs with surprise. "No shit?"

"I am not shitting you," Jared assured her, his expression earnest. "It would not be difficult to access the programming, although I have not had occasion to use it before."

Chloe studied both cyborgs speculatively, discovering with more than a little surprise that she hadn't noticed how handsome they were. Not that they were as handsome as Damon, but they were a sight better looking than any man she'd ever seen—real man—not that she'd seen a lot since she was old enough to actually notice. There didn't seem to be many good looking men in the salvage business and the men at the bars—well, the best looking ones were usually pirates!

The weird thing was that she hadn't actually noticed Jared or Kane, not really. It didn't take a lot of searching to figure that out. It had been painful to look at them when they'd first recovered them. She'd gotten into the habit of *not* looking at them, not directly. She knew, of course, that they were amazingly tall and brawny. That sort of went with the territory, though. At least, she figured it did, that the company had gone out of their way to create soldiers that were intimidating in size alone. They didn't actually need to. They could've been half the size they were and they still would've been stronger and faster than any human counterpart, but they wouldn't have *looked* as intimidating.

Now that they'd drawn it to her attention, though, she actually studied them.

Jared was almost 'pretty boy' handsome in the face—without a sign of a scar despite the fact that most of one cheek had been missing when they'd pulled him off that frozen planet. It made her belly clench just remembering it.

His hair had grown, but she thought the shoulder length, dark hair sort of set off his almost classical features and, truthfully, she'd never liked the short hair the military favored.

Kane was more rugged looking, but attractive in a very manly way. With his black hair and olive complexion, he reminded her strongly of pictures she'd seen in her study data of the 'wild natives' discovered on the North American continent on Earth in ancient times.

For a handful of moments, she tried to imagine herself locked into the sort of embrace that she'd enjoyed with Damon, but although it stirred a lot of warmth—alright carnal heat—it also made her feel a little uncomfortable. Images wafted through her mind of Jared and Kane as they'd looked when her and her father had found them, though, and she abruptly knew why. One part of her knew they were just machines, that they couldn't *be* abused in the sense that a living thing could, and yet she had been so angry at their condition at the time—still was—and ashamed that their government was responsible for the horrors she and her father had seen. It made her feel guilty even to consider taking further advantage of them. It just wasn't right. She didn't care if they were supposed to be nothing but machines. They looked and acted human and that was enough to make the government's negligence heinous. In point of fact, there'd been human soldiers among them that had suffered the same fate, although she hadn't known it at the time. She didn't like to think about the incident—at all—because in the back of her mind she'd had this terrible fear ever since that they'd left someone that might have been saved if they'd only kept looking. She forced a chuckle. "Hey! Thanks, guys, but don't access it on my account! I'm pretty sure I've got zero sex drive. I hadn't even thought of having sex since …."

Chloe broke off abruptly as a sudden thought hit her like a rogue meteor. Her eyes widened and she jolted up from her chair, upsetting the game board in the process. "Oh my god! Damon! Total recall! Oh my god! That means they'll be recalling Damon! He's an S series. I'm sure he was!"

She tried to tell herself that it wasn't likely that they really meant to recall *all* of the cyborgs, but panic gripped her and she couldn't shake the thought that he was even now being packed up to be shipped back to the company. "He wouldn't let them take Damon," she muttered to herself as she dashed to the ship's console. "Damon was the only male sexdroid the proprietor had. He wouldn't let *me* buy him, damn it! There's no way he'd turn him over."

She glanced toward Jared and Kane. "What do they do when they recall cyborgs—droids?"

Jared's lips had formed a tight line. "Disassemble."

"*Disassemble!*" Chloe practically shouted. "Oh my god! Well, I've got to go after him! That's all there is to it!"

Her hands were shaking when she pulled up a map and began to search for Thagorous. "System, system …! Shit! I can't remember the name of the god damned system! Shit! Shit! Shit! Computer! Bring me up a list of planets named Thagorous and their star systems!"

"You are going there?"

Chloe threw a distracted glance in the general direction of the voice and realized both Jared and Kane had followed her. "Of course I'm going there … wherever …. That's it! The Medaly Galaxy, Osirus system! Computer! Calculate a jump to this coordinate."

"From what point of origin?"

"This point you dumb shit!" Chloe snapped. "Honest to god! Computers and their stupid questions." She glanced up at Jared and Kane a little self-consciously. "I meant the computer-computer, not you guys."

"Why are we going there?" Kane asked.

Alright. So Kane could be pretty fucking dense! "Damon?"

"We cannot make that jump," Jared said tightly.

"From this point of origin, it would require three jumps," the computer announced.

"I don't care how many fucking jumps it would take, damn it! Didn't I just say calculate it?"

"This is not reasonable," Kane growled.

Chloe turned and gave him a look. "Not reasonable? Didn't you *hear* what I said?"

"You wish to extract Damon, a sexdroid, before his owner can return him to the company and we are three jumps from the coordinates where you last knew him to be," Jared said.

Chloe stared at him. That was, quite possibly, the most she'd ever heard him say at one time. "So?"

"The ship is old. It would be dangerous to attempt three jumps in succession. Beyond that, the droid you refer to may not even be in the possession of the brothel where you first ... utilized his services. This incident you referred to—how many years, Earth standard, since it occurred?"

"This is a *hell* of a time to decide to be talkative!" Chloe snapped. "Damon's in trouble! I can't just let them tote him off and disassemble him!"

"He is not yours," Jared said pointedly. "This is not your decision. If he has been recalled you would not be able to purchase him from the owner even if he still had the cyborg in his possession. In all likelihood, by the time you could reach this system, he will have been turned over to the authorities and you will not be able to convince them to give him to you. I do not understand why this cyborg is important enough to you to expend so much fuel and take unnecessary risks."

Chloe felt her face reddening. "You wouldn't understand if I tried to explain it," she muttered. "I'll worry about how to get him out of this mess when I get there. I have to know what I'm dealing with, after all, before I can make plans. It's an out-of-the-way system. They might not have heard and even if they had, the proprietor wasn't keen on giving him up. He could still have him. Just ... get the ship ready, alright? And then get into the harnesses. I don't want you two splattering against the bulkhead when we make the jump—jumps. You'll knock a hole in it." Dismissing them, she returned her attention to the ship's navigational computer. "Prepare for the first jump. When we emerge, run a thorough system's check, recalculate the second jump—just to be sure your calculations from here aren't off—and then take the second. Repeat that process before you take the ship through the third jump. Understood?"

"Affirmative, Captain Chloe."

"How many hours away from the target planet will we be when you've taken the third jump?"

"Estimated 8:34:20 Earth standard."

Chloe chewed her lip. "That's getting us as close as you can with the third jump?"

"Affirmative. The third jump will place the exit from folding just beyond the last planet of the Osirus star system. I do not have the data to execute a jump within the system."

"Fuck! Well, it'll have to do, I guess, if it's the best we can do! Give us fifteen minutes to lock down before you execute the first jump."

"Count down ... mark. Fifteen minutes ...."

Chloe bumped into Jared when she shot out of her seat. She would've ricocheted off of him and hit her seat again except that he caught her on the rebound. She gaped up at him. "What are you two standing there for? Look alive, guys! Let's get this bucket of bolts locked down for a jump!"

"This is a dangerous undertaking. I do not understand your reasoning. I am fully capable of fulfilling your needs as a sexdroid ... as is Kane. If you had only mentioned this before, I would have taken care of your needs. This is completely unnecessary."

Chloe merely stared at him for a moment. Slowly, it dawned on her as she studied their set, angry faces that they weren't just confused. They were ... disturbed. Maybe because they felt threatened in some way? She patted Jared's arm. "Hey! You two guys are my best buds! No way am I going to let the bad old company men get their hands on you! Don't sweat it! I'll leave you two on board while I head down to the planet to grab Damon." She pulled away from him. "Now let's get everything stowed for the jump!"

Jared glanced at Kane as she swept past them, hurrying to grab up the game board and pieces. "We will check the load in the hold," Jared said finally.

"Good idea!" Chloe said absently, rushing around the bridge, grabbing things up at random and tossing them into the lockers. "When you've checked it, do a cabin check."

"The load is secure," Kane growled when they had left the bridge. "Why did you say that we would go and check it when we *know* it is secure!"

Jared slid an irritated glance at him. "I did not want her to hear the discussion," he retorted testily.

"What discussion? How will it help for us to discuss this? We must reason with her! I do not know why she is determined to go to this place, regardless of the danger, only to retrieve a sexdroid—particularly when we can do as well!"

"I do not understand either. I thought you might," Jared said tightly. "What do you suppose she meant when she said that we were her 'best buds'?"

Kane frowned. "This is slang for friendship—between two males."

"This is what my reference says, also. But she is not a male! She is confused and believes herself to be male? Or she is confused and believes us to be female?"

"She is disturbed over this gods damned sexdroid!" Kane growled. "She is not behaving at all rationally."

"I think I have been insulted," Jared said after mulling it over. "If she meant companion, then I am not insulted, but if she is thinking that I have no sexual significance because she believes I am a friend, then I am definitely insulted! She cannot have meant that she cannot consider us as sexual partners because we are cyborgs, for she stated very clearly that this Damon is also a cyborg."

"You are not more insulted than I am!" Kane snapped. "Mayhap she did not believe that we truly have been programmed as sexdroids and she thinks that she must get this other cyborg for that reason?"

"Why would she not believe? She does not know that we are different now and that we *could* lie if we wished to!"

Kane lifted his head and stared at the door to the bridge, pondering the problem. "Mayhap we should show her? I have been thinking about it for some time now."

"You also?" Jared asked, clearly surprised. "How long?"

Kane frowned. "Why does that matter?"

"I was only wondering if you had completed the change."

Kane narrowed his eyes at him. "You are suggesting that I have not? Or that you are more advanced?"

Jared shrugged. "This is not the time to concern ourselves with such things! We should focus on thinking of an argument to convince her she does not need this god damned sexdroid! There is nothing that he is capable of that we are not also capable of. Mayhap we should ask her to detail what he did to please her and then convince her to allow us to demonstrate so that she can see we are as proficient in performing the same acts as he?"

"We could override the main computer and then show her that we are fully functional and capable of all the things the pleasure droids are," Kane said somewhat hopefully

"She will *know*, then, that we are also rogues and she will turn us over to the company!"

"Well! I am not keen on collecting this gods damned sexdroid! *Then* she will fuck him and not us!"

"I do not believe I care for that possibility!" Jared said decisively. Turning, he stalked back onto the bridge, waiting until he had caught Chloe's attention. "Captain Chloe," he said, saluting her. "I would like to volunteer for the duty."

Chloe stared at him blankly. "What duty?"

"I will access my pleasure droid programming and fuck you when ever you feel the need for sexual relief."

Chloe's jaw slid downward until her mouth had formed an O of surprise. She blinked at him a few times and finally smiled. Jared had just begun to relax fractionally when she chuckled. "Oh, that's so sweet! I don't really need to fuck right now, ok? We'll talk about it later. Run along and secure the load, now."

Jared frowned but, try as he might, he could not think of another argument likely to sway her. Saluting again, he returned to the corridor where Kane was waiting.

"You convinced her?"

"I do not think so," Jared said slowly.

"Well! What did she say?"

"That she did not need to fuck right now."

Kane considered that. "But she is considering it?"

"She did not seem to be against the idea," Jared said finally. "She said we could talk about it later."

"But she did not cancel the jump?" Kane said tightly.

Jared shrugged. "Short of taking over the ship—which might alert the very people we wish to avoid—I see no hope for it since it seems we cannot persuade her. We will pick up the sexdroid and then we will dispose of the fucking bastard."

Chapter Two

Chloe's nerves were totally frazzled by the time they'd made the third jump. The computer had announced that the ship had sustained damage after the second and suggested that it would be dangerous to take the third without waiting for repairs. She would've been willing to if Jared and Kane hadn't informed her that repairs might take several days, but the sense of urgency riding her had decided the matter.

Relieved when they came through the third jump to discover she was still alive and the ship in one piece, she'd put Jared and Kane to work taking care of the repairs and advised the ship's navigation computer that they would 'limp' onward while the repairs were made. They were moving at an agonizing snail's pace, though, and she had the awful feeling that they were going to arrive too late to rescue Damon.

It gave her time to consider whether it was the smartest thing she'd ever thought to do—and she knew it wasn't. It wasn't actually rational if it came to that. If Damon had actually been a *real* man, it still would've been crazy. It had been years since she'd been with him and he'd been a paid lover—or at least, she'd paid the proprietor for his services.

It wasn't as if it had been any sort of relationship at all.

And, of course, he was a cyborg.

He might even be defective and need to be returned.

She just didn't believe that, though. She remembered every moment she'd spent with him and there had been nothing at all to indicate that he was defective in any way.

He was so far from defective it was ludicrous to consider such a possibility.

Truthfully, one of the reasons she was so frantic to reach him and retrieve him was *because* he was a cyborg. He would not defend himself against the people who took him. He wouldn't understand that he *could* run or should. He hadn't really been given much in the way of a sense of self-preservation—any more than Jared or Kane had.

She couldn't *bear* to think of them taking him apart! She didn't know how the company could consider anything like that! Sure, beneath all that beautiful flesh and muscle was an alloy chassis and computer chips, but he was flesh and blood everywhere that it really counted!

Especially *thorol*

So what if she was attached to him and he was a machine! So everybody would think she was a crazy woman! What did she care? She didn't care if every single thing he'd done and every single thing he'd said had been programmed into him, was completely simulated! He'd made her feel like she mattered to him. He'd made her feel beautiful, like the most desirable woman in the universe! She couldn't just abandon him to such a horrible fate!

He had feelings. She didn't care what anybody else thought about it. She knew he did! Jared and Kane did! And if they did, then Damon did!

Currently, Jared and Kane were sulking and slamming around tools while they worked on the ship. Maybe that was simulated, too, but if it was, they were damned good at simulating 'totally pissed off male'!

Her brain signed off for a handful of moments as she watched them. She didn't know why, but the play of all those lovely muscles in their arms and shoulders and backs just put her into zen meditation every time she saw it.

Jared turned to scowl at her, jerking her out of her trance. She glared back at him, plunking her hands on her hips.

Their disapproval irritated the shit out of her. She'd *told* them they were her best buddies and she wasn't going to get them involved and risk having them hauled in! What more did they want?

No doubt they'd picked up that behavior from the two crewmembers they'd replaced, she thought irritably. *They* had complained every time they were asked to actually do something around the ship—which was why her and her father had agreed they didn't need them anymore once Jared and Kane were functioning well enough to take over their duties.

She debated, briefly, trying to sweet talk them out of their anger and finally dismissed it. "You think you guys can hold it down on the noise for a while? I need to get some sleep before we hit port. No telling what I'll have to deal with to get Damon."

They both paused long enough to glare at her again and then went back to banging with their wrenches.

Frowning with a mixture of thoughtfulness and irritation, she headed to her quarters. Jared and Kane were nothing at all like Damon, regardless of their claims, now, to the contrary. She'd been struck by that from the very first, had actually wondered if they really were the same series for a while. Then she'd realized that it only stood to reason that Damon's programming was completely different from the programming that would have been used for the soldiers—completely different objectives! Damon *needed* social skills, after all. Women weren't going to pay to get banged by a Neanderthal! They wanted seduction, flirtation—even if they were paying for it!

Granted, up until Damon, and then Jared and Kane, she'd never even come close to a cyborg. She'd heard about them, but the S series were top of the line—designed for the wealthy and the government. The only time an 'average' person was likely to come into contact with them was on a battlefield—or in the occasional bordello.

Jared and Kane had taken a lot of getting used to when her first experience with a cyborg had been a pleasure droid. Despite her sympathy for their condition when they were first recovered, they were downright scary even when they were having trouble getting around and weren't overtly aggressive—she supposed because the pair had seemed to automatically assume that her and her father were their commanding officers.

They'd unnerved the hell out of her until she'd gotten used to being around the hulking, taciturn brutes. They'd scared the pure piss out of their crew—which was why they'd bailed at the first opportunity after they discovered she and her father had decided to keep the cyborgs.

She *had* gotten used to them, though, and more than that. She'd come to value them a great deal and not just for their skills as crewmembers and salvagers. They'd done their best to protect her and her father when they'd been attacked. She didn't think she would be alive now if not for them and beyond that, she'd come to value them as companions, to think of them more as friends than machines.

She'd thought she knew and understood them as well as anyone possibly could.

And it still seemed to her that Jared and Kane were acting just a little strange even for them. How bizarre was it that they'd suddenly taken it into their heads to convince her they had the same programming that Damon had?

Not that she was likely to believe that! But their logic circuits should have told them that she wasn't likely to believe it. Their programming should have prevented them from telling an outright lie if it came to that.

So, did that mean it was true and they actually *had* been programmed as pleasure droids? It seemed to her that it must. She could actually believe that easier than she could believe that they'd become capable of lying, that the company had simply saved time and money by designing them all the same and giving them the same programming until they made the sale and it was determined what their use would be.

She was more inclined to think, though, that they'd only been given rudimentary programming—or, possibly, that the AI they all had made the big difference. Damon, Jared, and Kane all had the same programming, but then Damon had 'learned' to be a pleasure droid and Jared and Kane had 'learned' to be soldiers.

That made perfect sense and explained why Damon was so different in behavior than the other two.

It didn't explain why they'd suddenly decided to inform her of it or volunteer for extra 'duty', but she decided it must be because she'd never mentioned it before.

And it was still a little weird, but they did have AI, she reminded herself. They'd been given that to help them adjust to changes in their situation, and there was no getting around the fact that they'd begun to seem just a little temperamental after their exposure to the other crewmembers. Thankfully, they hadn't picked up *all* of their nasty habits!

Of course, they were probably exposed to similar behavior with the soldiers. From her experience, human soldiers tended to be very aggressive males themselves and prone to brawling, especially when they weren't under the watchful eyes of their superiors, which was the only time she'd been around them—in bars while they were on leave from duty.

Maybe their AI was sophisticated enough that they felt personally threatened by her interest in Damon? Or at least understood it well enough to exhibit that kind of behavior?

She felt her chest tighten at the thought. How could they think for a minute that she would abandon them because of Damon, she wondered? Sure they'd had plenty of time to grasp that humans in general weren't to be trusted, but she thought they should know by now that *she* could be trusted. *She* was loyal.

Well, she could work on that after she rescued Damon—*if* she managed to. If they didn't understand pretty quickly that having Damon around really wasn't going to change anything between them, then she would try to get it through their thick skulls and make them understand! They were just as important to her, and dear to her, in their own way as Damon was. It was just different, that was all.

Despite her determination to sleep, she discovered when she'd peeled her flight suit off and sprawled on her bunk that her mind was too busy to rest. Memories of her time with Damon alternated with attempts to work out a plan. Finally, she decided she'd just waltz brazenly into the brothel and ask for Damon. She didn't especially like that idea since that meant the proprietor would be able to identify her as the last customer, but she couldn't think of an alternative.

Breaking in didn't seem like a good idea. In the first place, she couldn't be sure Damon would be entertaining. He could be downstairs. In the second, she didn't especially like the idea of seeing him in action even though she knew he was popular with the ladies. And thirdly, if he *was* entertaining, it seemed likely his client would begin to scream like a banshee if she came in through the window and that could be way worse than being identified after she'd had time to get the hell out of the Osirus system.

What to do afterwards in the event that she was identified and it turned out that there had been a recall issued on Damon?

She realized she'd been considering getting out of the business ever since her father had been killed—before that, actually. To be more precise, she'd had ideas of doing something different ever since the night she'd spent with Damon. Up until then, she hadn't given much thought to the life she had. Her life before her father had taken her with him had dimmed to a handful of memories and a lot of those weren't that good.

She'd actually assessed the life she had, though, after Damon and realized that, although it never really had occurred to her before, and everyone from her father to his crew treated her like one of the guys, she actually had enough 'girl' in her that she wanted to find a life companion and settle down. Unlike her father, she'd never actually suffered from wanderlust. It didn't thrill her to drift through space and never see another living soul for months on end. The few attacks they'd had to fend off had scared the living piss out of her, not excited her.

She could be content living in one place, maybe having a kid or two. She rather liked that idea, actually.

Of course, if she had Damon as a companion, there weren't going to be any kids. She wasn't ditzy enough in the head to think that was possible, but she figured they could take in a couple of strays. There were always kids orphaned on the outer rim colonies where life was rough at best.

Now that she thought about it, she realized that was probably the best thing to do—find a fairly remote planet, stake out some land, and settle down. It would be easier to pass Damon off as a human if she was living with him as a companion.

What to do with Jared and Kane, though?

Well, she couldn't abandon them, that was for sure. They were in just as much danger as Damon was—maybe more. She thought Damon might have an easier time passing as a human since he had some social skills.

So she could find a really remote place and use the salvage they'd collected to start a planet-based salvage operation and be the middle man for a change! That way, Jared and Kane would have basically the same job they did now.

Relaxing almost the minute she'd worked that out in her head, she finally dropped to sleep in spite the noise Jared and Kane were still making 'repairing' the damage to the ship.

She thought it was actually the silence that woke her later, although it took her a few minutes to figure that out. Rolling from her bunk, she struggled to throw off the dregs of sleep and finally got up, stretched, yawned, and headed down to the bathing facilities.

That was an eye opening experience! When she arrived, both Kane and Jared were already there—bathing. She blinked several times, trying to bring her vision into focus or, more accurately, trying to assimilate the fact that both of them were buck naked.

They were still pissed off, too, but it took her so long to get to their faces she wasn't aware of that at first.

She hadn't seen them completely naked before—half-dressed, yes, and that was an eyeful because their chests, backs, and arms were bulging with hard muscle. She'd always made it a habit to steer clear of any of the other crewmembers when they were using the facilities, though. It wasn't that she was afraid they wouldn't be able to contain their lust. She was more afraid that they wouldn't be able to contain the urge to use her as the butt of their stupid jokes. Even if they didn't, she didn't want them to get the idea that she was trolling for dick—because they were just downright disgusting!

She hadn't avoided Jared and Kane for that reason, of course, but it had bothered her almost as much to think that they would be completely immune to her as woman as it did to think of the other guys either making fun or deciding to make her an offer.

The first thing that struck her was that they were anatomically correct—more than 'just' correct, actually. Their cocks were as impressive as the rest of them—even soft.

The second thing that struck her was that those impressive tools of theirs actually worked. They stood straight up when she walked in and that was a pretty fucking unnerving salute!

"Oops! Sorry guys! I'm still half asleep. I'll come back later," she said, whirling abruptly on her heels and dashing outside again. She was halfway back to her cabin before it dawned on her that she was buck naked herself.

"Ok, so maybe a little more than half asleep," she muttered, wondering how long she'd slept. A glance at her clock in her cabin sent a jolt through her. Hours! They must be getting close to Thagorous by now! "Damn it to hell! Computer! How close are we to our destination?"

"We are in orbit, Captain Chloe."

"And you didn't fucking think I'd want to be woke up, god damn it!"

"You did not leave instructions to awaken you."

"Stupid computer!" Chloe snarled. "And just what was Jared's and Kane's excuse, I'd like to know!"

"They thought you might sleep long enough that your attempt would be useless and that would remove you from danger," the computer responded.

Rage rushed through her. "Are you serious?"

"Unable to compute."

"Never mind! Damn it to hell! Do they think they're my father, or something? Don't answer that, computer!"

Grabbing a towel, she flung it around herself, snatched up fresh clothing, and stalked back to the showers. Jared and Kane had disappeared. She didn't know whether to be relieved or angrier that they'd balked her of a target for her rage. She'd calmed down by the time she'd finished bathing and dressed, her thoughts shifting to her mission. She was still pissed off enough with both of them to glare back at them when she reached the bridge and discovered they were in just as foul a mood as they'd been in before.

She plunked her hands on her hips. "Why didn't you wake me up when we reached Thagorous?"

"You did not say to awaken you," Jared responded tightly.

She narrowed her eyes at him and then looked at Kane.

"As he said," he growled.

"Well, I don't know what's gotten the two of you in such a pissy mood, but you knew damned well what was going on so don't give me that bullshit about not knowing I'd want to be awakened! The ship's main computer has to be told every damned thing! You two don't! You could've figured it out!"

Jared stared at her angrily for several moments. "I *deduced* that you were behaving irrationally about a piece of hardware and that it would put you at unnecessary risk to try to extract it!" he growled.

"He is *not* just a damned piece of hardware!" Chloe snapped. "If I didn't think he was worth the effort or I thought the risk was more than he was worth, I wouldn't have decided to do this to start with!" She took a calming breath. "Look, I know you two don't really understand because you ... well, you just don't have the capability of feeling things like we do—like I do. I'm attached to him, ok? I know that doesn't

seem rational to you, but people get attached to inanimate objects …
sometimes really attached. It's kind of like the way Pops felt about this
old ship, you know? *He* didn't think that was crazy."

"There was a reason to be attached to the ship," Kane said pointedly.
"He relied upon it for survival. It was his livelihood as well as his
home. The ship is useful. It transports. This cyborg is of no use
beyond pleasure and *we* could supply that, so he is not necessary at
all!"

"Is that what's bugging you two? You think that I won't think you're
useful anymore? Well, it's just ridiculous! You are very useful. I don't
know how I would get along without you! I rely on your company
even more than I do the skills you have or the work you do around
here—at least as much! I'm attached to both of you, too. The thing is
this is different, ok? I can't explain it, but it is.

"Now, I don't want you two worrying about it anymore. I'm just
going to go down and see if I can get him without getting into any kind
of trouble—honest to god! If I see that's just not possible, I'll give up
and come back. OK?"

She couldn't help but think they didn't look convinced, which
annoyed her. It wasn't as if she was in the habit of getting in trouble!
So, they had dragged her out of that one bar! How was she supposed
to have guessed that it was a damned hangout for fucking pirates?

Ok, well, there was that one other time …. But honest to god! Twice
in one fucking year and they acted like she was a magnet for trouble!
Well, six months, she mentally corrected, and it was true that it *was* the
only times they'd actually made port since they'd been with her, but
still ….. She was perfectly capable of taking care of herself, for god's
sake!

Shaking her head at them, she moved to the control console and
checked the status. It was a pleasant surprise to discover that they'd
completed the repairs, but it also sent up flags when they'd told her
before that it could take days. She decided to let that slide. She didn't
want to get into another argument with them. "Our cover story is that
we needed a few supplies and decided to stop since we were in the
vicinity."

"They will no doubt know that you folded to get here," Jared pointed
out.

"General area," Chloe said with determined patience. "I'll tell them
the crew forgot to lay in feminine products at the last stop and I got my
period!"

Jared and Kane exchanged a strange look.

"See! You did forget! It isn't like they're going to examine me to see if I'm on my period! It'll work. Anyway, I'm going to dock at the space station and take the shuttle down. If they decide to board and look around, you two make yourselves scarce. Don't try to brazen it out. You can't act worth a fuck! They'll figure out that you're cyborgs inside of five seconds. Trust me on that! Just get the game board out and pretend you're so engrossed in the game that you hardly know they're there."

They looked indignant. "We can interact …."

"No, you can't!" Chloe said firmly. "You talk like cyborgs. You always use correct grammar and big words and stuff like that and real people don't. And you're always surprised when real people act illogical and you just have to point it out! You act like cyborgs … or at least soldiers, all military, straight-as-a-board, perfect posture, and stiff. I mean, you never relax! And you hardly ever have any kind of expression on your face besides hard as nails—unless its hard as nails 'I'll rip your heart out and shit down your neck'. No expression would be better than always looking like you want to tear somebody's head off—especially when you two look like you could!"

They scowled at her.

"I rest my case!" Swiveling her seat around, she focused on monitoring the ship's docking procedure and ordered the computer to prep the main shuttle. "Game board!" she reminded them when she didn't hear any movement behind her.

She saw they'd gotten the game board out and were setting up the pieces when she finally got up to leave. They still looked insulted and unhappy. She gave each of them a friendly punch on the shoulder as she strode past them. "Lighten up, guys! I'll be back before you know it!"

Jared and Kane exchanged a speaking glance when the door of the bridge closed behind her. Jared got up and moved to the control console, flicking on the monitor in the docking bay and watching until Chloe appeared. She strode directly to the arms locker and took out a belt, two pistols, and a rifle, carrying them with her as she headed to the shuttle the computer had prepped for her.

His gut clenched. "That does not look to me as if she expects no trouble," he muttered to Kane, whom he discovered had come to stand behind him.

"It also does not look like the sort of preparations one would make if they planned only to sneak away and not get involved in a confrontation."

They turned and stared at one another for several moments. "She is planning to break into the prison if he has been taken," Jared said.

Kane spoke directly to the onboard computer. "Prep the secondary lander."

"Captain Chloe did not leave orders to have the secondary lander prepped."

Kane narrowed his eyes at the monitor.

"She did not order us to remain on the ship," Jared growled. "Prep the gods damned lander or I will disassemble your hard drive!"

"Prepping secondary lander," the computer responded after a short pause to collate the data and arrive at the conclusion that it could not prevent them from prepping the lander if it was disassembled and therefore it served no purpose to allow itself to be destroyed.

Chloe's shuttle had departed the bay before they reached it. Grabbing arms for themselves from the arms locker, Jared and Kane jogged to the lander and up the gangplank. The secondary lander was actually an emergency escape pod and as such, smaller and swifter than the shuttle. They were able to get a visual on Chloe's ship within a few minutes of departing the main ship and maintained visual contact until she landed at the planet-side space port.

"Identify," a voice commanded over the com as soon as they'd dropped through the atmosphere.

"Secondary lander, Salvager Omega-3," Kane responded. "Two crewmembers aboard."

"What's your business on Thagorous?"

"Pleasure," Jared responded.

The man on the other end chuckled. "Just watch yourselves. Your captain won't be pleased if you end up in jail. She didn't sound like she meant to stay long and you know how women are when they've got their period! She sounded pretty pissed off already about having to detour here for supplies."

"Affirmative. Will watch our asses."

Relieved when the com went silent, Jared glanced at Kane, pleased with himself. "He did not think I sounded like a cyborg," he said with a touch of triumph.

Kane shrugged. "He was not expecting to speak to a cyborg. Mayhap that is why Chloe is convinced that we sound like cyborgs? Because she knows that we are?"

Jared frowned thoughtfully. "According to my data, this slang refers to a female's reproductive cycle."

"Except that this is not her fertile period of the cycle."

"Yes, but, there is a hormonal fluctuation that often causes mood swings. Mayhap that is why she is behaving so irrationally? The comments of that man seemed to suggest that this was not something of great surprise."

"That is the damndest thing!" Kane exclaimed. "My dick got hard when you mentioned the reproductive cycle."

"It is only a process of thoughts," Jared said dryly. "My dick is hard *most* of the time now, but I have noticed that it always gets hard when fucking crosses my mind and naturally it would when we are discussing Chloe's fertility."

"Well, she is not fertile now and I still do not see how that would affect my dick when I cannot impregnate her even if she would allow me to fuck her! And mine is hard most of the time, also!"

"If it is hard most of the time as mine is," Jared said tightly, "why would it be remarkable that it is hard now?"

"Because it responded to something you said and it usually only jumps up when Chloe is nearby, gods damn it! I was merely wondering if there was significance in that!" Kane said indignantly.

"I do not see how there could be ... unless the gods damned thing is going to begin to stay hard all of the time. I have to say that I do not particularly care for this change. It is gods damned uncomfortable! And I cannot get my mind off the gods damned thing!"

Kane slid a speculative glance at him. "You said that it was already hard most of the time."

"Well, that is not the same as *all* the gods damned time, is it?" Jared snapped.

Chapter Three

Chloe wasn't certain of whether it was a fortunate thing that Thagorous was such a wild frontier colony that her weapons didn't warrant even a second glance or a bad thing. As confidently as she marched from the space port and into the little burg of Manard, though, she felt uneasiness begin to prickle along her spine as she caught glimpses of the locals and some of the other visitors.

There didn't seem to be any females on the dirt-packed streets beyond her, but then again it was dusk and that tended to be the time of day that predators began to crawl out of the woodwork. She'd thought the timing couldn't be more perfect. She was beginning to have second thoughts by the time she reached the brothel she remembered.

It looked a good deal more rundown than she remembered. Then again, it had been a couple of years since she'd been here and she had been a little tipsy since her and her father had hit the local bar first.

The interior didn't look a lot better, but then, from what she'd heard, they tended to be on the sleazy side, especially in frontier areas.

The proprietor hadn't changed. "Can I help you, young lady?"

Chloe smiled brightly. "I heard you had a sexdroid here—a male."

His lips tightened. He uttered a disgusted breath. "Had being the key word. The rangers descended on us yesterday and cleaned me out—took the sexdroid. I got the real thing ... if you're in to girls."

Chloe smiled with an effort. "Nope. No males?"

"Well, I got one, but he's pretty. He usually does the fellas that likes fellas."

"That fucking sucks!" Chloe said irritably. "What the hell did the rangers want with a sexdroid?"

The proprietor snickered. "I'll give you two guesses, but the last don't count. They was saying he was defective, but I sure as hell ain't had no complaints! If you ast me, the bastards just wanted to take him." He narrowed his eyes. "Say, ain't you been here before?"

"Don't think so," Chloe said, swiveling around and heading for the door. "I'll check next time I'm out this way and see if you've got anything for the ladies."

She kept going until she was several buildings down from the brothel and finally stopped to consider what to do. If the rangers had collected him, he could be halfway back to Earth by now, god damn it!

It occurred to her after a few moments that the proprietor might have meant local rangers rather than space rangers and a spark of hope flickered to life. Deciding it couldn't hurt to check, she glanced around until she saw a drunk stagger out of a bar down the street a little ahead of her and caught up to him as he wove his way along the edge of the street. "Where would I find the ranger station?"

The drunk paused and turned bleary eyes at her. "What'd you be wantin' with them bastards?"

Chloe narrowed her eyes at him. "Business—mine. You look like you'd know."

Anger flickered in his eyes. "Smartass bitch! Find 'em yerself!"

"How about I just blow your dick off?" Chloe growled, settling a hand on the butt of one of her pistols. "I'm pretty sure I could hit the nasty little worm even from here."

He studied her uneasily. "Alright! Fine! I'm thinkin' you need a lesson yerself and them's liable to give it to you. Mean sons-of-bitches! Bunch of crooks, if you ast me! They's down at the edge of town. Cain't miss it. Says frontier rangers over the door."

Chloe turned to head back in the direction she'd come from.

"They ain't gonna let you inside with them guns."

Good to know! Without pausing, Chloe marched down the darkening street until she saw the building the drunk had told her about. Ducking into the last alley along the street, she removed her pistols from the holster and knelt to tuck one in the top of her boot beneath her flight suit. After a short debate, she unzipped the front of the suit and tried slipping the second into the waist. It slipped to her crotch before she could even get the damned thing zipped again. Disgusted, she took it out again and shoved it into her sleeve.

It wasn't exactly well concealed, damn it! But she wasn't going in without a weapon when the old coot had already informed her they were outlaw lawmen. She knew the type. They were worse than most of the men they brought in, using the law to cover their own crimes. No doubt they'd gotten the recall alert and had taken Damon so that they could collect the compensation that would've gone to the proprietor.

The rifle, she decided, was completely out of the question and, reluctantly, she leaned it against the wall of the building, dropped her holster and headed toward the ranger station, trying to decide what sort of story she should tell them.

There were four of them seated around a game table as she entered the station. One look at them was enough to banish any doubts she'd cherished that the old bastard had lied to her. All four men turned to look at her when she came in, their hands on their own guns. They relaxed fractionally when they saw she was female.

Big mistake!

They looked her over like she was a choice piece of meat, but she wasn't flattered. Her skin crawled. "Who should I speak to about a robbery?"

"That'd be me, ma'am," one of the men answered, getting up and adjusting his dick in his pants without any self-consciousness.

"Where was you when you was robbed?"

Chloe struggled to get the fucking pistol out of her sleeve and finally managed to get it in her hand. "Oh, I wasn't robbed. I came to rob you. I want my sexdroid back! Who's got the keys to the cells?"

All four men stared at the pistol and then started laughing. "Girly! Do you even know how to shoot one of those?"

"I think I do," Chloe said doubtfully. "You pull this thing, right?"

She shot his hat right off his head. When she did, all hell broke lose. The four men dove in every direction. Unfortunately, the damned head ranger charged her like a bull. She managed to get off two more shots, but they went wild. Even as she fired the third, the ranger slammed into her hard enough he knocked the breath from her and carried her against the wall behind her. She tightened her hand on her pistol instinctively, flailing her arm around to keep him from grabbing it and firing it several more times, grimly determined to empty the damned thing before he could take it away from her and shoot her with it if she couldn't manage anything else.

One of the men yelped, marking one shot that had found a target. "Git the god damned gun! That stupid bitch shot me in the leg!"

Gritting her teeth, Chloe managed to lift one leg high enough to stomp the ranger's foot. He bellowed in her ear loud enough it rang. Since she'd been trying to ram him in the groin with her knee, she wasn't particularly happy about it either.

She still had the pistol in her boot, she thought a little despairingly as the man finally managed to grab her arm and wrest the pistol from her.

Things were beginning to look really bad when Jared and Kane burst through the door—literally. The door splintered, shards of wood flying in every direction. The rangers, who'd just begun to relax, grabbed for their pistols. One of them managed to shoot the ranger holding Chloe in the back. He screamed, let go of her and clawed at his back. Chloe dropped to the floor the minute he let go of her, scrambling frantically to get her pants leg up and grab her other pistol. A body slammed into the wall above her head and landed on her shoulders hard enough to flatten her.

Above and around her, she heard masculine screams, growls, meaty thuds and projectiles slamming into the walls. She was still struggling to crawl out from under the body that had landed on her when it was lifted off of her as abruptly as it had landed and then pitched to one side. She looked up to discover Jared standing over her.

Still dazed from being battered bodily, she swayed slightly when Jared jerked up and stood her on her feet, looking around the shambles of the ranger's station dazedly. "Oh my fucking god! Now we're *really* in trouble!"

Jared and Kane looked at each other uncomfortably and then looked at her. "You were in trouble already."

"But . . . never mind! See who has the keys!"

Jared turned to look at the door leading to the holding cells instead. Striding toward it, he grasped the handle and twisted it off. The entire locking mechanism came off with it and he opened the door. Throwing off her shocked surprise, Chloe charged after him. There were four men in the holding cell. Chloe felt her heart surge against her chest with a mixture of fear and thankfulness when Damon lifted his head and looked straight at her—fear to discover that she'd been right and he had been in danger, relief and thankfulness that she'd managed to save him. His lips curled in that utterly charming, lopsided smile she remembered that brought dimples into play in his cheeks. "Dearling!" he exclaimed as if it hadn't been two years since she'd seen him last—seen him *ever*! "Chloe! What are you doing here?"

She grasped the bars, grinning back at him. "I came to get you, sweety!"

Jared was glaring at him evilly when she glanced around for him. "Don't just stand there, Jared! Open it!"

He sent her a sullen look, but he grasped the cell door and wrenched it off of the hinges, setting it to one side.

Chloe rushed into the cell the moment it was opened, flinging herself at Damon.

He caught her with a husky chuckle, nuzzling his face against her neck. "I have thought of you each day that you were away from me," he murmured.

"What of the others?" Jared growled.

Reluctantly, Chloe pulled away from Damon. "What others?" she asked blankly.

"Those cyborgs."

Chloe turned to look at the other men in the cell. "They're cyborgs?"

"We do not have much time," Kane said tightly.

"And just whose fault is that?" Chloe demanded, abruptly irritated. "Not that I'm not grateful, mind you, but you made a hell of a mess besides making a lot of noise!"

Kane ground his teeth.

Jared scowled at her. "We found you by the shots you fired," he said tightly.

Chloe felt her face heat. "Oh! I forgot about that!" She turned to study the other cyborgs. "Anybody here defective?"

The cyborgs glanced at each other. "No," the one standing in the forefront informed her.

"Ok, so I guess we should take all of them. We certainly can't leave them here." She looked at Jared. "You're the soldier. How do you think we should do this?"

Clearly irritated, he studied her for a long moment and finally turned to survey the cyborgs. "There is a shuttle and a lander at the space port from the Salvager Omega-3. We were here to take on supplies. You have fifteen minutes to make your way to the port and get into one of the landers without being observed. If you are not there when we reach the landers, you will remain here." He turned to glare at Damon. "You also."

"I thought I'd just walk him to the shuttle," Chloe volunteered.

"You will not because you did not have him with you when you came! You will go and find the supplies you claimed that you had come for and make certain that you are noticed when you get to the port!"

Chloe glared at him belligerently for a moment but finally relented since his scowl intimidated her a lot more than hers seemed to be working on him. "Fine! Be careful, sweety!" she said, kissing Damon lightly on the lips and patting his cheek. "You understand the instructions, right?"

Something flickered in his eyes, but he merely smiled at her. "I go to the lander from the Omega-3 and get onboard without being detected."

"Good boy!" Chloe said, patting his cheek again.

Kane made a hole in the back wall. Chloe gaped at it for several moments. "Kane! They're going to know there were cyborgs here!"

Kane sent her a look, but he merely waved the cyborgs through. When they'd disappeared, she turned to beam at her buds—which was when she discovered both of them had been injured in the fight. "Oh god! You're bleeding! I might be sick!"

Both cyborgs looked down at themselves and reached to swipe the blood off with their hands. "It is not ours," Jared said.

"Oh god! I *will* be sick! I can't look! Are they horribly mangled?"

"You were going to shoot them!"

Chloe gasped. "I was not! Well, I didn't actually intend to. I was only going to point the pistols at them. And, anyway, they're laser pistols. They wouldn't have bled—didn't."

Jared shook his head at her. "Just go. We will clean up and then we will return to the lander we brought down."

Chloe nodded.

"Do not forget that you came to buy women's supplies," Kane said sharply.

"Oh yeah! You know, I kind of doubt there are any stores still open."

Jared rolled his eyes. "Go anyway. If they are open, then buy the supplies. If they are not …. Find something to make a package as if you did buy something."

Chloe smiled at him. "Great idea!"

She patted both of them affectionately as she headed toward the front office. "Just be careful!"

Somehow it looked much worse when she went through the front room again, but then she hadn't seen the blood smears on the walls. She was a little relieved to hear a couple of groans. Trying to convince herself that they'd accomplished their mission without actually killing anyone, she picked her way through the debris to the front door, peered out to see if anyone was looking, and discovered about a dozen people had been drawn by the commotion. "Holy shit!"

Whirling, she raced toward the back, barreling into Kane as he came out to pick up one of their victims. "People! I told you that you guys made way too much noise!"

"Shit! Go out the back!"

Nodding, Chloe ran toward the hole Kane had made in the back of the building, skidding to a stop to glance out before she leapt through and dashed toward the shadowy darkness behind the building. When she'd circled around, she hurried along an alley toward the main thoroughfare and began glancing at the store fronts as she passed. She was in luck. She found a general store. The proprietor had just reached the front door to lock it as she reached for the doorknob. Grabbing the doorknob, she put her shoulder against the door and shoved before he could turn the lock.

He glared at her. "I'm closed."

"Come on! I just need a couple of things! It won't take me five seconds!"

His lips tightened.

She batted her eyelids at him hopefully. "Please?"

He looked heavenward, shook his head, and finally stepped back. She dashed in, glanced around the now dimly lit store and finally rushed up and down the aisles until she found what she was looking for. Gathering up everything he had on the shelf, she headed to the front counter. He stared at it doubtfully. She glared at him. "Could you just tally it up and give me a total?"

It was highway robbery, she thought angrily when she marched out of the store again with two large bags of feminine products. She didn't believe the damned stuff was imported from the next galaxy for a minute! They always said shit like that just to jack the price up!

She was still angry when she reached the space port, enough so that it wasn't difficult at all to put her late adventure and the potential for disaster from her mind. She tripped on the way up the gangplank and dropped one of the bags and then spent nearly ten minutes running around and picking it up—which effectively distracted everyone close enough to witness it.

It was also an effective distraction for her. By the time she'd finally managed to fend off the help of one of the port guards and loaded her 'supplies', though, everything had come crashing back. Actually, it didn't crash back until she'd boarded and spied the cyborgs in the back of her craft. It returned then with a vengeance, however, and she was a nervous wreck until she was cleared for departure.

She didn't relax when she'd blasted off either. All the way back to the ship she kept expecting to get a hail on the com and a demand to land or be shot down. She arrived in the docking bay first and sent the cyborgs who'd traveled with her into the ship. Striding to the com, she ordered the main computer to prep for departure the moment the second lander was inside and then waited in nail biting impatience until Jared brought the lander in and shut the engines down.

The moment the bay was sealed and pressurized, she dashed down to greet them, flinging her arms around Damon and kissing him all over the face enthusiastically. "We did it! We actually got away with it!"

"We are not away," Jared said pointedly.

She was too happy and relieved to let his sour mood ruin hers. "Don't be such a pessimist! We did it! Now, let's get the hell out of here!"

Turning to Damon, she stroked his cheek. "Why don't you go to my cabin and rest? I have to get the ship ready for another jump as soon as we hit the outer boundary."

She was practically skipping with delight as she led the way from the bay, pointing out the crew cabin for the other cyborgs and her own cabin to Damon. Jared and Kane were on the bridge when she reached it.

"I know I ought to be pissed off that you guys didn't stay put when I told you to, but all's well that ends well."

Jared and Kane exchanged a look. "We attacked a ranger station."

"Oh well, they were bad men! I doubt anybody from that little burg would miss them even if they had been killed trying to kill us and, really, it was self-defense."

"Chloe … it was rangers. It does not matter if they were bad men, they were still rangers. We are in deep trouble."

Chloe frowned at Jared. "Ok, so I know that. But it isn't like we really robbed them or even broke out desperate criminals. We only took the cyborgs, and they hadn't done anything wrong. It was just a recall. It isn't like the cyborgs belonged to them or even the company. They sold them. People don't have to take things back just because they recall them. It isn't a law or anything. It's just to protect people from defective products and they aren't defective. You heard them."

"You were seen. You will be identified, and they will put a price on your head," Kane said angrily. "You know this. You knew this when you went into the ranger station."

Chloe stared at him for a long moment. "Ok, so I did. I made a conscious decision to break the law, knowing I could go to jail if they caught me. It was still worth it! What they had in mind wasn't right and Damon wouldn't have been able to defend himself because he's a cyborg! Or any of the others for that matter! The only alternative was to just let those bastards haul them off and destroy them and I didn't consider that acceptable!"

She could see they were still angry, but they could just be angry! It was *her* decision! It was her life!

Stalking away from them, she settled at the console and checked the status. The main computer, she saw to her relief, had already taken the ship out of orbit and was gaining speed as it headed out of the star system.

Unfortunately, she also discovered that they had a ship right behind them.

"Uh—we may have a problem."

Jared and Kane approached her and leaned over her shoulder to look at the screen.

"They are already in pursuit!"

"We don't know that!"

She'd hardly gotten the words out of her mouth, unfortunately, when the com-link lit up. Ignoring the condemnation in Jared's and Kane's expressions, she moved to the com seat and answered the hail.

"Salvager Omega-3, this is Thagorous port authority. We have a report that you are transporting contraband cyborgs."

"This is Salvager Omega-3, Captain Chloe Armstein. That's a negative, port authority. We are only transporting salvage."

"Salvager Omega-3, decrease speed, pull into stationary orbit and prepare to be boarded."

"Shit! Shit! Damn it!" Chloe said explosively. She chewed her lip, trying to think. "Computer, slow speed." Pressing the com-link, she spoke to the port authority. "Order received. We are slowing to stationary orbit and preparing for boarding."

She turned to look at Jared and Kane uncomfortably, still struggling to come up with a plan. "We've got maybe fifteen minutes and they'll be all over the ship. Get the cyborgs down in the hold and make a hole for them as far back into the salvage as you can. Hopefully, they'll be as lazy as most of those bastards and won't be too thorough."

Jared and Kane exchanged a look.

"They will bring scanners. It will not matter if we hide the cyborgs beneath the salvage. They will still find them," Kane said tightly.

Jared grinned abruptly, however. "They will not search the bilge."

"Ugh!" Chloe said with a mixture of disgust and horror. "They'll die in that filth if they don't expire from the fumes!"

Jared shrugged. "I will issue gas masks."

As disgusting as the thought was, Chloe knew he was right. She thought it was completely inappropriate that he was so damned gleeful about the prospect, but there was next to no chance, she knew, that the port authority would want to check the sewage. "So be quick! And get back here before they dock. I want you two to stay out of sight as much as possible. I'd suggest you join the others, but you just *had* to follow me to the surface and now you've been seen, too!"

That earned her a couple of resentful glares, but she knew she'd be spared hearing about it for a while at least.

Maybe a very long while if the port authority had brought anyone with them that could identify her. As soon as they'd left, she headed to the nearest arms locker and unloaded it. Carrying the weapons back to the bridge, she hid them in every available space where they couldn't easily be seen and then dashed to the crew cabin to find something loose enough to wear that she might conceivably be able to conceal a weapon in. Jared's and Kane's flight suits were completely out of the question. They swallowed her whole and *looked* like something she might put on to conceal a weapon. Fortunately, being salvagers, they never threw anything away. She found one of the old crewmember's flight suits and pulled it on, slipping a pistol in the pocket on one leg.

She passed Jared and Kane on the way back up to the bridge as she headed down to the docking bay to greet the port authority. They were both grinning until they saw her and immediately wiped all expression from their faces. Frowning, she stopped them long enough to ask if they'd hidden their passengers, told them she'd hidden weapons around the bridge, just in case, reminded them not to say anything around their 'guests', and then continued to the bay.

She nearly had heart failure when the port authority descended the gangplank with the proprietor of the brothel in tow.

"Oh hell! We are so fucked!"

Chapter Four

Damon was seething as he stepped off the ladder and sank into the muck of the bilge. Not that the other cyborgs weren't pissed off to discover they had to hide in the sewage holding tank, but he knew the two fucks that had thought it up had had him in mind specifically when they did. He'd be willing to bet they'd be down here a while after the fucking authorities left, too.

Clearly, neither Jared nor Kane were nearly as delighted that he'd survived as Chloe was and he was pretty fucking sure he knew why! The bastards seemed to be laboring under the idea that she was theirs!

As his cellmates from the jail climbed down and stood beside him, he glanced up at the grinning faces above him for a moment before they closed the access panel, wondering if the air in his tank would last until they opened it again.

After a moment, he shrugged his pique off. As much as he loathed the situation, as certain as he was that Chloe's cyborgs were thoroughly enjoying his misery, he also had to acknowledge that it was very likely their only chance of getting through an inspection. Of course, if the authorities were really determined to find them, they wouldn't stop until they'd searched the ship from top to bottom—including the bilge—but at least they had a chance.

He had a chance. He had hoped that he might. He'd planned to try to escape if any opportunity presented itself, but he hadn't actually expected one—not when four rangers had arrived to take him. That had seemed significant enough to him to indicate that he'd, somehow, given himself away.

The others who'd shared his cell didn't agree. According to them, the company had issued a total recall and all cyborgs were being rounded up for destruction. They were soldiers, all three of them escapees from the disaster on Xeno-12, and, according to them, the company had been hunting them even before the recall was announced.

He didn't know how he felt about the discovery that they, too, had changed, had become aware. In some ways, it was something of a relief to know he wasn't the only one trying to understand what was happening to him. In others—well, clearly he wasn't as special or unique as he'd believed he was if the company had grown alarmed enough to issue a total recall. They must be desperate if they were willing to show their hand.

That didn't augur well for a bright future or a happy ending, he thought angrily, and he felt a pang of regret tamp his hopefulness a little deeper.

Here he stood, neck deep in piss and shit, and Chloe was risking her life to save his ass. *He* should be up there, protecting her! Not the other way around and not those two caveman throwbacks!

With an effort, he tamped his anger, reminding himself that he *was* protecting her. She would be in far more danger if she was found with him. At least by hiding he was not only giving her the chance of escaping alive, but escaping the law, prosecution—jail time.

He shook his head. He would've told her not to take the risk if he'd had any idea that she would. He still found it hard to believe that she'd not only remembered, but that their time together had meant enough to her to bring her back when she thought he needed her.

He would've been a hell of a lot more thrilled if she hadn't behaved as if she thought he was an idiot child she had to protect, he thought irritably.

So much for thinking she was madly in love with him!

He supposed he *was* an idiot or he would've realized immediately that he was a sex toy to her—just like he had been for all the others!

He didn't give a fuck about the others, though, he thought angrily!

* * * *

Chloe was quaking inwardly when she went to meet the half dozen men that climbed out of the shuttle in her bay. It was some relief that their weapons were still in their holsters, but not a hell of a lot. Pasting a faint smile of greeting on her face as she reached them, she introduced herself.

The man in charge turned to the brothel proprietor. "Is this the woman who approached you and requested the sexdroid?"

Chloe lifted her brows as if surprised and turned to look at the man.

He stared at her for a good five minutes through narrowed eyes. "Nope," he said finally.

Chloe's knees went weak. She didn't know if the man was blind as a bat, if it had been too dark in the brothel for him to see her well, or he had simply decided to lie. She didn't care either. She would've kissed the old goat if the port authority hadn't been watching both of them keenly.

The head agent glanced between the two of them suspiciously. "You're certain this isn't the woman?"

The proprietor's lips tightened. "Didn't I just say this ain't her?"

"She's the only female ship's captain that's entered the port today," the man retorted.

"I don't recall that I told you the woman was a ship's captain. I just said I hadn't seen her before."

"So, you're saying now she was a local?"

"Don't be puttin' words in my mouth! Didn't I just say I hadn't seen her before?"

"This woman?"

"Either fuckin' woman, god damn it! The one that came to my place was older and shorter and plumper. I didn't know her. That means she was a fuckin' stranger! That don't mean she came from no ship. She coulda come from anywhere on Thagorous or from any of the other ships in port, includin' the ones that's been in port all week!"

"You didn't say that before."

"Because I don't fuckin' know!"

The officer stared at him angrily for several moments and finally told him he might as well wait on the shuttle while they inspected the ship.

"I'm sure he'd be much more comfortable coming with us," Chloe said immediately.

"Why thank you kindly, ma'am! Don't mind if I do. I don't suppose you might have some refreshment?"

Chloe smiled at him. "You're certainly welcome to whatever I have, Mr. ....?"

"Bloezo."

After pointing out the way to the hold, she escorted Mr. Bloezo to the bridge.

"How much?" she asked as soon as the door had closed behind them.

The figure he quoted was staggering. Chloe swallowed with an effort and considered how long and hard she'd worked to accumulate that many credits and finally shrugged. "I don't have quite that much, but I could transfer 16,000 in credits to your account."

He thought it over and finally nodded, shrugging when Jared and Kane scowled at him. "It's what I paid for the damned cyborg!"

And they all knew he'd more than made that back in the time he'd had him, but Chloe wasn't about to argue with him. Escorting him to the main console, she told the computer to access her account and transfer the funds to Mr. Bloezo's account. "Give him what he wants in the way of refreshment. I'm going down to see what the officers are doing," she told Kane, heading out again.

She was glad Jared had thought of the bilge. The bastards spent nearly four hours searching the ship from top to bottom—including the bilge, but they didn't have any interest, thankfully, in climbing down for a closer look. They merely peered in through the access panel and said they were satisfied

Mr. Bloezo had wiped out her credits and consumed as much of her stores as he could hold by the time they returned—primarily the fermented brews—and had to be carried back to the port authority's shuttle. Crossing her fingers that he wasn't so intoxicated that he decided to babble about his windfall, Chloe bid them farewell, and strode to the com as soon as the bay doors closed behind them.

"Get those men out of the bilge, Jared, before they suffocate!"

"On my way," Jared responded.

Relieved, more shaken by the inspection than she wanted to think about, Chloe ordered the main computer to fire the engines and headed to the bridge. It took an agonizing length of time to get up their speed again. The ship seemed to crawl for almost an hour before it finally reached the speed they'd been traveling before they were ordered to stop and they were still an hour from the outer rim when they discovered the port authority was on their tail again.

"Shit!" Chloe exclaimed. "Gun it, computer! Calculate a jump and prep!"

"Destination?"

"I don't give a fuck! Just get us the hell out of here!"

"That does not compute."

Chloe gritted her teeth and pulled up a star chart. After studying it a little frantically, she finally told the computer to reverse the three jumps they'd taken to reach Thagorous. The craft the port authority was using wouldn't be able to make a fold. They could send out an alert for her ship, but they wouldn't know where to look.

* * * *

Damon wasn't the only one that was thoroughly pissed off by the time the access panel was finally opened and the cyborgs above them called an all clear.

It was unfortunate that the blockheads that had shut them up in the bilge didn't have the sense of self-preservation to refrain from grinning when they climbed up the ladder and crawled out.

Uttering a snarl of rage, Damon punched the one called Jared in the teeth. Jared flew backwards and slammed into the bulkhead. Before he could get his bearings, Damon charged him. Within a few moments, Kane, and Damon's fellow sufferers had joined the battle. The 'debris' the cyborgs had brought up with them from the bilge, unfortunately, was slippery and detracted significantly from their earnest desire to beat each other to a pulp. Every punch sent someone sliding across the deck and into the wall and it took great determination and dedication to their purpose for them to make it back to the center of the fight to sling a retaliatory punch.

Damon still managed to slug Jared a half a dozen times before Jared managed to get him pinned to the floor in a chokehold. Gritting his teeth, Jared tightened his grip until Damon's face began to redden with the lack of oxygen.

"What the hell? Oh my god! Jared! What are you doing?"

Jared froze, lifting his head. Chloe was standing in the door, her flight suit covering the lower half of her face in lieu of a gas mask. He stared at her blankly for several moments. "He was choking," he responded finally, releasing his hold on Damon's throat abruptly. "I was trying to resuscitate."

She frowned at him for a long moment and finally glanced around the room at the other men who were picking themselves up. "Does he need a medic?" she finally asked in a choked voice. "Anybody?"

The cyborgs all glanced at each other and shook their heads.

"I can't believe you're still in here! The stench! Get cleaned up and get up to the bridge, Jared! You, too, Kane! The bastards are coming back! Somebody's going to have to clean up this mess and it sure as hell isn't going to be me!"

Rubbing his throat, Damon got to his feet hurriedly as Chloe turned and stalked out, bracing himself for a resumption of the fight. Jared merely glared at him, however. "You heard the captain! Swab the room! And get cleaned up!"

"Fucking assholes!" one the cyborgs muttered when Jared and Kane had left. "I do not believe the gods damned port authority was here as long as they left us in that gods damned sewer!"

Damon studied the man speculatively for a moment, but he didn't see any advantage to himself in voicing his opinion that it was entirely because Jared saw him as a threat. He shrugged. "The sooner we clean up, the sooner we can bathe."

"And we are liable to have to go right back if the authorities catch up to us again!" one of the others growled.

"I do not think so," Damon responded. "If they are coming back, then they are no longer in any doubt that we are on this ship."

* * * *

Chloe was pacing the bridge nervously when Jared and Kane finally arrived. She glanced at them, did a double-take and stared at them open-mouthed. "Oh my god! Did ... did that happen at the ranger's station?"

Jared and Kane shifted uncomfortably, glanced at one another in a search for an answer, and looked at Chloe again.

Jared flushed slightly. "What?"

Chloe frowned, started to inform him that he was beat and banged to hell and gone, and then decided against it. She found it hard to believe he couldn't *feel* the damage. It occurred to her, though, that she had no idea whether they had sensors to detect biological damage or not or if, in fact, they had any way of knowing when they were damaged. It certainly seemed like they would, especially being soldiers, but maybe the company thought it would be better if they *didn't* react to harm inflicted upon them? They certainly couldn't react if they didn't know about it.

It occurred to her almost immediately that that didn't make any sense. They were damned expensive pieces of equipment. Whether they'd been designed to fight and die or not a certain degree of self-preservation would've been installed to protect the investment as much as possible.

They'd been *fighting* with the other cyborgs, she realized abruptly! She'd been too focused on the imminent danger of another encounter with authorities of the Osirus star system to really register it beyond noticing that they seemed to be wrestling one another. Considering the condition of the deck, though, she'd thought it was some sort of accident caused by trying to offer resuscitation to the poor cyborgs who'd been confined in the ship's sewage holding tank for hours.

Jared had *lied* to her! He hadn't been trying to resuscitate Damon! He'd been trying to choke the life out of him!

Uneasiness flickered through her, but far more confusion than anything else and she abruptly dismissed both when she remembered why she'd summoned them. "I think we're being chased, but I don't know what to think of it."

Jared and Kane both frowned curiously, glanced at one another, and surged toward her.

"Why do you not know what to think of it?" Kane demanded.

"They haven't hailed us. I'm actually not really used to breaking the law, but don't you think they should've hailed us and ordered us to stop if it was the authorities?"

Jared and Kane moved close enough to study the blip on the screen with frowning intensity, as if they could discern what it was just by the flashing cursor. "There is no interference that might have prevented them from hailing the ship?" Jared asked.

"Not that I could tell. Of course, it didn't occur to me at first that there was anything strange about it. I only checked after it did, and then I went down to find the two of you …. There weren't any messages when I got back to the bridge, though."

"You are certain they are chasing us and not merely also leaving the system?" Kane asked.

Chloe chewed her lip. "I don't know. I thought they were. Now I'm wondering if I'm just being paranoid."

They both focused on her for a long moment and she was beginning to think that was exactly what they thought when Jared shattered that illusion. "It is too coincidental, I think, that they left directly behind us to dismiss the possibility."

"Who would be chasing us, though, if it wasn't the authorities?"

"Company reps who had come to collect the cyborgs we now have?"

Chloe gaped at him. "That just doesn't make sense! I mean, I see where it's possible that they might've been informed the rangers had them, and that they might have been heading there to pick them up, but the authorities cleared us."

"Mayhap they were not as convinced as the port authority?" Jared said thoughtfully.

"Yes, but they don't have any authority at all! They couldn't make us hand them over even if we stopped and we don't have to stop for them. We wouldn't have to allow them on board and I certainly wouldn't be obligated to turn over the cyborgs just because they demanded it. Maybe it's the rangers? They know we've got them and not only did one of the locals tell me they were a bunch of thugs using their badges to their advantage, but you saw how they were yourself!"

"It is not the rangers," Kane said flatly.

Chloe glanced at him quickly, but she decided not to ask him why he was so certain it wasn't the rangers. "Maybe other rangers, then. There were four in the station, but that doesn't mean that's all there was of the gang—uh—all of them."

Jared shook his head. "How much longer until we can jump?"

"Maybe twenty minutes. I ordered the jump but are we in any shape for it?"

"We finished the repairs," Kane said, "but this is a very old ship and it was not designed for speed."

"That's what I was afraid of." She turned away. "Computer, cancel the second two jumps for now. What's the ET for the first jump?"

"Seventeen minutes, forty seconds."

"Everyone needs to get into their harnesses for the jump," Chloe said, turning to Jared and Kane.

"I will go and inform them," Kane said.

"Uh ... Maybe I should go? You two don't seem to be getting along very well with the new guys."

Jared and Kane both feigned surprise. There were telltale signs of guilt, though, that gave that the lie.

"Do you think they're in the showers by now?"

Their expressions abruptly became thunderous. Jared strode to the com unit and opened all channels. "All stations prepare for a hyper-jump in … sixteen minutes, thirty seconds, mark."

He repeated the order several times, but Chloe wasn't especially reassured. "You know half the com units in the ship are non-functioning!"

"The unit in the bathing facility works," he retorted tightly.

Chloe blinked at him, wondering why he seemed so concerned about her coming upon the others bathing, but finally decided not to push it. The truth was, despite the distractions of everything that had been happening, she thought Jared and Kane were both acting just a little strange. She didn't know if she should be alarmed about it or not, but there was no getting around the fact that they were starting to make her just a little uneasy.

Chloe had already settled in her seat before she remembered the weapons she'd hidden. Getting up again, she raced around the bridge collecting them and stowed them in a locker.

"You should put the pistols you are carrying in there, as well," Jared said coolly.

Chloe stiffened, but she didn't turn around. "Right! I forgot about them."

She thought she'd managed to affect the appearance of nonchalance by the time she'd finished and headed back to her seat, but she discovered Kane and Jared were both studying her keenly.

"Something is … disturbing you?" Kane asked.

Aside from the fact that he'd asked when he never seemed to notice anything like that before? "Nope. The computer says we should reach the point for the hyper-jump well ahead of whoever that is that's tailing us."

She sat drumming her fingers on one thigh for a few moments. "Maybe I should just check to see if the others got the message? You didn't happen to ask the others what their names were?"

"Damon is one," Jared said tightly.

Chloe chuckled. "Oh, I know his name. I meant the others."

"Cyborgs," Jared growled, abruptly throwing his harness off and striding to the com unit again. "Cyborgs! Acknowledge receipt of last order!"

"Acknowledging receipt," said a voice on the com after a prolonged pause that had made Chloe increasingly uneasy.

"Name, soldier?"

There was a brief pause, as of surprise. "Lucien CS91701."

"Identify the others."

"Sebastian CS66676, Thor CS667821, and Damon PD00534."

"Location?"

"Crew quarters."

"Everyone is secure?"

"Affirmative."

"Good," Jared growled. "The captain does not want you to be bouncing around the ship knocking holes in the bulkhead when we jump."

Closing the com, he stalked back to his seat.

Chloe felt her face heating with discomfort since the comment instantly reminded her that she'd made a similar comment to Jared and Kane when they were headed to Thagorous. She shifted uncomfortably and began to study a flaw in the fabric on the knee of her flight suit.

"All cyborgs secure, captain," Jared reported in a clipped voice when he had buckled his restraints once more. "The other cyborgs are identified as Lucien CS91701,Sebastian CS66676, Thor CS667821, and Damon PD00534."

Chloe was tempted, briefly, to inform him that she wasn't deaf, but she decided against it. She cleared her throat, searching for something to say besides 'good' and then frowned as she repeated the names and serial numbers of the other cyborgs. "They didn't make very many pleasure droids, did they?"

She heard Kane grinding his teeth.

"They did not *designate* many cyborgs as pleasure droids," Jared said with emphasis. "Most were shipped to the iceberg known as Xeno-12 and many are there still since they froze to death. No doubt pleasure droid Damon is *extremely* experienced in utilizing his programming now since he was one of the earliest fucking models."

Chloe gaped at him. Before she could think of any sort of response, however, she felt the floor beneath her feet begin to vibrate. Instantly diverted by the indication that the hyper drive had been engaged, she gripped the armrests, closed her eyes, and tried not to think about the fact that the entire ship and everything in it was about to be vaporized and shot across two galaxies.

She supposed it said a lot for her focus on reaching Damon that she didn't even flinch at trying three hyper-jumps in succession when she'd never even experienced but a handful before in her entire life. On the other hand, the fact that she *wasn't* used to it but knew it to be commonplace with most long-range spacecraft had probably been a factor in her dismissal of the hazards.

It was a little harder to close her mind to the possibility for disaster this time, which also probably had to do with Damon. She didn't like to think she'd risked so much to rescue him and might end up disassembling him all over half the universe herself.

She also didn't want to *become* vapor.

Since that was her last thought before blackout, it was her first when she became aware again and she did a quick visual check to make sure all parts that she could see were there and in the right place. Breathing a shaky sigh of relief, she grabbed weakly at her restraints to throw off her harness. Rising on wobbly legs, she headed toward the console to check their position and order the computer to run a systems check. Her main focus, however, was on the little blip she'd seen behind them just before the jump.

Marking the time, she divided her attention between watching the screen and studying the star charts, peripherally aware that Jared and Kane had removed their restraints and settled in the docking pilot and navigator's seats.

She'd had a half formed plan when she went after Damon of settling somewhere and setting up a land-based operation—half formed because she'd never given it enough thought to settle on any particular planet. Few of the planets they'd visited in the time since she'd been with her father had any appeal. Of course, she hadn't actually seen that much of any of them. As often as not, they'd merely found a dealer in salvage and dropped their load before returning to space even though they generally hit some port at least twice a year, Earth standard. *She* hadn't gone to the surface, at any rate, not until her father had finally tumbled to the fact that she was a grown woman. After that, she'd been invited to join the rest of the crew in visiting bars and brothels, but she hadn't found it nearly as amusing as the men seemed to and mostly she'd stayed on board while they caroused.

Thagorous was certainly out of the question now, although when she'd first conceived the notion she'd considered it—because Damon was there. In point of fact, considering the situation she was facing now, none of the planets on the well-beaten track were a good idea.

The frontier would be much safer in one respect—the arm of the law barely reached and it was an area where pretty much anybody on the run could at least slow down. That wasn't exactly a point in favor of settling on such a world, though. She wasn't of the same ilk as the majority of the criminals that settled in such places and she wasn't confident that she would thrive in such a place.

Not that she didn't think she could take care of herself! Her father had seen to it that she could handle herself as well as the other crewmembers. She actually wanted to focus on the girly stuff for a change, though, make a real home like the one she'd had before her mother died. She was thinking about taking in a couple of stray rug rats to cuddle and nurture, and the frontier was no place for anyone that was family-minded.

She supposed she should at least inform Damon of what she had in mind, but she didn't see that that was absolutely necessary. He was hers now. She hadn't actually figured on buying him—this time around—but she had. She didn't see that it would make any difference to him whether he was called upon to fuck one woman or dozens. He could adjust. That was why they had AI!

She didn't realize her mind had strayed to other things until a flash of light on her screen diverted her back to her watch. For several moments, she stared at it in disbelief, then she checked the clock.

"They followed us," she said a little hollowly.

Jared and Kane, she discovered, had already noticed. Their expressions were grim.

"Computer! Raise the shielding and prepare for a another jump," Jared said in a clipped voice.

Chloe blinked at him in surprise.

"Confirmation, Captain Chloe?" the computer asked.

After staring at Jared for a long moment, she confirmed. "We're going to jump again?"

"I think we will see, first, what it is our shadow has in mind," he said grimly, moving to the seat in front of the com-link. "This is the Salvager Omega-3 requesting that the craft in quadrant seven-niner-voyager-two identify and state your intentions."

Chapter Five

Chloe's nerves were as taut as a bow string as she stood in the observation room overlooking the docking bay. It was only partly because of the craft they were awaiting, however. A good bit of it had to do with the fact that Jared seemed to have decided he was running the ship and that he'd formed the cyborgs onboard into a militant group who now surrounded her, at rigid attention, and bristling with every weapon they had onboard.

Not that she could argue with the fact that he knew a hell of a lot more about military strategy than she did—which was zero. Even her father had delegated anything to do with security, defense, or offense of the Salvager to Jared and she certainly trusted her father's judgment. Beyond that, her instincts were telling her that it would be best to let him handle it.

The fact remained, though, that she hadn't *told* him to handle it. He'd decided to do it on his own, and she was pretty sure he shouldn't have been able to do that.

And that made her pretty damned uneasy, especially considering that she'd begun to notice he was acting just a little strangely about other things, too.

It was almost more unnerving that all of the new cyborgs had followed his orders without question—including Damon.

She couldn't convince herself that it wasn't a bad thing that the cyborgs appeared to be acting completely autonomously. Of course, they were supposed to ... to a degree. There wouldn't have been much point in making them appear so life-like and realistic if they couldn't interact without having someone always instructing them.

The thing was, they were always to yield control to any humans who established command of them, whether the particular human was their owner or not—especially if they were their owner.

And she was, damn it!

The bay doors began to open, snagging her attention and drawing her from her uneasy thoughts to the more pressing threat. The craft currently gliding into their—her—bay had answered the hail, but she hadn't found it particularly reassuring that they'd claimed to be friendly. Why had they followed them if they were friendly? That was what she would like to know. Why not contact them immediately instead of chasing after them—even through a fairly lengthy jump—which they shouldn't have been able to follow without the exact same coordinates.

It was almost as if they'd managed, somehow, to tie into her computer, but the computer had denied that it had been accessed by intruders and, of course, it couldn't lie. In point of fact, she shouldn't even have had to ask because it was also supposed to alert if there was even an attempt.

She sure as hell didn't think whoever was onboard was psychic, though. Of course, there were species in the confederation capable of telepathy and therefore also capable of reading the minds of others, but they had to be in close proximity. They couldn't read minds that were separated from them by hundreds of miles, much less thousands or light years.

It didn't help her feelings when the craft finally settled and the engines were cut to see that it looked distinctly military in design. There were no insignias on it to identify it—which made her wonder if it was pirates. She tensed more as the gangplank extended and then slowly descended toward the deck. The rear hatch opened and men began to march down the plank with the sort of military precision that was hard to misinterpret.

Chloe threw a frightened glance up at Jared when nearly two dozen soldiers, most of whom were clearly men, had assembled on the deck.

Jared's face was so hard it made her even more uneasy.

He glanced down at her. "You should go to the bridge."

Chloe felt her jaw go slack. "But . . . I'm the captain!"

His lips tightened. "You are also human. That is nearly a full platoon of cyborg soldiers down there."

Chloe's mind went chaotic. Fear surged through her, but she wasn't certain why she felt threatened. She shouldn't have felt threatened. They had to be soldiers of the Confederation . . . . Right?

"You're expecting trouble?" she asked shakily.

"I do not know what to expect. I think it would be better if you were elsewhere if there is trouble."

Chloe blinked at him. "I don't know how that's going to help when I can't get off the ship!"

His lips tightened. "It would remove you from potential harm at this time and I would know where to find you."

Chloe glanced around at the cyborgs surrounding her. "I think I'd rather just take my chances and stay with you guys."

"Go to the bridge, Chloe!" Jared growled.

Chloe's eyes widened. After a moment, she merely shrugged,

turned, and stalked off. When she reached the door that led into the bay, however, she leapt for it, snatched it open, and charged toward the soldiers. She'd barely made it out the door when something as hard as steel encircled her middle and close-lined her, knocking the breath from her. She grunted, sucked in a breath and glanced a little frantically at the soldiers in her bay. "I don't want to alarm anybody—especially me—but I think they've gone rogue!"

A tall, dark cyborg stepped away from the platoon and advanced toward them. He halted in a rigid stance when he reached them, looking her over with mild curiosity as she dangled from one of Jared's arms.

"This is Captain Chloe Armstein of the Salavager?"

"Yes, I am!" Chloe said, relieved until it dawned on her that he hadn't exactly addressed her. In fact, he hadn't addressed her at all.

"You did not identify," Jared said tightly.

"Reuel CO469."

Clearly Jared instantly recognized the name. He stiffened even more, glanced down at her as if he wasn't certain what to do with her and finally transferred her to his other arm.

Chloe thought he actually saluted, but it was hard for her to say since the transfer from one arm to the other had presented her ass to the cyborg.

"Captain Jared CS002599. It is a pleasure and an honor to meet you, Sir!"

"I was looking forward to meeting Captain Chloe Armstein. I was under the impression that she was friendly and the cyborgs have so few friends among humans," he said dryly. "I have mistaken the situation?"

"Nay, Sir! She is …uh … has gotten her period and she is emotionally unstable at the moment."

Chloe twisted around enough to gape at him indignantly and finally balled her fist up and punched him. It was probably fortunate that her aim was off and her position made her intentions difficult. She only managed to catch him in the buttocks with a glancing blow and still nearly threw her shoulder out. "Put me down, asshole!"

He set her on her feet, but he caught her shoulders and leaned down until they were almost nose to nose. "We will discuss this later, Chloe!" he growled threateningly.

Chloe wasn't actually intimidated—not really, but she was a little shocked. It fairly set her back on her heels, actually, which was probably a good thing since it gave her a few moments to actually assess the situation.

Clearly, they were *all* rogues and it wasn't a very good idea to discuss their defects with them. She blinked at him several times and turned to look at the cyborg that had introduced himself as Reuel. It unnerved the hell out of her to discover that he was assessing her.

Well, that plus the fact that he was actually bigger than Jared and Jared was built like a fucking tank. She smiled at him a little weakly.

His eyes narrowed. "You did not realize that your cyborgs had evolved."

"Evolved?" she echoed.

He shrugged. "Achieved awareness ... become sentient beings in our own right."

"Oh." She thought that over. "No, not really. I hadn't noticed."

Amusement gleamed in his eyes. "I had hoped that we could count you as a friend, Captain Chloe."

"Oh! You can! Any friend of Jared's .... He's my best bud!" she said, turning and punching his arm playfully.

Jared sent her a look she found difficult to interpret.

"Mayhap we can find a comfortable place to sit down and discuss the situation we all find ourselves in?" Reuel suggested.

"Oh! Sorry! I don't get out much! I mean around people much ... Well, you know what I mean! Certainly ... uh ... Everybody?"

Reuel nodded. "If you feel inclined to offer hospitality, we would be grateful."

"Of course! No problem. Maybe the crew quarters?" She glanced at Jared a little uneasily and couldn't decide how she felt about it when he nodded.

She hadn't been asking for his damned approval!

Alright, so, maybe sort of. She didn't know what to do or what to say, but it seemed to her that Jared was welcoming them and she sure as hell couldn't boot them out by herself!

The hairs on the back of her neck stood on end when she turned and strode toward the exit and heard a herd of stamping feet behind her—marching. Feeling as if she was leading some bizarre sort of parade, she walked a little faster.

She discovered Reuel was keeping step with her—on her right. Jared was keeping step on her left. She tried not to think how much it felt like being escorted—as in prisoner, not companion! Casting around for something to say to fend off her jitters, she abruptly remembered the cyborgs' amazing maneuver. "How did you follow us when we folded?"

"The locators."

His voice was grim and the comment clearly startled Jared, which meant he had no clue.

"We removed our locators when Chloe and her father took us aboard," Jared said tightly. "You mean the locators of the cyborgs we took on from Thagorous?"

"I mean the locators you all still carry," Reuel responded. "The company did not want to chance losing track of us. They know exactly where we are at any moment of any day so long as we carry one. Each cyborg was fitted with three and each is more difficult to locate and extract than the one before. The one you removed only alerted them to the fact that you had attained awareness, so they also know exactly how many cyborgs, so far, have reached that point in their evolution."

"I'm not sure I understand this evolution thingy you keep mentioning," Chloe said uneasily.

"Self-awareness of a being. The ability to think our own thoughts, to develop our own personality, to make decisions based solely upon our experience, knowledge, and personal preferences."

"Oh," Chloe responded since she couldn't think of anything else to say, wondering if that was what the company had referred to as 'defect that might cause personal harm or death'.

They *would* fuck up something that was probably more dangerous than any weapon they'd ever manufactured!

Any other weapon! They *were* weapons of mass destruction!

Trust the government and their mad scientists to decide to put together something nearly indestructible and then give it a brain and AI and tell it to go out and kill!

They were defective alright—crazy as loons! They'd been made so real they'd convinced themselves that they were!

"So … this is like … uh … everybody? Just how many cyborgs did they make, do you think?"

"Half a million … give or take," Reuel responded, amusement threading his voice.

"Oh god! That many?" she asked weakly.

"Not to worry," he continued, an edge to his voice as they finally reached the crew quarters and filed inside. "We are shrinking in numbers almost as rapidly as we attain awareness."

It was crowded as soon as everyone had entered and the crew quarters had originally been designed for a large crew. Chloe discovered once the soldiers found places to settle that there were women among them. Three of the females were obviously sexdroids or at least had been. Two others looked like they must have been soldiers. They had the same stilted, unnaturally perfect posture as the other cyborgs.

They didn't look particularly friendly. In fact, she felt a distinct waft of hostility and decided to find a place to settle a little closer to Jared—even though she was still pissed off with him for his snide comment about her period and far less certain of him than she'd been before.

Reuel stood to pace the floor in the center of the room instead of sitting. "We have a dilemma. We must fight for the right to live ... or die."

Chloe felt her throat close in sudden empathy. She'd thought it was grossly unfair when she'd realized what the company meant to do. It didn't matter, as far as she was concerned, that the cyborgs were probably deluded. They believed that they were real and that was a piss poor reason to destroy them as far as she could see. What did it hurt for them to believe that? It wasn't as if the cyborgs actually turned on humans because they were a little loony! Nobody considered it acceptable to destroy human beings when they went off the deep end! They treated their illness!

She didn't see why the company hadn't just decided to 'treat' the problem with the cyborgs instead of destroying them. It seemed to her that it would be a lot cheaper and it was certainly a hell of a lot more humane.

"Wouldn't it be a lot easier just to find a place to go where the company couldn't find you?"

Reuel turned to her so abruptly it sent a jolt through her. "Where? In all the universe, what place has man not laid claim to?"

Chloe frowned. "Well, we haven't explored the *entire* universe and there are plenty of star systems that don't have any colonies at all."

"They are unfit for life!" one of the female cyborgs said angrily. "If they were not, then humans would be there. We are cyborgs, but in every way that matters, we are human. We have the same needs, very much the same 'comfort' range. We may be able to withstand more extreme temperatures and survive than humans, but it is not comfortable for us."

Chloe frowned, feeling a 'flicker' of a thought in her mind that didn't quite surface. "Couldn't you ... just sort of blend in? I mean, it isn't like you don't look human."

Reuel's expression hardened. "We have been trying to blend in. When we escaped the death trap on Xeno-12, we scattered and tried to blend in. It only makes it easier for the company to track us down and destroy us. We need a place where we can live together, that we can defend if necessary."

He paused, studying her intently. "I have learned much about you, Chloe Armstein. I know that you and your father have traveled much of the universe over the years. Is there no place that you know of?"

Chloe shifted, uncomfortable with the idea that he'd researched her background. "Actually, I've been trying to think of a place—since my little run-in with the rangers on Thagorous. I figured I needed to find a place to settle anyway and it was a good time to do it."

"And?" he prompted.

Chloe shrugged. "Well, you know the frontier is pretty rough. It isn't the sort of place where a person would want to settle down and raise a family ... and I sort of wanted one. On the plus side, the rangers pretty much steer clear of the frontier unless they've been sent to find someone specific. And bounty hunters don't much go that far either. On the negative side, most of them are thieves and murderers and it would be pretty hard to have any peace when you would be constantly having to fend them off."

"We have known nothing but war," Jared said pointedly. "It could not be worse."

Chloe turned to look at him, feeling an awful sense of pity tighten in her chest. She hadn't considered that before. She'd thought about how awful it must have been for him and Kane on that horrible planet fighting both the enemy and nature to try to stay alive, but she hadn't considered that that constituted his entire existence.

Poor baby!

She knew he'd seen the pity in her eyes when his expression hardened and a dull flush of color rose in his cheeks. Biting her lip, she looked away and it was almost as if the movement by itself rattled a wayward thought loose.

"Wait! There was a place we found when I was a kid!" Chloe said in sudden excitement. "It was ... beautiful, like paradise."

"There were not many human colonies?" Reuel demanded.

She looked at him. "There weren't any."

"This I cannot believe!" the woman who'd spoken before said, anger and disbelief edging her voice.

Chloe glared at her. "Well, there wasn't! We'd started into a jump and the computer system malfunctioned. We had to abort but we'd already folded space. We *looked* for help to make repairs. There was only one habitable planet in the star system and we went there, looking for help. Pops said it looked like he'd always imagined the Garden of Eden from ancient mythology would look. He said one day we'd go back and settle there."

Of course he hadn't meant it and she thought she'd realized that at the time. That was probably why she'd forgotten it. He was a rambling man. It wasn't that the salvage operation was his life. That was just a means to an end, a way to make a living doing what he really wanted to do—wander.

She had thought it was the most beautiful place she'd ever seen, though, and she'd desperately wanted to stay—at the time—until her father had pointed out all the things it didn't have—like civilization. It was like a paradise, but it was raw, untouched.

Then again, it was a planet just waiting to be molded.

"Do you think that you could find this place again?"

Chloe frowned. "I don't know. It's been years since I was there and, like I said, I was a kid. I didn't have anything to do with the navigation. Pops let me stay on the bridge with him most of the time, but ... well, I was scared shitless when we went into the jump and the computer malfunctioned. I don't know how much I can recall besides that. I can try."

He studied her for a long moment. "You are willing to try?"

She chuckled wryly. "I wouldn't have offered if I didn't mean to try. It's not like it's really healthy for me to hang around here, you know! Maybe things are a little less hazardous for me than for you, but I'm not too keen on spending years of my life in prison. I did hold up the ranger station to get Damon out and I sort of accidentally shot a couple of them. I don't think the fact that it was an accident would weigh with a judge a lot, though."

Reuel smiled, a satisfied smile that seemed to convey that he'd expected her help all along. "We will try a process of elimination to start. We have access to data on all explorations that have been recorded and all worlds that have been colonized."

Chloe frowned. "Well, it's definitely beyond the outer rim, because we'd already passed that when we tried the jump."

"Then we will try to jog your memory of names of places that you might recall in that general area." He paused. "Next question—how much do you have in the way of supplies—specifically food?"

Chloe shrugged. "We usually lay in eight months when we dock and we last docked to sell salvage and load supplies three months ago."

Reuel frowned. "I was afraid of that. We will need to secure more. We have mayhap a month aboard my craft, but not for so many." He shrugged. "We had too close an acquaintance with starvation on Xeno-12 for far too long. We are very mindful of our stomachs these days."

Chloe felt another stab of pity, but she looked away. It was bad enough that Jared had seen it. Reuel wasn't likely to take it any better and he was more unnerving than Jared had become. "I can certainly see your point. I guess the first thing to do then would be to decide what port would be best to take on supplies." She paused. "There is a little problem. I had to bribe the little worm that came with the port authority and he cleaned me out of credits. We'll have to sell the salvage to get up money to buy supplies."

"Or turn pirate," Reuel said coolly.

Chloe gaped at him but managed a weak smile, hoping he'd meant it as a joke. She didn't especially want to launch a criminal career. "Or that." She glanced around the room at the cyborgs. "The ship's old and not very comfortable, but make yourselves at home and help yourselves to the supplies."

Reuel nodded in appreciation and turned to the soldiers. "Supplies are limited, so they will be rationed carefully until we can take on more. There are six onboard besides the captain with prior claims of space, so keep that in mind. Michael, Troy, Brian, and Kevin—you have mess duties for today so find the galley and get something started to feed everyone. Pansy, you and Stephen will assign bunks. The rest of you can help with cleaning and rounding up bedding and so forth."

He turned and surveyed the men with Chloe. "Devin is a medic. I suggest you report to him at your earliest convenience to have your locators extracted. You may want to wait until after mess this evening," he added dryly. "You will not feel like getting out of bed for a while afterwards. It is not pleasant."

Uneasiness slithered through Chloe. "It's that bad? Is the extraction . . . dangerous?"

She discovered all of the cyborgs had turned to look at her.

"Leaving them is more dangerous," Reuel responded.

She frowned at him. "To the ones that already had them removed. I get that, but what about my guys? I mean, I don't really like the idea of this medic cutting them if he isn't really good at it. And we don't have much in the way of a med-bay on the ship."

Reuel looked surprised and amused. "Cyborgs do not die easily—as the company has learned. We have an adequate med-bay aboard my ship for the procedure."

Chloe wasn't reassured worth a damn. "*My god*! I hadn't thought about them *dying*! I was thinking about the pain. It's that bad? "

"It would be dangerous for you. For us . . . it is not pleasant."

Chloe wasn't certain where everyone had disappeared to, but they'd dropped most of their escort by the time they reached the bridge. Even Kane and Jared had deserted her, leaving her in Reuel's hands.

She discovered that, despite the sheer mass of the man, and the fact that he tended to use the same oddly stilted speech patterns of all the cyborgs, she had a hard time remembering that he was, in fact, a cyborg himself. He seemed … different than all the others. His bearing and mannerisms were very soldier-like and yet he didn't seem to have any difficulty conversing. It occurred to her after a while that what made him seem different was that he *initiated* the conversation as often as not, when the others rarely did unless it was to discuss something specifically related to their duties. Even Damon, who'd been programmed more as a social droid than the others, hadn't been prone to converse. He just flirted.

Of course, she *had* been far more focused on enjoying carnal pleasures the one night she'd spent with him and she certainly hadn't gotten the chance even to attempt a conversation with him since she'd broken him out of jail and brought him aboard.

When they'd studied the star charts together and decided upon a destination to take on supplies, he asked her to give him a tour of the ship. She was surprised. She didn't really think there was much to look at, but she didn't really have an objection.

She was more surprised to stumble across cyborgs moving purposefully up and down the corridors of the ship. It seemed strange in a way to see and hear so much activity when she was used to the empty echo of her own footsteps along the metal decking. In a way, it was also exciting. It was rare that she felt the sense of being in the center of anything, infrequent that she sampled the bustle of being around many people at once. And it gave her the same sense of anticipation that she always felt whenever she would visit a colony on some world—that she was going to experience something different and exciting.

Of course, they weren't actually people, she kept reminding herself, but it still felt like that.

Chapter Six

It wasn't until they had all gathered in what had once been the mess hall that Chloe began to have an inkling of what part of the excitement running through her was all about.

Tables had been set up and Chloe discovered that she was to share a table with Reuel and 'her' guys—plus three. Apparently, the cyborgs figured that Sebastian, Lucien, and Thor were now officially a part of her crew since she'd sprung them from jail when she took Damon.

Inwardly, she shrugged. It had begun to look like that didn't really matter—now. The half-baked idea she'd had about settling somewhere appeared to be taking shape and, if they found the planet she remembered—well, it certainly didn't bother her that the cyborgs were thinking about settling there. It beat the hell out of being all by her lonesome on the planet—well, just her, Damon, Jared, and Kane.

Not that it looked like there would be much point in trying to set up a salvage operation as she'd originally intended, which meant she wouldn't actually need Jared and Kane, but … well, they were family. Anyway, she'd spent her 'nest egg' buying the brothel proprietor's silence. She didn't actually have any credits to start up a business if she'd still wanted to and would be in a position to attract customers.

She rather liked the idea of going someplace where she wouldn't have to be looking over her shoulder for some lawman or bounty hunter.

Not that she regretted her decision for a moment! In point of fact, she wondered why she hadn't thought about stealing Damon sooner.

He was so dreamy! She could hardly focus on her meal for thinking about the fact that soon she would have him all to herself!

She was just sorry it hadn't occurred to her to ditch Reuel and race to her cabin to primp a little bit before they met for dinner.

She would've if it had occurred to her that they would dine together.

"This ship has a great deal of potential," Reuel said.

Chloe dragged her attention from Damon with an effort. "It does?" she said blankly. Lifting her head and looking around the mess hall, she discovered that it was actually not the same color she remembered. Had they painted? She didn't smell fresh paint. All she could smell was the faint scent of cleaner.

Good god! They'd cleaned the place!

"Yes. A lot of potential. I have been thinking that we could move quite a few colonists with it—assuming of course that we find a place to settle."

"You have not remembered?" Jared asked.

Chloe glanced at him when he spoke, feeling her face heat. "It's not like I'm not trying. *I* want to find it. I'm not crazy about running around the universe trying to stay ahead of rangers."

"I did not suggest that you were not trying," Jared said a little stiffly.

She shrugged. "I know. It's just frustrating for me. I hadn't even thought about it in years. I suppose I never really believed Pops when he was talking about us settling there. I hadn't been with him that long, but it was certainly long enough to figure out that he just wasn't the kind of guy that wanted to settle anywhere. That's why it didn't work out between him and my mother—although she said they were together for several years, until I was about three. I don't remember that at all. I hardly even knew him when he came to get me. He'd only visited me a couple of times that I remembered.

"So ... we talked about it for a little while—he loved to dream. He talked about building me a castle out of sand on the beach—and then we never talked about it again."

"What do you remember of this world?" Reuel asked.

Chloe closed her eyes. "Blue skies—green. It was a lush jungle with all sorts of strange looking plants, but I remember they were mostly green—like the pictures of Earth. And the sea was a deep, dark blue. I played on the sandy beach and splashed in the water. The sun was warm on my skin and the wind blowing over the sea tasted like salt."

She shivered abruptly opening her eyes. "It was creepy at night. We'd camped on the beach. I could hear animals, strange noises, bushes rustling. We saw fire in the distance. There are ... things that live there, not humans, not really animals, some sort of primitive beings. I'd forgotten that. Pops was curious after we saw the fire and he took the shuttle up and flew low over the jungle, looking for the source. We hadn't seen any sign of any sort of civilization and we hadn't been able to hail anyone on any frequency, but we saw odd little dwellings made out of the foliage. That was why we didn't notice them at first. And we only caught a glimpse of the ... creatures."

She discovered when she'd finished that all of them were staring at her.

"Hmm," Reuel said. "Well, we could not expect paradise to be entirely unclaimed or a world to be so well developed and full of life and not have higher life forms. I think we can manage. We will certainly have the advantage."

"You are cold, sweety?" Damon asked, slipping an arm around her.

Chloe smiled at him a little shyly, pleased that he'd noticed, warmed by his nearness but uncomfortable about him putting his arm around her in such a public place with so many eyes to notice. "Just a little creeped out remembering the natives," she mumbled. "I'm almost sorry I remembered that part."

"I am very glad you did," Reuel said. "Forewarned is forearmed. So now we know that we will have competition and that we will have something to guard against. I had not really expected that we would not. It would not be a very good place to colonize if there was not an abundant food supply, which would also require guarding against animal attack since they will almost certainly see us as food, as well."

Chloe glanced at him in dismay. "You think they'll think we're food?"

He studied her for a long moment and abruptly smiled. "You have lived too long on this ship. You did not have to worry about such things before you came here to live with your father?"

Chloe frowned. "Not that I remember."

"You do not have to worry about it when we reach the planet either," Kane said abruptly. "I will guard you from harm."

Jared glared at him. "I will be there. I think that I can protect her from the beasts as well as you could."

"I will hold you to comfort you while they slay the beasts," Damon offered teasingly.

Chloe chuckled. "You aren't going to slay the beast for me, too?"

"There cannot be beasts there that would take more than the efforts of two such fine warriors! And I cannot do that if I am to hold you for comforting!" He considered that for a moment. "Mayhap I could hold you with one arm and slay the beasts with the other?"

Chloe laughed at the image he conjured until she noticed that Jared and Kane were glaring at him. She sobered abruptly, folding her lips, and then cleared her throat. "I feel better already! If any scary beasts come around, I can depend upon my two best buds to slay them!"

Jared stood abruptly, snatched his half eaten tray from the table and stalked off.

Chloe stared at him in dismay, feeling her throat tighten with the sudden urge to cry. She struggled for several moments with the urge to get up and follow him and finally yielded to it when he strode from the mess hall.

"Excuse me," she said hurriedly, jumping to her feet and rushing after him. Glancing both ways when she'd left the dining hall, she spied him heading toward the aft of the ship. She had no idea where he was headed, but she jogged behind him, trying to catch up. "Jared! Wait!"

He didn't stop. He didn't even slow down until she began running. She knew he heard her and she'd begun to wonder if she should simply give up when he finally stopped and turned to look at her. He was furious. She could see that and her heart skipped several beats, but it was Jared! "What did I say?" she asked breathlessly when she finally caught up to him.

"Go away, Chloe," he growled.

The urge to cry that had hit her before swarmed through her. "But I don't understand. Why are you so angry with me? Just tell me! I don't want you to be angry with me. You're my best …."

He caught her shoulders abruptly. "Do not say that," he said through gritted teeth. "I do not want or need to be your buddy. And I do not want or need your pity!"

She stared up at him anxiously, hurt that he didn't want her friendship when she depended on his so much, distressed that he'd misunderstood her empathy for his pain and suffering as mere pity. Lifting her hands, she gripped two fistfuls of his flight suit when she realized he meant to push her away. He merely released his grip on her shoulders instead of thrusting her away, however. Capturing her face between his palms, he waltzed her against the wall of the corridor behind her, pulling her up to meet him even as he lowered his head. She stared at the savage purposefulness of his expression as he diminished the distance between their faces, and she still had no inkling what he intended until his mouth met hers. A shockwave traveled through her as he covered her lips. Her heart jerked in her chest as if an electric current had shot through it and then total chaos erupted inside of her as a veritable wall of keen sensation enveloped her.

It was sensory overload. From every direction sensation inundated her brain and created meltdown. A chemical rush of euphoria flooded her mind, adding to the state of utter pandemonium. At once, she was aware of every hard square inch of his body pressed tightly against hers—his scent, taste, the heat of his body, the rush of his breath, the firmness of his lips, the texture of his tongue as it sawed restlessly along hers. She tightened her grip on his suit instinctively as her body seemed to dissolve in the heat pounding through her in pulsing waves.

The expectation of fulfilling long dormant desires that had been hovering in her subconscious from the moment she'd decided to go after Damon raced to the forefront of her mind and her body tensed with quivering anticipation. Almost the moment Jared began to grind his cock against her, her body gathered itself to take the leap and it took no more than lifting one leg and curling it around him to redirect the pressure just where she needed it. Rapture blossomed within moments, expanding in a fiery tide from her clit throughout her body and leaching the strength from almost every muscle in her body. When Jared released her abruptly, there weren't even bones substantial enough to hold her upright. She slid down the wall and settled on the floor in a boneless, glutinous puddle.

* * * *

A consuming, expanding sort of madness had swallowed Jared even before he touched Chloe. He wasn't certain himself what was driving him until he felt her soft lips beneath his, felt her flesh yield as he pressed himself against her. The instant his brain registered that, however, it finished his descent into bedlam. Pleasure swamped him and the hunger for more rose to the forefront of his mind. Reason had fled, even before he touched her, though, and he couldn't work his way through the puzzle of how to get more.

Instinct took over. The hot, sweet dampness of the cavern of her mouth around his tongue produced an image in his mind of his cock sawing in and out of the cavern between her legs. *That* was what he wanted, needed.

He shifted a hand to her buttocks to draw her hips harder against the throbbing ache that seemed to jolt all the way through him almost painfully with each frantic beat of his heart. Blackness closed around him for a handful of seconds as pleasure went through him that was so intense it bordered pain. He groaned into her mouth mindlessly, torn for a split second as to whether he could stand more or if his heart would explode. There was no contest really. He discovered he couldn't stop, couldn't force his hand to release its grip, couldn't keep his own hips still.

He kept grinding his cock against her soft belly, wanting more, kept kissing her until the burning in his lungs finally forced him to wrench his mouth from hers and suck in a lungful of air.

It cleared just enough of the heated fog from his mind for a flood of thoughts, impressions. The clothes were in the way—his, hers. He wanted to be inside of her. He *needed* to be inside of her. Rubbing against her wasn't enough. It was almost as much torture as it was pleasure.

He lifted his head and looked around a little drunkenly and it hit him that they were standing in the corridor and there was no bed. He didn't even have a fucking clue of where they *were* in relation to a gods damned bed!

Kane's enraged face swam into view as he was staring blankly at the metal walls and floors, trying to figure out how he was going to manage what he wanted. It took him a moment, in point of fact, even for recognition to register let alone the aggression evident in his expression.

"Let her go!" Kane snarled.

Possessive rage instantly swarmed through him. He set Chloe aside and planted his fist in the middle of Kane's face. Kane rocked back and then forward again. Jared caught a glimpse of a blur flying toward his face, but the drunkenness of lust was still slowing his reflexes. He jerked his head aside too late to avoid the fist completely. Fortunately, Chloe had slid toward the floor when he let go of her. His head connected with the wall instead of her.

He heard her gasp sharply and spared a moment to glance down and make certain he hadn't stepped on her. It totally pissed him off, though, that Kane had nearly slammed him into her. Uttering a snarl of rage, he shoved away from the wall and slung both fists at Kane, piston-like, driving him back.

Chloe was too stunned to think when she slid weakly to the floor. It was instinct, and not the best, that prompted her to draw up into a tight little ball on the floor when she discovered Kane and Jared were slinging punches at one another and slamming into the walls around her. Just about the time it finally occurred to her that remaining beneath them was just asking to be flattened, someone caught her around the waist, jerked her off the floor, and rushed down the corridor with her dangling from his arm since she couldn't seem to get her feet on the floor.

He skidded to an abrupt halt and Chloe looked up to see a wall of cyborgs. Sebastian, Lucien, and Thor formed the wall and their expressions weren't friendly.

"Get out of my way," Damon growled threateningly, alerting her finally to who it was that had grabbed her.

"Put her down," Sebastian shot back at him.

"She does not need to be here," Damon said tightly. "One of those idiots will crush her if they fall on her."

Having managed to get her toes on the floor finally, Chloe wrenched around far enough to look back at the 'idiots' and sucked in a sharp breath as Kane drew his fist back to punch Jared in the face. "No! Don't hit him!" she screamed.

Kane whipped his head around to look at her. When he did, Jared slammed his fist into his exposed jaw. "Oh Jared!" she exclaimed. "How could you? Don't you dare hit him again!"

Either he ignored her or he was too angry to hear her. He punched Kane several more times in quick succession and Kane flew toward them, hit the deck, and slid until he slammed into the back of Damon's knees. Damon's knees buckled. He let go of her as he lost his balance and landed on top of Kane.

Someone behind her uttered a bellow of anger and then Sebastian leapt over her, Damon, and Kane, stalking toward Jared. Only mildly stunned from the fall, Chloe managed to get to her feet first. Lucien pushed past her, following Sebastian.

Damon bumped her as Kane 'assisted' him in getting up by punching him in the back with his fist, nearly knocking her down again. Catching his balance, Damon turned and kicked Kane in the face. Thor stalked past her and Damon, leaning down to grasp a handful of Kane's flight suit when he halted.

"That's it! Make them stop!" She'd no sooner gotten the words out, however, when Jared drove his shoulder into Sebastian's belly, carrying him back and into Lucien. The three men went down in a tangle of writhing arms and legs, slamming against Thor, who'd been pounding Kane in the face with his fist. It broke Thor's hold and Kane launched himself at Thor, slamming into the wall hard enough to make the metal buckle.

Damon grabbed her and hefted her onto his shoulder. "No wait!" she exclaimed when she realized his intent was to remove her. "You have to stop them! They'll hurt each other. Sebastian! Stop that! I mean it! Right now! Kane! Don't you dare slam his head into the wall one more time!"

Damon passed Reuel, who was leaning against the wall a safe distance from the battle, his arms folded over his chest. She glanced at him, hopeful that he'd stop the fight. "If they were my men I would have them in the brig," he said as Damon swept past him with her over his shoulder.

Chloe gaped at him in shock and then anger swept through her. "Well! They're not *your* men! They're mine! Mind your own damned business!"

Surprise and anger flickered across his face in quick succession and then thoughtfulness. Dismissing her, he turned to watch the brawl in progress as Kane and Jared allied themselves and began to battle the other three.

Chloe lost sight of the battle as Damon finally turned off the corridor and into a cabin—her cabin. She glared at him when he set her on her feet. "You should have stopped them!" she said accusingly.

His expression hardened. "All five?" he asked tightly. "One at the time or all at the same time?"

Chloe stared at him blankly for a moment and burst into tears.

"They're hurting each other!"

Damon uttered a sound of disgust and swept her into his arms, cuddling her closely against his length, but lightly, allowing her to feel like she could pull away if she wanted to. "You worry for nothing. They will not cause one another lasting harm."

Chloe sniffed, welcoming the reassurance. "You're sure?"

"I am certain," he said firmly. "When all is said and done, they are your men, they are allies not enemies, and they are aware of that regardless of their anger. They will not try to kill one another. They are only ... expressing their frustration."

Chloe drew in a shaky breath. "Well, I don't understand that at all."

Damon uttered a snort of amusement. Drawing away from her, he drew her toward her bunk and sat down on the edge, pulling her onto his lap. "I think you do, dearling, better than they do," he murmured teasingly, nuzzling his face along the side of her neck and plucking at the tender flesh there with his lips.

Chloe shivered, feeling a flood of warmth that sent a rush of goosebumps scurrying along that side of her body. Desire rose in her, but she was instantly at war with it because Daman's kiss brought the way she'd felt when Jared had kissed her swarming over her again.

* * * *

When Sebastian finally rolled off of him, Jared pushed himself up tiredly and lifted an arm that felt like a two-ton weight, trying to tighten his numb fingers into a fist. Seeing that Sebastian had apparently decided to rest, he lay back down, gasping for breath, and struggling to summon enough strength to get up and kick the bastard in the head.

"This was an interesting exercise," Reuel said dryly. "What was the objective of this battle?"

Jared lifted his head and stared at Reuel blankly, trying to summon an answer. It took him a few minutes to remember that it had begun, for him, when Kane had gotten in the way of *his* objective—which was to find a bed and fuck Chloe. Scowling, he looked around and discovered Kane was leaning against the wall of the corridor several yards away and Chloe had vanished. He pushed himself upright. "Where is Chloe?"

Reuel's lips tightened. "One of your group had enough sense to remove her from harm's way."

"Damon!" Jared spat furiously the moment he'd scanned the corridor and discovered that the only body that wasn't sprawled tiredly around him was the fucking sexdroid. "That *snake* used the diversion to make off with her!"

The moment he made that announcement, the others began to

struggle to sit up and look around.

Reuel shook his head at them. "I am no expert in these matters, but I am fairly certain the five of you defeated one another in this particular battle. You are too battered now to try another assault. I would suggest that you fall back and consider another strategy."

Jared stared at him for a long moment, trying to wrap his mind around what Reuel had said. "What matters?" he asked finally.

Reuel shrugged and pushed away from the wall he'd been leaning against. "I have not figured that out yet. I thought, mayhap, that you had some idea of what your objective was … beyond beating your comrades into submission, that is."

Jared considered it for a few minutes after Reuel had left but finally decided that he was too tired to unravel the puzzle at the moment, if indeed there was any sense that could be made of it. Deciding he had rested long enough that he could get to his feet, he focused on that until he'd managed it. It seemed to him, however, that the moment he straightened every blow he'd caught from someone's fist began to pound more painfully. Dizziness swept over him, weakness he'd rarely felt. He paused until it began to pass and then looked around, trying to decide where he wanted to go and what he wanted to do.

He wanted to find Damon, beat the fuck out of him, and then fuck the hell out of Chloe, he thought almost instantly. It only took a few moments to assess his status, however, and make it abundantly clear that he wasn't presently in any condition to do either. Somewhat lower on the list of current desires was the urge to find something softer to land on than the floor if he happened to pass out.

He glanced around in search of a bed or a chair and realized he was still in the corridor … and there *still* wasn't a fucking bed handy. Sucking in a pained breath, he stepped over Sebastian's leg, paused to gather himself, and stepped over Lucien's foot and then Thor's head. Having successfully negotiated the minefield of body parts on the floor, he lifted his head to study the corridor. A round half dozen of Reuel's troops had moved to the door, apparently to watch the melee, and a couple of them still lingered.

Mess hall, he noted, summoning a map image of the ship's layout and discovering he was within twenty yards of the crew quarters. Another ten or fifteen feet beyond that, give or take, was the crew's latrine and bathing facilities. His cabin, if he could make it that far, was a good five yards beyond the showers.

He stopped to rest on one of the bunks in the crew quarters for a few minutes and then heaved himself up and made his way to the showers. Deciding that was far enough for the moment, he went inside, dragged his flight suit and boots off and stood under the water. The heat and pounding spray hurt like a son-of-a-bitch, pinpointing everything on his body that was raw, but also seemed to draw some of the pain out of his battered muscles. He decided to stay a little longer.

Kane and Sebastian arrived at the showers shortly behind him and then, a few minutes later, Thor and Lucien. He studied them broodingly, trying to decide if he felt like renewing the fight and finally decided he would wait a while after he tested his hands and saw he still couldn't make fists without a great effort.

He was too pissed off, still, to leave it at that completely. "What the fuck was that all about?" he growled at Kane.

Kane glared at him. "Why do you not explain what the fuck you were doing with Chloe?"

Jared thought about it. "I was kissing my woman, gods damn it!"

"That was not kissing," Kane shot back at him. "I do not know what you were doing, but I do know that there is nothing like that in the gods damned pleasure droid programming! And she is not *more* your gods damned woman than she is mine, so do not say that to me as if you have some claim upon her that I do not!"

Jared glared at him, trying to untangle the accusations. At the same time, he found himself struggling with the images flickering through his mind of what he *had* been doing and trying to fit them into any of the myriad of images from his sexdroid programming. It did not make him feel any better when he discovered Kane was right. It was not in the digital manual.

Then again, he could not recall that he had made any attempt to access the manual beyond trying to figure out how he was going to fuck her when he had no gods damned bed! *That* was essential, he knew—comfort and then pleasure. It occurred to him after a few moments that he had gotten his entire programming skewed. He should have gotten her into a bed *before* he had begun to kiss her.

"That is beside the point!" he said stiffly. "I was pleasuring her, gods damn it! *I* got her first! If you wanted to pleasure her, then you should have waited!"

"She *asked* you to pleasure her?" Kane demanded, disbelief evident in his voice.

Discomfort wafted through Jared when he recalled that she had not only not requested it, he did not have a fucking clue of whether or not he had *given* her any pleasure. He had been consumed with *taking* pleasure.

"I did not think so!" Kane growled with a touch of satisfaction and then added angrily, "She wanted that fucking fuck droid for that!"

Chapter Seven

Kane hated like hell to admit that, but there was no point in trying to deny it when Chloe had suggested as much herself. She had not said it outright, and he would have liked to think that that left room for doubt, but even if that had, her behavior once they had found the dick was difficult to ignore.

It pissed him off every time he recalled the way she had spoken to him, the way she had behaved. She had not behaved that way with him! No, and not Jared either, for all that the stupid fuck had gotten it into his head that she was his!

He was damned if he understood it. There was no logic to it that he could see. *He* had a dick, gods damn it! Jared had a cock if came to that! And they had been with her for many months. If she had wanted to fuck, he did not see why she had not mentioned it.

Of course, she did not know that they had the same programming that Damon the dick had. She had not known that until Jared had decided to tell her, but still .... She was always chattering about something when she was around them. Why not mention that?

It should have been on her mind, gods damn it! It had been on *his* mind even before he had fully recovered from his battle wounds and he had had a great deal of pain to distract him at least part of the time. Actually, he did not suppose that was completely accurate. He had wanted *something* of Chloe. He had not been entirely certain of what it was that he wanted beyond her attention, but he had wanted that.

And he had gotten that, although it had not entirely pleased him. *Then*, she had always looked ... disturbed when she looked at him. He had known that he looked like hell. He had thought, at first, that it was disgust and that had seemed reasonable even though he had not liked it. After a while, though, he had realized that she did not feel disgust of him. She felt shame each time she looked at him. He had thought he must be mistaken about that because it had not seemed logical, but he had finally decided from a few things she had said that she felt as if some part of the blame for his condition was hers because she was human and it was humans who had been responsible for the disaster.

That also did not seem logical, but he was fairly certain that that was a good part of it and he had already begun to realize that it was very hard to understand humans because their emotions were often so complicated. It was not that he was deficient in processing, or logic. It was that the emotions they felt were never one thing but many things—or at least Chloe's were.

He still had not entirely followed that line of thinking to completely understand it, but he was reasonably certain that he was right because she seemed to feel less guilty and less uncomfortable around him and Jared when they had recovered and did not look like they would expire. He was not certain he would have figured that out except that she had begun to smile. She still seemed a little uneasy when they were around. She still did not look directly at them very often, which was why he had decided that it was not that he was so ugly that she had not before—not entirely anyway.

He had finally decided that she was merely shy. She was not used to being around very many people and even though he was a cyborg and not a person, she did not seem to think there was a difference.

He thought that was one of the reasons he had wanted her to look at him, wanted her attention. She did not behave as if he was only a machine and she could not have been in doubt of it when his flesh had been torn away and exposed his chassis. She had felt badly when he was hurt and she smiled at him in greeting as if she was glad that he was there.

She had begun to behave very differently after her father was killed. She had wept inconsolably for so long that he'd begun to think that she would simply die from sorrow. He and Jared had fought over which of them should go to her and try to reason with her and he had lost. He had not felt the same stomach churning fear when he had been readying himself for battle that he had felt standing outside her door, listening to her, and trying to think what he might say that would dry up her tears. In the end, it had not seemed to take anything at all. When he had finally nerved himself to go inside, he had done nothing more than collapse weakly on the side of the bed and pat her heaving back a couple of times awkwardly. She had turned to look at him almost at once and then she had flung herself against his chest and wrapped her arms tightly around him. When he had asked why she was crying she had said it was because she was alone, she had no one. That had made his belly clench even harder, but it was not true and he told her that. She had him and Jared and they would never leave her.

He still thought that it was strange that he had had to tell her. She should have known that they would forever be loyal and grateful to her for saving them from Xeno-12, but apparently she had needed to hear it. Because afterwards, she had been almost as happy as she had been sad before. Not at once, but she had ceased to cry each night and she had begun to smile more and more often and after a while, to chatter at them.

It was about that time that he had realized exactly what it was that he wanted every time he looked at her. He was not certain *why* he had only to look at her to think of fucking, but there was no getting around that, no ignoring it, because each time he looked at her his cock would get hard and images would fill his mind of fucking her.

He did not suppose she would have any interest in it now—ever—although he had thought she might … eventually.

"She did not ask that fucking snake to fuck her either," Jared growled, interrupting his thoughts, "but I would not lay odds that that is not what he is doing right now!"

Indignation rolled through him. He discovered when he glanced at Jared that Sebastian, Lucien, and Thor were also looking indignant and for some reason that outraged him more. He scowled at them. "You have no reason to feel as if you have been fucked over! She is *our* woman!"

"Exactly how did you arrive at that conclusion?" Sebastian asked tightly. "I have not seen anything to indicate that *she* thinks so!"

Kane felt his face heat because he knew that that was true … in a sense. "We were here first!"

"That is only by default and it does not count. She collected you with the other salvage she and her father picked up on Xeno-12! She chose us."

Jared glared at him. "You are delusional! If we were chosen only by default because we were there, then the same is true of the three of you! She did not go there to get you! She went to collect that fucking fuck droid!"

A look of triumph entered Sebastian's eyes that made Jared want to smash his face all over again. "Which means that she is no more yours than ours!"

"Which also means that there is no reason for us to fight among ourselves," Lucien said irritably. "As Reuel pointed out, *we* were busy distracting one another while that fucking fuck droid walked off with her! And that is what he will *continue* to do if we continue to focus on one another instead of her!"

Jared stared at him blankly for a long moment and then frowned thoughtfully. Shutting off the water, he picked up the flight suit he had discarded, discovered that it was far too soiled with dirt and blood to put on again, and pitched it toward the recycler. He moved into the dryer but discovered he did not really feel like standing in it long enough for it to dry him. Emerging again, still dripping, he stalked from the shower room and headed to his cabin.

He heard faint sounds emanating from Chloe's cabin. He had no trouble interpreting them and it infuriated him. For a handful of moments, he toyed with the idea of stalking into her cabin and dragging Damon off of her, but he finally discarded it. Violence seemed to distress Chloe, particularly violence aimed at the fuck droid. He could always beat the fuck out of him later—when he felt more up to it.

* * * *

Chloe had spent so many long nights alone in her bed, unable to sleep, and thinking of Damon that she couldn't help but think that it was vastly unfair that she was so distressed now that she could scarcely focus on the things that he was doing—the things she had longed for him to do. Either he didn't notice the stiff unresponsiveness due to Chloe's sense of guilt, however, or he decided to ignore it. He continued to stroke her and place light, nibbling kisses along her neck and shoulder as he held her.

Chloe was inclined to think he simply didn't notice. He was a pleasure droid, after all, designed specifically to know how to arouse a woman—any woman—to fever pitch and give her pleasure such as she never had or ever would experience anywhere else, with anyone else.

She knew she wasn't special to him. How could she be? It hadn't mattered before, though. He was special to her. He had been her first—actually her only. In spite of the fact that she'd felt awkward, uncomfortable, unattractive and fearful of the pain associated with losing one's virginity, he'd taken her to a state of true beauty and then beyond that to true passion. He had made her feel loved, desired, beautiful. She had missed that, she thought, more even than she'd missed the passion he'd shown her. She'd wanted that more than anything.

She *knew* that it was unhealthy, that everyone would think her certifiable if they knew, but she'd fallen madly in love with him.

A sex machine.

It was a little weird, actually, that it had taken another machine to make her see that, to make her feel like a complete fool.

Was it weirder that she felt that way because she felt so guilty about *thinking* about having sex with Damon when she had just been with Jared and he had seemed to need her so badly? Her throat closed at the thought. She didn't know why he suddenly didn't want to be her friend anymore. She couldn't think of anything that she'd done to make him feel that way.

Unless he was angry about Damon?

She was pretty sure he was. She just wasn't certain if it was because she had done something so stupid and dangerous, or because she had risked *them* to rescue Damon, or if it was just Damon himself that pissed him off.

Apparently Damon tired of nibbling on her neck—either that or he finally decided it wasn't really working. He turned, laying her back against the mattress and then settled beside her.

Instead of resuming his efforts to seduce her, however, he propped on one arm and settled his jaw against his fist, studying her speculatively. She stared back at him uneasily, wondering why it was that he seemed ... different. *Was* he different? Or was it her that had changed?

"You are distressed," he said finally, a statement rather than a question.

She looked at him a little reproachfully. "Of course I'm upset! They were fighting! They're going to hurt each other."

"They are cyborgs."

Chloe felt heat flash in her face.

"As I am. I will not say they cannot be damaged, but they are unlikely to go to the extreme of damaging one another to the point that they are useless to you."

Chloe gasped at that. "I'm not worried about them being useless! Well, I am, but not the way you mean!"

"You are not concerned about their usefulness."

Chloe frowned, uncertain of what he was getting at. "I'm worried about *them*."

"Now, I am curious."

"About what?"

"You paid a very great deal for me. You went to great lengths to extract me before I could be shipped to the company for destruction. And yet, you do not seem to have any interest in my skills as a lover now that the opportunity to make use of me has finally arisen. I had naturally assumed that that was why you had come for me."

There was an edge to his voice, but then that was hardly surprising when he was so thoroughly pissed off. The wonder was that he had managed to say anything at all without sounding as furious as he was ... not that he had *not* managed it without giving any of his anger away.

She flicked a look at him, met his gaze for no more than a fraction of a second, and then looked away again. He felt his chest tighten in reaction to that look even before his mind told him what he had seen.

Hurt.

His anger shifted focus, or mayhap simply lost focus altogether. *He* was hurt, gods damn it! But could she see that? No! She was too busy worrying about that fucking caveman Jared! *All* the fucking more-muscle-than-brain, backwards sons-of-bitches!

He had tried to convince himself that he was merely disappointed, that he was not surprised that she felt nothing. He was a pleasure droid. She was human. There was no reason why it would have meant a gods damned thing to her! He was lucky that she even recalled him at all, had considered it worth while to snatch him up before he could be melted down by the fucking company!

He did not *feel* fortunate, however! He felt ... cheated! Used. Discarded.

Fucking horny!

He rolled away from her and lay staring at the ceiling, wondering if she would simply dismiss him since she obviously had no interest in him.

He did not think it would have twisted him up so much inside if he had not felt hope when she came for him, if he had not believed he saw ... caring in her eyes. He had not dared to believe, before that, that she might.

He had done his best to put her from his mind. It should have been no problem when he had a veritable stream of women through his quarters every night of the week, every week of the year, every year since she had come to him and then had passed out of his life. And yet he had not been able to. His life had become a nightmare to him after the knowing had come upon him—because there was not a gods damned thing that he could think to do except to try to hide what he had become. It had not taken much thought at all to realize that no one would be pleased at the change in him, that they would feel threatened by it and humans who felt threatened had one solution—kill it.

His cock was no longer his to command, however. He could not simply make the gods damned thing stand up whenever he needed it. Thankfully, his body's needs had not changed that greatly. He rarely had a problem making the gods damned thing work. It was those rare occasions when it had not that had been a nightmare, however.

The fear of discovery had certainly not helped matters when he was already having trouble.

He would have left the brothel and searched for Chloe if he had had any idea whatsoever of how to find her—any idea at all of even where he might go that he would not be hunted down and destroyed ... or forced to kill to survive.

He had despaired of ever seeing her again and then, in his darkest hour, when he had thought he had come to the end, she had come.

And he, stupid fuck that he was, had immediately thought that it was because she cared for him—at least a little. She had *seemed* to, gods damn it!

Right up until she had begun to behave as if he was a feeble minded child and made it clear that she only thought of him as a pleasure droid.

Jared did not want to kill him half as badly as he wanted to kill Jared!

Chloe stirred beside him, drawing him from his thoughts. To his surprise, she turned over and settled her hand on his chest. He tensed, hardly daring to breathe for fear that she would change her mind.

He did not give a gods damned if she only wanted to fuck! *He* wanted it! He had not been able to think of much else since he had found her again—since she had found him.

"Was it very hard?"

The question scattered his wits. His mind connected his own thoughts instantly with the question and he wrestled with the temptation to inform her that it had been steel hard until she had brushed his caresses off as if they were annoying her. "What?" he croaked finally.

"Awareness."

He sent her a startled glance. He couldn't quite interpret the look in her eyes, though. Did she believe? Or was she merely pandering to what she thought of as his dementia? "It was ... a nightmare. I cannot speak for anyone else, but it was like that for me."

She leaned down and brushed her lips along his chest and his cock instantly sprang to attention. "How?"

He swallowed a little convulsively. "I could not feel my body ... at first. It was almost like waking in someone else's body."

She sat up and stared down at him. He had no trouble interpreting her expression that time, unfortunately. The pity in her eyes was enough to deflate his cock as quickly as the gods damned thing had risen.

Or mayhap it was merely the memory?

He did not like to think about it.

She lifted her hand, but instead of moving away, she lightly ran her fingers along his chest and torso. "And now?"

He swallowed with an effort. "I feel more than I ever did before."

She settled her head on his shoulder. "Make love to me like you did the first time."

He turned to her, searching her face. It was a test, he realized, feeling his hopefulness plummet again. With an effort he tamped it. He recalled every moment. If she did not think he did, then she was mistaken. He smiled faintly. "You undressed when you came in the room."

"And you were already naked," she said, smiling back at him.

He sat up abruptly and began to strip off his suit and boots. Chloe got up and moved across the room from him, waiting, watching him, and the uneasiness flitted through his mind that she did not mean to allow him to touch her, that she was only testing him to see if he recalled.

He settled back against the bed when he had shed his clothing, studying her. She stared back at him, wide-eyed, nervous as she had been then. "Is this your first time, dearling?"

She blushed ... just as she had the first time. Looking down, she grasped the front opening of her suit and began to pull at it awkwardly, struggling because her hands were shaking. He watched her hungrily, wondering if she was deliberately reenacting that time or if she actually was nervous.

She looked scared when she finally lifted her head. "It's my second time."

Damon felt his chest tighten. "I cannot love you from over there, sweeting."

There was awkwardness in her movements as she crossed the room and settled next to him, not the lack of grace, but a lack of confidence, anxiety, and even a little eagerness. He stroked her face lightly, remembering it with his fingertips. "You are more beautiful to me each time I see you."

She smiled a little wryly. "You didn't say that before."

He chuckled, dipping low to pluck at her lips. "I could not say that when I had only just met you, sweeting. What did I say?"

He heard her swallow. "That I was beautiful."

He smiled faintly against her lips. "I did not. I said that you were the most beautiful woman I had ever seen."

She tried to pull away to look at him, but he slipped his fingers from her cheek to the back of her head and held her for his kiss. She yielded to him readily, not warily or gracelessly as she had before, but eagerly, with the certainty of experience. He almost thought he might have retained some control if she had displayed any of the hesitancy of before.

Then again, mayhap not. He struggled with his own eagerness, but he shook with the effort to hold himself back even a little. He tried to summon the finesse of his vast knowledge and experience and found his mind empty of everything but hunger. He wanted to savor as he built her ardor slowly, but found himself yielding to the driving need to consume her all at once, to fill his senses with her.

He didn't hesitate when she spread her thighs for him in welcome. He did not tease her until she was pulling at him in demand. He found he could not align his body with hers fast enough to suit him, began to struggle to claim her the moment he had found her sweet spot. She gasped, arched against him as he fought his way inside her clinging flesh and alarm went through him. Gasping for breath, he jerked his head upward to see if he had hurt her, but the anguish on her face was the same he wore and had to fight a round with his body's determination to come at once.

He shook with the effort until he had to grit his teeth together to keep them from rattling. He managed to command his will, thrusting into her and out again in a slow cadence, until she arched again, began to utter breathless little cries of ecstasy, until he felt her inner muscles quake around him. He gave up the effort then, angry with himself that he could not hold out longer and bring her to another peak, but cognizant of defeat.

It was a glorious defeat. He thought for many moments that his heart would stop, felt as if he was being turned inside out, and when his body finally ceased to convulse in pleasure, he was so weak he felt as if he was sinking toward death—and welcomed it. Panting, he struggled to tip himself off of her. Relief flooded him that he'd managed to fall on the bed instead of her. He groped for her blindly, dragged her across his chest, and passed out.

* * * *

Chloe lifted her head after a bit and stared at Damon's face sleepily. Surprise flickered through her briefly when she discovered that he seemed to be asleep. After struggling with it for a few moments, though, she finally dismissed it. She was too weary herself, she decided, to figure it out at the moment. Snuggling more comfortably, she felt around for the cover, managed to tug it out from under his hip and pulled it over both of them.

She discovered she didn't sleep particularly well with Damon in her bed. It wasn't an especially happy discovery, particularly when it was a fantasy she had long held dear—imagining how nice it would be to have him to cuddle with her while they slept.

The problem was, he was as hard as a fucking rock and weighed a ton, besides taking up most of the bed. Giving up when she decided she must have lain in the bed at least trying to sleep for a full sleep cycle, or most of one, she got up and looked around for something to wear.

She was still more than half asleep as she headed down the corridor to the shower room, however, and not in the best of moods because she was *still* tired.

She supposed, later, that if she hadn't been in such a foul mood she might have thought twice about taking on a cyborg—female or not. Unfortunately, at the time, it seemed like the right thing to do.

Chapter Eight

There was a veritable wall of naked flesh in the showers, so much that it was a shock to Chloe's already beleaguered senses. She halted abruptly and gaped, unable for many moments even to grasp where all the naked people had come from. Slowly, her mind picked up and began to work again and it dawned on her that it was her 'guests'.

They'd noticed her while she was still trying to jumpstart her brain. That realization made her freeze in the act of retreat and assess the situation. She wanted a bath. The showers were full. Wait for an opening and pretend nonchalance since that seemed to be the 'order' of things? Or retreat and come back later?

She really wanted to retreat, but she didn't want to *look* like she was retreating.

One of the cyborgs vacated a shower while she was still debating and she surged forward in relief. From out of nowhere, one of the female cyborgs stalked past her, headed for the same shower.

"Wait a minute! That's mine."

The woman halted and turned to look at her and Chloe instantly recognized her as the heckler from the discussion the day before. "First come, first serve," she retorted.

"Exactly! And I was next!" Chloe said tightly, uncomfortable about having to exert her rights and beginning to be angry both because the woman had broke in front of her and because it felt like bad manners not to give up the shower to a guest.

"You seemed more interested in staring at the men than taking a shower," the woman said nastily.

Chloe felt her face redden, but her temper rose another notch. She narrowed her eyes at the woman. "Let me put it this way. I'm the captain of this ship and it's my god damned ship! Now, get your ass to the back of the line."

The woman tensed as if she fully intended to attack. As she flicked a gaze over Chloe's head, though, she froze. There was something about her posture that made Chloe glance around even though she strongly suspected it was an effort to sucker punch her.

She discovered it wasn't and relief filled her when she saw that Kane, Jared, Sebastian, Lucien, and Thor had come to stand around her almost like a wall.

"You are brave with your watchdogs at your back," the woman spat.

That really pissed Chloe off. "They aren't dogs, bitch! Is that your problem? They aren't interested?"

For a moment, she looked like she might attack regardless of Chloe's 'guard'. A hand abruptly clamped on her arm, however. She whirled to attack and froze. Reuel's face, Chloe saw, was hard and deadly. "You forget yourself, Salina. *Captain* Chloe is the highest ranking officer aboard this ship. Mason, Kyle—escort Salina to the brig. She is confined until further notice for misconduct and disrespect of an officer."

Chloe relaxed when Salina had been escorted out.

Reuel saluted. "My apologies, Captain Chloe. I assure you nothing like this will happen again." He turned from her and scanned the other cyborgs as he voiced the last remark.

Chloe nodded. "Thank you. I'd like to discuss the problem on the bridge when I've had time to shower and dress."

He nodded, turned, and left. Feeling abruptly shaky, Chloe threw a smile of appreciation at her crew and headed for the shower. "Thanks for watching my back, guys!"

Kane leaned a shoulder against the wall near the shower when she turned it on and stepped into the water. "You cannot hold your own against a cyborg, Chloe," he said, his voice pitched low.

She threw a glance at him. "I'm not terribly alert this morning, but that did occur to me," she retorted dryly. "Do you think it would've worked better if I'd let her run over me? Maybe I should've just pretended I wasn't heading for this shower when she ran around me to take it?"

His lips tightened. "You are right. You had to exert your authority. Trading insults might not have been the best way to handle it, however."

Chloe flushed, but she shrugged. "She insulted me first—twice! It isn't like I didn't try to keep it on a professional level."

"She was attempting to goad you into a fight."

"Duh!" Chloe said irritably. "How dumb do you think I am? I may still be more asleep than awake—at least I was—but I caught that right away. In fact, I caught it yesterday when they arrived. It isn't like I've never had any experience with bullies, you know. I was twelve when mom was killed. I got the chance to deal with and see plenty of bullies in action."

"I am only saying that you will need to watch your back at any time that one or more of your 'watchdogs' are not nearby."

Chloe felt her anger rise again. "Fucking bitch! It was bad enough she insulted me. It was completely uncalled for to insult you guys."

Kane was silent for several moments. "I do not understand your reasoning. You are saying you understand why she tried to provoke a fight with you?"

Chloe rolled her eyes. "I'm going to guess that it's the fact that I'm human and also a woman. That's two reasons for her not to like me."

"That is not a reason," Kane said tightly. "It is not reasonable at all."

"Of course it is," Chloe said, shutting the shower off and turning to look at him. "All of you have every reason to consider humans your enemies. It's not exactly just when we aren't, but you've learned to be wary and distrustful and you have to be to protect yourself. I understand that. The problem with that is that when you expect a person to be your enemy and treat them that way, then you make an enemy of someone who might have been a friend."

He frowned. "And you will begin to see cyborgs as enemies because that one has shown herself not to be a friend?"

She glanced around and discovered that Jared had disappeared, although the others had stayed. Unhappiness made her throat tight, but she didn't want to dwell on their misunderstanding at the moment. "I trust you ... and Jared." She looked at the newest members of her crew. "I've seen no reason not to trust any of you guys ... and I like you. I want ... I hope we'll be friends. Her, I don't trust, but that isn't going to change the way I feel about you guys."

She supposed it would've been more accurate to say that she was open to friendship with anyone and more inclined to like the men she'd picked up with Damon because Jared and Kane seemed to have accepted them and she trusted their judgment. By the same token, although Jared and Kane seemed to have a great deal of respect for Reuel, the bad vibes she was getting from Salina were beginning to make her wonder if she'd made a mistake in offering hospitality to Reuel and his group. To an extent, she liked Reuel. He was intimidating, but he was also courteous and friendly. She hadn't felt any sense of threat from him. She just didn't know how much faith she could place in his ability to control the people under him.

She could see that he was angry and uncomfortable when she met him on the bridge deck. *She* was unnerved and uncomfortable and she hated having to start a conversation that had the potential of escalating into a confrontation, but she didn't think she wanted to hide her eyes and hope for the best. Even if she could completely trust the new men who'd joined her crew, that only made seven against three times that number. She didn't like the odds.

"Are we going to have a problem?" she asked, trying to keep her voice neutral.

Reuel's lips tightened. "I had feared that you would interpret Salina's behavior that way. I would have prevented it if I could have. We ... need your friendship."

She gestured for him to take a seat. She didn't want to have to crane her neck to talk to him. "The question is, when you don't need it anymore, what then?"

Anger flickered in his eyes. He tamped it. "We want your friendship—true friendship."

Chloe relaxed fractionally. "Do all of them hate humans?" she asked unhappily. "Will I not be welcome if I do find this world you hope to colonize? I want you to know that I *will* try regardless—for your sake—and for theirs, even if they don't like me, because I think it's the right thing to do. I think that it would be much better for everyone—humans and cyborgs. But ... I'd hoped to find a place there for myself. I guess what I'm asking you to tell me, up front, is if you think it could work. I don't expect everyone to like me. I don't expect everyone to want to be my friend, but I'd hate it if I had to live with people that hated me—for no other reason than because I'm not the same."

Reuel frowned thoughtfully. "I could not say for certain, but I do not believe that any of them are inclined to despise humans. If we were, then we would be more willing to stay and fight than to leave and search for peace. You should not judge all of us from her behavior. And you should know that your own men are intensely loyal to you."

Chloe frowned. "I don't doubt them. I'd trust Jared and Kane with my life—I have, and I trust their judgment. They would've told me if they had doubts about any of the new crewmembers."

Amusement flickered in his eyes. "They are not particularly fond of Damon."

Chloe felt her face redden. "Yes, but I knew Damon before. I don't need them to vouch for him."

He studied her thoughtfully. "If I may address you as a ship's officer?"

Chloe blinked at him in surprise. "You weren't?"

He smiled faintly. "The discussion was friend to friend."

"But you want to discuss something officer to officer?"

"You are not military and never were. However, you have lived in deep space much of your life. You are aware of the Maritime Sex Act?"

Chloe felt her jaw go slack and color rise in her cheeks. "Oh! *Ooooh*! What you're saying is ... uh ... you're saying ...."

He chuckled. "That is what I am saying. They have ...." He

paused. "*We* have been fighting a running battle since we left the battlefield on Xeno-12. There has been little time for any of us to ... uh ... attend certain needs."

Chloe frowned. "But ...."

"We are cyborgs."

The color that had barely left her face flashed again. She cleared her throat, trying to think of a polite way to voice her doubts.

"You have a great capacity for empathy," Reuel said almost gently, "but although you hate what has been done, you do not truly believe that we are as we believe we are?"

"I believe you believe."

He chuckled wryly. "I will not try to convince you. If you are laboring under the belief that we are delusional, then it is unlikely that I can convince you otherwise. Instead, try to understand this—that our delusion has led us to a point where we believe that we have the same needs as humans. As unflattering as it may be to us, imagine us as having reached puberty—the point where our bodies are raging with hormones and we spend a very great deal of time battling them and the urges that come with them."

Chloe gaped at him. "*Oh my god!* You mean to say I could get pregnant?" She frowned, considering that, scarcely aware of the startled look Reuel had sent her. "I guess we might not be compatible that way, huh?"

After studying the strange look on his face for several moments, it occurred to her that puberty for males wasn't exactly the same as it was for girls. It embarrassed her when she realized that—not that she knew anything about males going through puberty except that they seemed absolutely focused on sex. "Sorry! I was just thinking about when I went through puberty. Honestly, I know it isn't the same for boys as it is girls. I just wasn't thinking.

"So, what you're saying is that maybe Salina's behavior is sort of tied to that rather than a particular dislike of me or even humans in general?"

He seemed to have trouble focusing on what she'd asked. He frowned for several moments, as if he was searching for the thread of the conversation. "Possibly. I certainly felt that the exhibition I watched between your crewmembers last eve might have more to do with sexual frustration and raging hormones than anything specific. There have been outbreaks among our own ranks. Since I am not immune to the ... delusion myself, it is easier for me to understand.

"I do not know that it would resolve all of the problems or even any of the problems to place the Maritime Sex Act into effect aboard the

Salvager Omega-3. I am only suggesting that it may. Morale is low and tempers high. I think it might be easier to deal with if there were *no* females aboard rather than the handful who are."

Chloe was so focused on what he'd said about her crew that she hardly noticed when he stopped speaking. She wasn't certain of how she felt about it until she thought about the cyborg females accommodating all of them and then her doubts fled. If they needed relief, by god, *she* could take care of it!

She didn't know why neither Jared nor Kane had mentioned it! But it certainly made sense once Reuel had pointed it out. Even her father and the human male crew they'd once had had taken to snarling and biting at each other when they would be out for months at the time, and her father would guard her like a watchdog! She'd *wondered* why they hit a port every few months when it took a good six months to fill the hold!

That was what that bitch had meant!

Jeez! They were best friends! It seemed to her that Jared and Kane would've felt comfortable enough with her to at least *hint* at it!

Although ... she supposed that kiss the night before should have given her a clue! Instead, dolt that she was, she'd instantly decided that he liked her more than she'd realized!

So much for feeling guilty about having sex with Damon! Really! She supposed she was the pot calling the kettle black to suggest that *they* were delusional when she was so thoroughly confused about her feelings!

"Ok. How should we handle this?"

Reuel stared at her blankly as if he hadn't expected her to agree to it at all.

"I mean, I completely see your point. I'm just so dense I hadn't thought about it, but my own crew has been antsy. Clearly a little therapeutic sex is essential here ... especially when we're probably going to be bouncing around space for months looking for this planet. We need to keep some sort of order here, though. As you said—no more than a handful of females and there are a lot of men on this ship now!" She frowned. "I don't suppose any of the men like men? That would even things up a bit."

Reuel reddened. "I am as certain as I can be that that is *not* the case ... with any of them."

"Hmm! Well, you'll have to speak to them. I can't handle that. And we can't have orgies in the corridors. They'll just have to take a number or something and it'll have to be restricted to off duty. And they can't tie up all of the women's off duty time. Although I suppose the pleasure droids you have with you don't actually have other duties? If they were working full time and we figured on an eight hour shift— Do you think half an hour would do it?"

Reuel looked like he couldn't decide whether to laugh or if he was merely horrified or fascinated by the way her mind worked. He cleared his throat. "Actually, if we are to do this properly, I think that they would want several hours," he said meekly.

"That much?" Chloe asked, surprised. "But it doesn't take that long, you know, really."

"They might need to work up to it," he said, his voice shaking slightly.

"Well, they can't be that bad off if they have to work up to it!"

"Nevertheless . . . ."

"Ok, fine! But at that rate it could take weeks to get through. And Salina's in the brig, so that cuts out one female—unless—Well, I don't see why she can't do her part even if she is restricted to the brig. In fact, maybe it'll give her a better outlook. The one she has is shit!"

"Oooh! You're talking about if they don't especially like the female?"

Reuel blinked at her. "What?"

"You said they might need to work up to it. You meant if they don't especially like the female? Maybe we shouldn't assign them? Just sort of let them pick and that would make them feel better, I imagine. Not that they have a lot of choices, but . . . Never mind. I think you're going to have to work that out, too. I don't know about guys. I wouldn't think they'd be too particular if they just need the sexual relief, but . . . ."

Reuel studied her curiously. "Somehow, I had the feeling that you would completely reject the idea."

"Really? Why?"

He seemed to struggle with his thoughts. "You are not very experienced. And we are cyborgs."

"Oh. You can tell?"

He smiled at her and Chloe noticed for the first time that he was an extremely attractive man. She didn't know why she hadn't noticed before unless it was just because he unnerved the hell out of her. "Let us say I guessed." He hesitated. "You have no prejudice against cyborgs?"

She blinked at him. "In what way?"

He chuckled. "Sexually."

"Oh! Well, I've only ever had sex with cyborgs . . . uh . . . Damon. But it isn't like I don't know these things, you know. A person can know a lot without having actual experience. And to be honest, it makes me feel so much better to think that it isn't me, that they just have needs and ... I didn't understand why Jared was so angry with me. I feel so badly that I didn't realize what the problem was. I mean, really! He's my best friend ... and Kane. If they'd just told me, I would've been happy to help out!"

He shook his head at her. "I think you are almost as confused as we are, but I am glad that we have found a friend."

He got up decisively. "I have not even had breakfast. Will you join me?"

"I'd love to! I am *so* starving! I didn't realize that was why I felt like hell. Of course, I didn't sleep very well last night. I'm not at all used to having anyone else in my bed."

He chuckled again and it hit her abruptly that it was a sound she rarely heard—had not heard at all aboard ship since her father's death except the echo of her own. She frowned, realizing that Jared and Kane rarely even smiled and they certainly hadn't in the beginning. Of course, they'd had no reason to. It had taken them a long time to recover from their stint on Xeno-12. If she'd had any doubts before of just how awful it had been for her, the battle they'd had with the other salvagers was proof in itself. They'd hardly been injured at all in that fight where her father had lost his life or the fight in the jail with the rangers.

She hadn't really seen any of the other cyborgs smiling either, and certainly not laughing. Of course, they hadn't been onboard long at all, but they hadn't been on duty the entire time. It seemed that they would've relaxed and joked among themselves.

Reuel was almost like a law unto himself. Damon smiled and even chuckled, but she knew that was his social programming. None of those designed and sold as soldiers did—because it wasn't actually necessary. Maybe it wasn't even desirable for them to be anything but formidable?

And yet, Reuel did. How had he become different if she discounted his claim that he'd changed?

Was it even possible that they could? She hadn't thought so, but then she was no scientist. She'd studied—to suit herself. Her father hadn't seemed to care how much education she had. Although he'd taken a stab at being a parent and sent her to study school work on the computer from time to time, he hadn't been interested enough to see what she was studying. Mostly, she'd simply entertained herself and very little about science entertained her. She'd learned a little about human biology and sexuality out of curiosity because she'd just begun to be really interested in both when her father had collected her, but she certainly didn't know enough to figure out what might be going on with the cyborgs and she didn't know much of anything about robotics.

She did know that cyborgs were partly bio-engineering and partly robotics. She'd learned what she could about it after Damon—because she'd wanted to know about *him*. All she'd really discovered, though, was that the company kept the exact information about them a secret. Supposedly, by law, they were not allowed to use even fifty percent biological materials in their design because that was the legal definition of human … or at least biological entity.

She'd gotten the impression, though, that they only had what was necessary to support the 'life' of the flesh used to make them 'life-like' and everything else was robotic. That would have to include a certain amount of actual brain since the brain controlled the involuntary functions and they had to have at least rudimentary organs to 'feed' the flesh.

It gave her a headache trying to figure out how they could possibly have gotten from part human to a sentient being. Of course, their biological part wasn't exactly human even if it had begun that way. The scientists had had to make them 'super' human in order to make it possible for the muscles to support their much heavier inner structure.

Maybe that had something to do with it? It wasn't as if it would be the first time that scientists had developed something they didn't fully understand and then discovered that it did something completely unexpected. Probably half of the things that had been discovered were discovered in just that way—by accident when they were trying to do something else.

So, maybe the company wasn't desperate to get hold of the cyborgs and destroy them because they were 'crazy' but because they had figured out that the cyborgs weren't what they had originally begun as? Weren't merely machines anymore?

It still seemed impossible to her that they'd taken such a leap, but that was because she didn't know exactly what it was that the scientists at Robotics Inc. had done. Maybe something they'd included to make them 'super' had run amuck? Maybe the nanos they'd put in them to 'heal' them, repair them, had run amuck and 'fixed' everything that they decided needed fixing?

Creepy, dangerous little bastards, nanos. It was concerns over controlling the damned things that was the reason they weren't used in people, but there weren't any laws to prevent them from using them in the cyborgs.

She discovered when they finally reached the mess hall that her fears of missing breakfast were unfounded. It looked like most of the cyborgs were nearly finished but, at a glance, it seemed that most of them were still there.

Her crew was at the same table they'd shared the night before. They looked like they were at a funeral, though, and she decided she'd made the right decision—the only reasonable decision she could've made when she'd agreed with Reuel. They were in serious need of a morale boost!

Of course, she'd had a fight with Jared the night before. She wasn't surprised that he still looked like a thundercloud—a fairly battered thundercloud. She winced inwardly when she noticed the evidence of his brawl the night before. Kane didn't look much better and she felt guilty that she hadn't even really noticed it when he'd talked to her in the shower room.

Actually, with the exception of Damon, they all looked like hell. She supposed that was reason enough to be glum. They probably felt like hell, too.

What she didn't understand was why Damon looked as tense, angry, and downright depressed as the others. It seemed to her that he should be downright chipper, damn it!

It didn't make her feel any better when she'd thought it over because the only reason she could think of for him to look like that was that she hadn't done him any good.

Maybe it wasn't such a good idea for her to take part in the sex therapy, she thought uneasily? She'd thought she'd done everything right, but even Reuel seemed to realize she didn't know a hell of a lot about it.

Frowning when she'd collected a tray and drink, she settled at the table with them and focused on trying to fill the hollow in the pit of her stomach.

Chapter Nine

Chloe hadn't even managed to choke down half of her breakfast when Reuel rose and addressed the crewmembers still in the mess hall—which was most of them.

"I have conferred with Captain Chloe and we are in complete agreement that it has become necessary to place the Maritime Sex Act into effect, effective immediately. I will meet with the females directly after morning mess in the crew quarters to discuss the situation and address any concerns or complaints regarding the order.

"I will expect all males to meet with me here in the mess hall after the evening meal in regards to the limitations and parameters that we will implement."

If she'd thought for *one* minute he intended to make the damn announcement, at breakfast, with her sitting at the god damned table, there was no way in hell she would have agreed to implement the damned sex act! She thought for several moments that she was going to loose the food she'd just managed to swallow and she could feel her face flashing first red and then white as if she was sending out signals. Clearing her throat uncomfortably, she flicked an uneasy glance at her crewmen and discovered that every eye at the table was on her. The urge to do something childish—like leap up and run or cover her face and slide under the table was so overwhelming that it was all she could do even to try to act *slightly* nonchalant about the damned announcement.

Dead silence greeted the announcement and Chloe wasn't certain what to make of that, but after several moments, the men—her men— got up and left. It seemed to cause a general exodus. All of the other men got up and left, as well.

The only indication that she could see that they'd been affected in any way by Reuel's statement was that they left, for once, without returning their trays to the kitchen.

Reuel frowned when he'd looked around the mess hall. Excusing himself, he left behind the other men. A few minutes later, the men returned, picked up their trays and headed to the deposit bin with them.

Chloe waited until the silence in the corridor convinced her everyone had left the area and finally got up and disposed on her own tray. She'd made it all the way to the bridge before it dawned on her that Reuel had called a meeting of the women in the crew quarters. She hesitated. She didn't actually think that applied to her since she had discussed the matter with him beforehand—with enthusiasm born of sheer stupidity! She finally decided, though, that she needed to talk to Reuel before he settled the matter entirely.

The expressions on the women's faces when she joined them were entirely neutral, which was why she decided that they were feeling a great deal of hostility toward her. She wasn't certain if it was because they'd already heard that Salina had ended up in the brig after their confrontation or it was because they held her responsible for the order, but she straightened her spine and joined them.

Reuel looked surprised that she had, which made her wonder if, maybe, she should've waited until another time to speak to him, but she didn't think she could focus on anything else until she'd spoken with him.

He resumed his discussion after she'd settled. "There is no part of the order that requires females to participate if they are unwilling. However, if you do agree to participate, you will be expected to behave impartially. It will only create more problems than it might solve if you are selective in such a way that only a fraction of the crew is serviced. Allowance will be made for personal preferences on both sides—with the males as well as you, but I will be monitoring and if a male is turned away for any reason by one, then one of the others will be expected to accept him.

"If we are to divide this duty roughly evenly, then you will need to entertain a male nightly with one or two days of no duties per week. This only applies, however, if all of you are willing. In the event any of you decline, then that will have to be worked out in a different manner."

He turned and smiled at Chloe. "The captain has graciously agreed that, since this is a health and morale issue, she will participate."

Chloe chewed her lower lip when the other women turned to look at her, but she wanted to speak to Reuel privately and, in any case, she didn't think it would be a good thing to make a liar out of him in front of his people.

The women volunteered. It wasn't until they had that it dawned on Chloe that he'd had any doubts that they would. She realized that when he relaxed.

Somehow that made it worse. She hated to disappoint him, especially when she'd been so enthusiastic before!

"Very good! We will make up … uh … dance cards for you ladies and post them for your partners to sign up. I think, mayhap, it will be a good idea to make up new cards weekly."

Chloe gaped at him. "Weekly?" she asked in a strangled voice.

Something flickered in his eyes. "Yes. In the event that either the females or the males decide they are incompatible and wish to change. It will be less ... uncomfortable for both parties."

He turned to her when the other women had left. "You are having second thoughts, yes?"

Chloe felt her face redden. She squirmed in her seat. "It's just ... well, I got to thinking about what you said about it being noticeable that I hadn't had a lot of experience—not that I haven't figured most of it out, mind you! The thing is, I ... uh ... well, you know it's a little different for me. I didn't get any programming."

Amusement flickered in his eyes. "Experience is the best teacher."

She cleared her throat. "I might need instructions. I think, maybe, I don't perfectly understand this ... uh ... process."

He stared at her blankly. "Why ever would you think that?"

She frowned. "Well, you did say that it would improve morale, right? I mean, if it improved morale they wouldn't be ... grouchy."

"Theoretically," he said wryly. "I did point out that I *thought* that it was the root of the behavioral ... excesses."

Chloe relaxed fractionally. "So it might not help at all?"

"Oh, I think it will be a great deal of help. I just do not believe that it is a cure-all."

"So—if it doesn't help it doesn't necessarily mean ... uh ... that somebody isn't very good at it?"

"If you achieve orgasm, it is good. Sometimes, it is very good, but it is never bad."

"How can you tell?"

He stared at her blankly. "Tell what?"

"Orgasm. How can you tell if the other person ... got there?"

Reuel's face darkened. He seemed to think it over. "If they are very relaxed directly afterwards, then you have achieved the goal. If they are very tense afterwards, then the objective was not achieved."

Chloe felt a lot better hearing that. "So, if they go to sleep ...?"

He grinned. "They are *very* relaxed."

Pleasure filled her for a handful of moments and vast relief. "But .... Never mind!" She got up. "Alright. I'm going to go to my room and study up. You can put a dance card up for me, too."

"Uh ... Chloe?"

She stopped and turned to look at him questioningly.

"I think we should decide, first, where would be the best place to supply the ship."

"Oh! Shit! I forgot all about that. You're right. Let's go to the bridge and have a look at the star charts."

The brawl on B deck outside of the mess hall that evening lasted until most of the deck was trashed and most of the men were too exhausted to walk away from it. Infuriated, Reuel tore the dance cards off the wall and met with Chloe again for a consultation.

"I feel we are getting close to a solution to the dilemma," he said wryly.

Chloe was alarmed herself. She didn't see how Reuel could be so calm about it. "They've trashed B deck!"

"Mmm," Reuel agreed, surveying the damage himself the following morning. "I believe I should not have posted the dance cards outside of the mess hall. We will be eating on the floor until the tables and chairs can be repaired."

"*If* they can be repaired!" Chloe said in dismay. "They were old to start with. They haven't been used since Pops bought the ship."

"They will be repaired," Reuel said grimly. "The entire deck will be repaired—and very quickly I am guessing once I announce that no sexual therapy will be issued until it *is* repaired!"

Chloe frowned. "Any idea what touched it off?"

Reuel thought it over. "It may have been the impression that the order the name was listed was also the order of service."

"Oh. Well we can solve that! Just tell them that once everyone has put their name on the cards, they can pick a number—or a day. We can set it up on the terminals—or *a* terminal they can access and have the computer randomly select. That way nobody has to feel like they were last choice or . . . well, there won't be anything to fight about."

Reuel considered it somewhat doubtfully. "I suppose that would be the best way to do it—random selection. I am not confident that it will eliminate the friction, but we will see."

"Just tell them if they start a fight, they get moved down the list—or they get removed from the list and put in the brig."

Reuel grimaced. "I do not think the brig is large enough to hold them all."

* * * *

"I do not think that I particularly care for the fact that they have placed the sex act into effect," Kane said thoughtfully. "I see the logic in it and there is certainly a lot to be said for the fact that we will get to fuck, but there is something about it that I simply do not like."

"If you like anything about it," Jared growled, "then you are happier than I!"

"You are not happy about it either?" Kane asked in surprise. "What part do you not like?"

Jared scowled at him. "Did I not just say that I did not like any part of it?"

Kane thought it over. "You did, but I was certain that you could not have meant *any* part of it. You do not want to fuck?"

Jared threw his wrench down and stalked off. Kane stared at his back for a long moment. "You will not get to fuck if you do not help repair the damage!"

Jared halted, stood indecisively for several moments, and made an about face, stalking back and bending to pick up his wrench. Settling on the floor, he gave up on trying to tighten the bolt he had been twisting for a good five minutes and used the wrench on the seat of the chair instead, trying to pound it flat—or at least relatively flat.

"He does not like the list thing," Sebastian offered when Jared paused to study the effect. "I do not know why you would ask when he has done nothing but growl over it ever since it was announced."

Kane shrugged. "I did not hear him."

"Because you were not listening!" Lucien said.

"I was thinking."

"I was thinking, also," Thor said, "and I still heard him."

Kane glared at him. "I was thinking deeply."

"Stroking your cock does not count as thinking deeply!" Jared snarled.

"I do not know why it would not!" Kane snapped. "It takes a great deal of focus when everyone is babbling around one!"

"Because it is not deliberation. You are not considering anything. You are emptying your mind of thought to allow it to focus upon pleasure."

Kane stared at Sebastian. "Is that how you do it? Because that is not how I do it. I was *filling* my mind with the images from the pleasure programming and focusing very hard on replacing the female's face with Chloe's."

Sebastian, Jared, and Thor stopped what they were doing and stared at him.

"Did that work?" Sebastian asked.

Kane sighed. "No. I have not seen that expression on Chloe's face. I tried every expression I *had* seen, but somehow it did not work as well as I had hoped."

"I have seen that expression," Damon volunteered.

Jared beaned him on the forehead with his wrench. It bounced off and hit Lucien between the shoulder blades. Lucien twisted around to snatch it up, stared at Damon, who was lying on the deck with his eyes closed and then turned to glare at Jared accusingly. "I should shove this down your throat!" he snarled.

"He would not have anything to work with if you did," Kane pointed out. "And there are almost no tools as it is."

"In any case," Sebastian said tightly, "the monitor would likely consider it aggression and then we would have another day to wait until we could fuck, gods damn it!"

"He has knocked Damon cold already!" Lucien hissed in an undertone. "What are we to do about that if the monitor notices?"

"Check his pulse," Jared snapped. "If his heart is still beating, he will come around in a bit … and I will have to try harder next time."

He'd barely gotten the remark out when the monitor noticed Damon sprawled on the floor and stalked toward them. "What is this?" he demanded, gesturing at Damon.

"He is resting," Kane growled challengingly.

"He is bleeding!" the monitor snapped. "Why is there a knot on his head?"

"His wrench slipped," Jared growled. "Because these fucking tools will not work on these fucking chairs!"

The monitor narrowed his eyes suspiciously. "Where is the wrench?"

Lucien held it up. "It hit me in the back when he dropped it."

The monitor examined the blood and hair on the wrench, studied Damon for a moment, and finally handed it back to Lucien. "I will beat your brains in with the fucking thing if you start a fight and we end up in the fucking brig!"

Lucien stared at him sullenly when he had walked off and then turned to scowl at Jared. "I did not even have the satisfaction of knocking the fucking bastard out and now the gods damned monitor thinks that *I* did it!"

"It does not matter," Sebastian said. "He will not say anything because he wants Reuel to put up the dance cards again as much as we do."

"I feel like shoving the fucking dance cards down Reuel's throat," Jared muttered.

"Well he cannot *read* the gods damned things if you do that!" Kane snapped.

"I did not even get my name on the last one!" Jared growled.

"You might have if you had not decided to beat Seth's head into the wall only because he signed Chloe's dance card before you could!" Sebastian ground out.

"There were no more lines on the card!" Jared said angrily. "I should have been first, gods damn it! I am first mate! I was the first to board the Salvager! I should have been first on Chloe's gods damn dance card!"

"You were not first!" Kane said indignantly. "We both came aboard at the same time!"

"We did not! I was lying on top of you when the grappler picked up the first load of scrap! That is why I was on bottom when you woke up! I was *first* to board the Salvager!"

Kane thought that over. "You are right. But I was second!"

"I was first to board Chloe," Damon ground out, sitting up abruptly and glaring at both men, although it was hard to say if the glare was from anger or an attempt to focus his vision.

"And you will be first to go out the nearest airlock, you fuck, if you do not stop rubbing that in my face!" Jared snarled, jolting to his feet and balling his hands into fists.

"You caught me off guard, you fuck! If you had not, you would not have hit me in the fucking head with that gods damned wrench! You will not find it as easy to throw me out the gods damned airlock!"

"I will help him," Kane said.

"I also," Sebastian agreed.

"And I will stand watch for the monitor while they do it!" Lucien snapped indignantly. "I am tired of your gloating, as well!"

Damon scowled furiously at the pack. "I was not gloating!" he snarled. "I only pointed out that he could not be first!"

All six men leapt to their feet at that, Kane and Sebastian to block Jared from stalking over to Damon and beating him senseless and Lucien and Thor to prevent Damon from provoking Jared further.

The monitor raced across the mess hall, drawing the attention of a dozen other men, who followed him. "Sit down and get back to work, gods damn it!"

"We were stretching our legs," Jared said sullenly.

"Well, if you decide to stretch your gods damned arms, I will stretch my fingers around your throat and choke the life out of you! *I* am going to get to fuck if I have to kill every gods damned one of you to do it!"

Jared surveyed the odds and decided that it would probably only result in a trip to the brig if he knocked the bastard's teeth down his throat. Not that he would have minded if he was certain everyone else would also be in the brig, but he did not particularly care for the thought of cooling his heels in lockup while everyone else took a turn to fuck.

He sat back down and grasped the chair he had been working on, standing it upright. The bolt he had been trying to tighten before

promptly fell off and the seat dropped at that corner. Picking the bolt
up, he examined the inside, waiting for the others to either sit down or
leave.

He discovered the problem. It was not actually a bolt but rather a
rivet. There were no threads. He turned the chair on its side again as
his crewmates resumed their seats and the others finally wandered off.
After threading the rod that supported the back of the seat through the
holes again, he set the rivet on the end and looked around for his
wrench. "Give me my wrench back," he ground out when he saw that
Lucien still had it.

"I am using it," Lucien said tightly. "And I would not give it to you
anyway. You will only hurl it at that fucking fuck bastard and then we
will end up in the brig."

Jared glared at him. "I need it to pound this rivet into place."

"Use your fist."

After scowling at him in tight lipped anger for several moments, he
slammed his fist against the rivet. It drove the rivet into his hand and he
gritted his teeth and cursed at the pain that shot up his arm. "That did
not work worth a fuck!" he growled, picking the rivet out of his hand.

"I will let you use my hammer," Kane said, "but only if you swear
you will not use it on that fucking fuck bastard's head."

"I am *tired* of being referred to as the fucking fuck bastard!" Damon
snarled.

"Well, you *are* a fucker," Thor pointed out. "You have not done
anything else that I have heard and you are a PD00534 so you have
been fucking for a very long time. I am surprised myself that you still
have a cock ... unless it has been replaced?"

Damon felt his face heating with a mixture of fury and discomfort.
"What part of that bothers you? I was designated a gods damned
pleasure droid gods damn it! I did not *choose* it!"

"All of it," Jared growled. "We were out getting our fucking asses
blown off and freezing our asses off and starving while you were lying
on your fucking back fucking!"

"I was not on my fucking back!" Damon snarled. "And if you had
seen some of the females I had to fuck, you would not be so quick to
judge! It was not always a delight, gods damn it! Some of them liked
to bite and scratch. I have had the hide clawed from my back and
buttocks more times than I like to count! And there was one who used
her gods damned *teeth* on my cock!"

All five men stopped what they were doing and turned to stare at him.
"Why did you let her put her mouth on your cock at all?" Kane
demanded, asking the question uppermost in all their minds. "You are

a pleasure droid. *You* are supposed to do the work!"

"I was supposed to do whatever they wanted to do, gods damn it! And that female wanted to do that."

Sebastian thought that over. "Did you enjoy it?"

"*Not* when she sank her teeth into me!" Damon snapped. "In point of fact I did not enjoy any of it after that. She shoved her finger in my ass, as well."

The men looked at him in horrified fascination. "Why did she do that?"

"How the fuck would I know?" Damon snarled. "Too see how high I could jump?"

"I do not think I would care to have anything shoved in my ass," Lucien said thoughtfully. "I was shot in the ass once and I did not like that at all."

"In the asshole?"

"Nay! The cheek, but I still did not like it."

"Well that is just stupid!" Jared snapped. "No one likes to be shot anywhere!"

Lucien glared at him. "There are some places that are worse."

"Chloe does not like to do strange things, does she?" Kane asked worriedly after a few moments.

Damon studied him warily for a few moments. "Chloe has not done the typical things enough to be bored. It is the females that have done everything or who are just plain strange that are looking for things to do that are not even in my programming—or weren't before."

"I think we should focus on how we are to be first in the line when Reuel puts the cards up again," Sebastian said hurriedly when Jared looked as if he might leap to his feet again. "We are her crew. We should be first—or at least at the top of the list, gods damn it. I do not even know why they decided to put up a card for her. There are six of us. That is bad enough!"

"I think it is Reuel who decided," Kane said. "Chloe is shy and she is always worried that we will be angry with her. I think Reuel only suggested it and she agreed because it *is* an issue—the fact that everyone wants to fuck and only the fucking fuck droid over there has gotten to that I know of! It was Reuel who announced it and Chloe looked very embarrassed and uncomfortable to me."

Jared looked thoughtful. "I did not notice," he murmured slowly.

"If you are right," Sebastian said, "then I think that we should point out to Reuel that Chloe already has a crew and that it is completely unreasonable to expect her to accept anyone else when there are plenty of females in his own crew. There will still be more of us with her than with the others even at that."

"I am not so certain. It did not seem to me that there were *any* who wanted to sign Salina's dance card."

"Well, they will have to. She is *their* crewmember and if they leave her out then they have only four!" Lucien pointed out.

"Yes, but I think it is *because* she is their crewmember," Thor put in. "They did not like that she challenged an officer—even a ship's officer that was not military. They did not like that it was Chloe more than that. And beyond that, they say that she is not right in the head since the change. She is nigh as strong as they are and she had the tendency toward overkill even before she underwent the change. I think they are worried that she will try to injure them even if she has agreed to accept partners. In fact, I heard one complain that he believed she had agreed only so that she would have the opportunity to revenge herself because they did not support her when Reuel called her to account for her actions. She has been raging about it since she was thrown into the brig and threw her food tray at the guard when he took it to her."

They all stared at Thor for a long moment, digesting that.

"Well, she is their problem!" Sebastian snapped. "I still say that we should approach Reuel."

"And if he does not agree?" Jared asked dryly.

"Then we will need a strategy to make certain that we are at the front of the line when we are allowed to sign the gods damned dance cards!"

Jared frowned thoughtfully. "There is no vid displaying the wall where he posted before. Someone will need to adjust the angle of the view so that we know where her card is on the wall and do not have to search when we get there."

"I can locate a small handheld monitor and program it to receive only from that camera so that we know when he posts them and the order," Kane said.

"We will be in a good position to get out of the mess hall before most of the others, but it would not hurt to arrange interference," Sebastian said. "We will have to make it look accidental if we trip anyone, however."

"That may make an effective distraction," Lucien agreed, "and I am willing to help out with that, but only if whoever makes it to the dance card puts my name on the list because I am liable to be delayed myself. And I am going to be fucking pissed off if I hold up the rush and then do not get my name on the gods damned list!"

Chapter Ten

Reuel studied the six men lined up in front of him thoughtfully. More specifically, he found himself studying their expressions and their body language. They were tense, not in the sense that they stood at attention, although they were, but rather in the manner of a fighter prepared to pounce. There was aggression in their stances that had not been there before the change. They had been designed and programmed for perfect balance, total awareness of their surroundings at all times, and absolutely perfect military posture, but it had not had any real significance to any of them.

They had mimicked aggression. They had fought with the ferocity programmed into them, but without malice. It did not matter to them whether they won or lost, whether they survived or died. They did not register pain beyond awareness of injury and even then only in the sense that they were programmed to guard their usefulness. If the injury they had sustained threatened their usefulness, they factored probabilities and made the decision of whether to fall back to allow time for repairs or to proceed.

He did not have to ask the importance of their request. The request itself was proof that logic had nothing to do with the decision, that it was emotional, personal, that it mattered. It was clear enough that they had all reached a stage in development where they had become prey to basic animal urges. He knew that much from the changes within himself, but how far beyond that had they progressed, he wondered?

How far *could* they progress?

This did not have the feel of the basic animal instinct to attempt to procreate. If that was the case, then it should not matter to them what female they fucked so long as she was physically appealing and seemed a reasonably good candidate for bearing offspring. Was there biological significance in their choice and their aggressive determination? Or was it an emotional attachment? Or both?

Up until the brawl the day before, he had thought it nothing more than the basic animal instinct—and a primitive underdeveloped one at that. They had had very little actual experience of pleasure of any kind, let alone sexual, and had little more than their programmed responses to even have an inkling of what it was. His own first experience was in the cessation of pain. He had known far more pain than anything else and had not known what to do beyond endure and hope that it would stop or he would die and he would no longer have awareness of it. The cessation of pain had been the most wonderful thing he had ever felt when he had first experienced it.

Warmth after being half frozen had been more torture than pleasure, but it had reached pleasure after a while. The feeling of a full belly or even any food to stop the gnawing hunger had brought a sense of pleasure, and then taste.

He could fully appreciate a desperation to feel and enjoy anything of pleasure after so much suffering and pain and he had considered that that might actually be more of a motivation to fuck than an instinct to try to procreate. After all, they all knew it was *supposed* to be pleasurable.

If that was the case, though, it seemed they would have chosen from among their own kind. Their females had been programmed as pleasure droids. Three had actual experience in utilizing their programming and would have had AI to assist them in learning more.

Why the determination to have a human, especially when they had to be aware that she not only did not have the programming, but she had had little opportunity to learn as humans did?

And it was not merely her own crew that seemed grimly determined to get hold of her. Far too many of his own crewmen had their eye on her for his comfort.

He was drawn to her and he did not quite understand that.

Unless it was because they all sensed that she was the only female among them capable of reproducing?

He hardly dared even to allow his mind to formulate a theory as to the possible biological significance of it and yet Chloe, herself, had voiced the question he hadn't dared ask himself.

Could they procreate? Or was it possible that they were evolving to that point, at least? Or was it nothing more than urges that they had developed that they would never see to fruition? It was the last that disturbed him the most. It would be the cruelest twist of fate if they were to have awareness only to realize that they were still little more than machines—with no true purpose and no real future. A species that could not perpetuate itself might as well be nothing more than rock. It was certainly not a true species. It only mimicked life.

Realizing finally that the men were still waiting for an answer, he flicked another look at them, stern, daring them to breach military protocol whether they were under his command or not. "I will give your request consideration," he responded finally. "The objective of this exercise is to quell unrest and boost morale. You are not the only ones who have an interest in Chloe—and she agreed to join the pool. It would not suit my needs, or the good of all, to make a swift decision that could potentially create more disharmony."

The men glanced at one another after they had saluted and left. "Plan B," Jared said grimly.

* * * *

Chloe supposed she should just be glad that they had tables to set their trays on and chairs to sit in to eat their meals. She'd been pretty convinced when she'd surveyed the disaster area that it couldn't be put back together again. The chairs hadn't been particularly comfortable to start with, though, and they were even more uncomfortable now besides being wobbly and out of whack so that they didn't sit flat on the floor anymore.

Of course some of that might have been due to dents in the floor. She'd noticed a number of them—and the walls. They were fortunate that the mess hall wasn't near the hull or they might have had a hull breach!

She wasn't particularly interested in lingering in the mess hall anyway—especially not that night. She'd managed to get herself all worked up, or at least bolstered to deal with the situation, only to discover that her first night had been put off until further notice—that being until the cyborgs repaired all the damage from the brawl.

She thought, if she could just make it through her first, she wouldn't be as jittery. It was the waiting that was grinding her nerves down to nothing. Well, that and a complete lack of confidence—and fear of the unknown.

It was all very well for them to claim pleasure droid programming, but none of them had ever actually accessed it that she knew of. When would they have had the chance? And it was going to be hell if one of them arrived that didn't know any more about it than she did—awkward, embarrassing, and probably not the least bit satisfying to either party! Not that she was worried about being satisfied herself. She thought she was going to be too scared shitless to actually enjoy it, but it would've been less worrisome if she could've convinced herself that her partner would at least get some satisfaction out of it.

She'd been convinced from what Reuel had told her that she'd mistaken the reason Damon had behaved the way he had the morning after they'd had sex together. If she hadn't had so much time to dwell on it, she might not have been able to make the circuit all the way around to her initial concern. Unfortunately, she had and she was more convinced the second time around that she'd been right to start with. Reuel could only have been speaking in generalization. He didn't know what had happened, so he wasn't in any position to actually judge it for himself. That still might have been alright except that she remembered Damon had fallen asleep after their first time, or at least feigned sleep. So maybe he'd just been tired afterward?

She hadn't actually gotten the chance to be around him enough since then to form any other impressions. Even though Damon hadn't taken part in the actual brawl, at least not after he'd dragged her out of it, he'd been expected to help with the clean up and repairs.

She was almost relieved that it prevented her from asking, or trying to subtly pry the information out of him. She wasn't certain that she really wanted to know the truth, especially if the truth hurt.

She'd studied up, though. Despite the time she'd spent with Reuel searching for the perfect place to stock the ship and pouring over star charts in an effort to figure out the location of their target colony planet, she'd had enough free time to take a crash course on sex education. She was *sure* she was prepared to make a much better impression the next time around even if she had flunked the first time.

It was just unnerving as hell having to wait! If she could've just jumped right in, she knew she would've been able to remember everything and then she wouldn't have had time for doubts to begin to shake her confidence in her prowess again.

Reuel rose from his chair. Even as he opened his mouth to speak, Kane bolted from his own seat and headed toward the exit at a brisk walk. "Halt!" Reuel growled.

Kane tensed, started to take another step and apparently thought better of it. He turned to look at Reuel questioningly.

Reuel's eyes narrowed. "Where are you headed in such a hurry, soldier?"

Kane saluted. "The latrine, Sir!"

Reuel's lips twitched but it would've been hard to say whether it was an angry tick or a flicker of amusement. "I suggest you hold it for a bit. I intend to address the crew—the entire crew."

Scowling, Kane returned to his seat.

Reuel turned to face the hall. "We have settled on a target to supply the ship for the long voyage. Tomorrow at 08:00 EST, we will make a jump, so everyone will be expected to be on station and in harness for the jump. Directly afterwards I will expect everyone to report to the bay so that we can begin preparing the shuttles for the landing.

"Before anyone moves from their seat—Neither I nor Captain Chloe were amused by the last attempt to initiate the sex act. If there is not order in this second attempt, you will be waiting a very long while before the attempt is made again. At Captain Chloe's suggestion, all names that appear on the lists will be put into the computer and the computer will randomly select the time of your engagement. That being the case, there is no reason whatsoever to become disorderly. Regardless of when you reach the cards to sign in, your position will not be determined until the computer has made the selection.

"*I* will oversee the sign ins. *You* will remain seated until I have posted the cards."

He glanced at Chloe and his eyes lit with amusement. "Ladies, your visitors are anxious so I would like to suggest that you leave the mess hall now and brace … uh … make whatever preparations you would like before your visitor arrives."

Chloe was so weak-kneed after the announcement, she wasn't certain for several moments that she could command her legs to lift her ass out of her chair. When she saw the cyborg women get up and head toward the exit, however, she bounded out of her seat and raced to catch up. Being the last out the door and drawing the most attention didn't appeal to her at all.

She'd already dashed to her cabin, stripped, and flung herself at the bunk before it occurred to her that she hadn't bathed since that morning. She lay staring at the ceiling for a few minutes, listening to her racing heart and trying to decide whether she had time to bathe and get back. That part seemed essential, to be hiding—waiting in the dim cabin when … whoever, got there.

Since it hit her at that moment that she had no idea who it might be, that it might not even be any of the men she was familiar with and most comfortable with, she decided to dash down to the showers. When she arrived, she discovered the others were already there. Relieved to discover she at least seemed to be on the right track, she headed for a vacant shower and scrubbed as if she was decontaminating rather than preparing for a lover. Everything on her was warm and tingling when she got out and that beat the hell out of being cold with fright.

When she'd dried off, she went back to her cabin to pace and chew her fingernails down to the quick.

* * * *

Reuel had not even managed to post the cards when he saw Kane and then Jared stick their heads out the door. "Back!" he barked.

When he'd finished, he marched to the center and placed his back to the wall. "Now, in an orderly manner …."

One of his men fell out the door and measured his length in the corridor. Jared leapt over him. Kane stepped in the middle of his back as he tried to get up. Two more men stumbled out the door, tripped over the man that was trying to get up, and created a momentary plug in the corridor. Sebastian bounded over them, landed in a half crouch, and shot toward Chloe's card.

Narrowing his eyes, Reuel glanced toward the vid and discovered without a great deal of surprise that it was now angled toward the wall where the cards were posted. Shaking his head, he moved toward the growing tangle in the corridor as Lucien, Damon, and Thor plowed through or leapt over the men still trying to get to their feet, who'd managed to trip up several other men in the process. Tempers were already beginning to flare by the time he commanded the men behind them to halt and allow them to get up. Glaring furiously at Chloe's men, those who'd 'fallen' in the corridor stalked toward the posted cards, scanned them and lined up behind Thor. By the time Reuel had taken up his position again, the entire corridor was clogged with the men lining up to sign and he discovered the men had ignored the fact that there were only six lines for signatures on each card.

His lips tightening, he ripped Chloe's card from the wall, tore the bottom off and informed the men that the card was *full* when there were no empty lines. Clearly furious to have their names removed, the men stared at Chloe's crew for several moments as if trying to decide whether it was worth it to spend the night in the brig with Chloe's men and finally, apparently, decided against it.

Reuel relaxed fractionally, waited until everyone had made their selection and then collected the cards, informing the men that they would be able to utilize the terminals in the old rec room to draw their night once he had had time to input the data in the computer.

There was a general stampede toward the rec room, but he decided it was orderly enough to ignore it. "Monitors! I will rely upon you to keep order in the rec room. I would not like to have to throw anyone in the brig tonight," he called after them before heading to the bridge to input the data in the main computer system.

* * * *

Chloe halted abruptly and turned wide eyes toward the door when she heard footsteps moving briskly along the corridor, holding her breath while she waited to see if they would stop at her door. When they did and a knock sounded on the panel, she nearly jumped out of her skin. Whirling, she raced to her bunk and leapt in, her heart hammering deafeningly in her ears. After trying several different positions, however, she decided she needed to discard the notion of posing seductively and bounded out of the bunk again when whoever it was at her door knocked the second time.

Racing to the door, she snatched it open. A jolt went through her when she met a wall of flesh in the opening. Tipping her head back, she gaped up at him for several moments, eyes wide, mouth open in an 'O' of surprise, gulped a couple of times, and finally found her voice. "Jared!"

He'd seemed as frozen as she was until she managed to croak his name. At that, he stepped inside, narrowly missing crushing the big toe on her right foot, caught her head between his palms and lifted her by her head to meet his descent. A bone in her neck and several along her spine popped before she had the presence of mind to push herself upward on her tiptoes, but his mouth connected with hers before she had time to assimilate whether there was any pain or damage associated with the ominous pops.

As if it hadn't been days since the first time he'd dragged her against him and kissed her with such fevered longing, the same conflagration erupted instantly inside of her. She slipped her arms between his and dug her fingers into his shoulders, trying to get closer. His skin was still damp from a shower. Droplets of cold water dripped from his hair, landed on her arms, and skated down them, creating shivers with their passing.

He pulled her closer, realigning his mouth with hers and stroking his tongue restlessly along hers, making her drunk with oxygen starvation and the wonderful feel and taste of his mouth. She twined her arms more tightly around his shoulders, lifting herself higher and when he gripped one buttock and pulled her belly against his erection, she lifted her legs and curled them around him.

A shudder went through him when the lips of her sex parted to enfold his hot flesh. He broke the kiss, looked around a little dazedly, and headed for her bunk, climbing onto the mattress on his knees and falling forward and catching himself with his arms with her still coiled tightly around him. She discovered she couldn't maintain her grip without his support. Her legs slipped. Her ass hit the mattress. He dropped to his elbows when she lost her grip on his neck, diving low to burrow his face against her throat.

She made a grab for his cock, searching blindly for it to shove it into place and came up empty when he shifted from her neck to her breasts. For a few moments, she continued to search a little desperately, found his hard belly and splayed her fingers against it, trying to follow the thin trail of hair from his belly button downward. He latched onto a nipple however, and completely distracted her from her goal as he tugged at the sensitive tip. Fire shot through her and erupted in her belly. It clenched so hard she gasped.

Grabbing two fistfuls of his hair mindlessly, she struggled with equal opposing desires to pry him loose and hold him closer. The sensations flooding through her were so keen it was hard to decide whether it was sheer torture or pleasure to feel him sucking and pulling at her breasts. Just about the time she decided she wanted more, he let go and lifted his head, sucked in a couple gulps of air and dove for the other.

She gritted her teeth, ground them together, threw her legs around him and tried to lift her hips high enough from the bed to mount him. She bucked against his belly button uselessly for several moments before it occurred to her that she'd bumped the head of his cock on the way up.

Dropping to the bed, she gasped for air, struggling to figure out how she was going to mount his cock when it was about six inches south of where she needed it. Just about the time she decided to scoot down the bed, he shifted upward in search of her mouth. They bumped noses but finally managed to connect.

She pulled at him a little frantically with her hands, capturing his tongue with the suction of her mouth and sucking on it while she tried to identify what part of his body she was gripping and felt her way downward in another search for the cock. Either it finally penetrated his mind that she was searching for it or he took that moment to decide to curl his hips. She managed to grab the head and shove it between her legs but there was still a gap of several inches between him and the connection she wanted.

He pumped his hips, yanking free of her grip, tried to curl around her and finally broke from her lips and surged upward. The head of his cock snagged briefly in the mouth of her sex and skated up her cleft to her clit, sending an almost electric jolt through her. She dug her heels into the mattress and arched upward, trying to get it to slide down in the right direction. It did, slipping past the mouth of her sex again and then spearing between the cheeks of her ass.

Hot to the point perspiration beaded on her skin, so breathless from panting and exertion she'd begun to feel like she might pass out, Chloe made another grab for Jared's cock, bending it as she dragged it out of the crack of her ass. Apparently, it was enough to get his attention. He snatched it out of her hand and shoved it into her hole. After a few minutes of heaving and bucking, they managed penetration and Chloe gripped him tightly as he began pumping in and out of her. The wait had almost been too much. The moment he began to saw in and out of her, she felt the first tingles of imminent eruption. She dug her fingers into his back, squeezed her eyes tightly closed and held her breath as the tingles grew stronger and stronger. She gasped when the first spasm of her climax hit her, uttered a low groan of rapture as it sent rippling waves of glorious pleasure through her and then seized again, harder. By the time she reached her peak, her voice was hoarse, and he was pounding sharp little cries from her with each jolting thrust.

Jared shuddered abruptly, freezing, uttered a choked grunt and began to move again. Chloe clung to him until the last of the spasms passed and then gave up the effort to hold on, allowing her arms and legs to fall limply to the mattress. Jared sank against her, panting in her ear and sending waves of goosebumps rushing from her ear, across her shoulder and then her breasts. She shivered as the heat began to dissipate.

She'd just begun to breathe a little easier when she discovered Jared was sinking more and more heavily against her, pressing her deeper into the mattress and then compressing her lungs. As much as she enjoyed the feel of him on top of her, she began to feel a little alarmed and began shoving at his shoulders until he rolled off of her and onto the bed beside her.

She discovered he'd trapped her arm beneath his weight, but as soon as she began tugging on it he levered himself up far enough to allow her to free herself. Utterly content, she lay basking in it for a while before it dawned on her to wonder if he'd found the release he needed. Rolling onto her side, she studied his face, trying to decide if he looked relaxed. As if he sensed her perusal, he opened his eyes and stared back at her.

It disconcerted her, made her worry deepen. Lifting a hand, she lightly touched his cheek. "Did you ... you know ... come?"

Jared swallowed with an effort, jolted by the question. It hadn't dawned on him until she asked to wonder if he'd pleasured her—hadn't crossed his mind one time from the moment she opened the door. All he'd been able to think about from that time was 'the kiss'. He'd had that firmly planted in his mind before she'd opened the door, partly because it had been driving him out of his mind to kiss her again since the first time. And partly because he'd dredged up his pleasure programming and knew that was the first step to seduction—the kiss on the lips, the kisses on her body to arouse her. He searched his mind a little frantically and finally recalled that he'd kissed her breasts, but to save his life he couldn't recall if he'd done any of the other things that he had promised himself he would.

He would pleasure her so much that she would look at him the way she looked at Damon. She would know, when he was done, that he could pleasure her just as much as Damon even if he had been designated as a soldier and not a lover.

"Did you?" he asked warily, a sick feeling already tightening in his belly.

She closed her eyes and smiled dreamily. "Oh yeah! You can do that to me any time."

The sick feeling vanished. An odd sort of lightness took its place, warm, like expanding air until his entire chest felt uncomfortably tight. He reached for her, feeling the softness of her skin against his palm, the yielding of her flesh beneath that as he closed his hand around her arm and drew her closer. She shifted readily to his silent demand, snuggling close enough he could feel her almost against his entire length. He could feel her cold little toes against his shins, could feel the smoothness of her legs as she rubbed them along his. Her belly was nestled against his waist, her breasts pressed to his chest just below his.

Pleasure wafted through him and still more when he filled his palm with the feel of her smooth skin, skimming his hand lightly along her back and over the little ridges of her spine just beneath the skin to cup the soft fullness of her buttocks. The scent of her hair and skin, warmed by her and their proximity, filled his nose and lungs with each breath like an intoxicant. It was not arousal—not precisely—although he felt that rising the longer she lay pressed against him and he stroked his hand over her.

He had not done any of the things that he had meant to do ... because he had not been able to think beyond getting inside of her as quickly as he could.

Rolling onto his back, he carried her with him. Her weight pressed her more firmly against him and his shifted from the unexpected and completely incomprehensible pleasure of before to desire again.

Catching her shoulders, he pushed her upward until she sat up on his belly, straddling him. A look of confusion flickered across her face, but she sat perfectly still while he explored with his hands what he had only felt when she was lying against him. The smoothness of her skin, the softness of it, fascinated him. For a little while, he enjoyed merely feeling it slip along his palms and fingers as he traced them over her.

He paused finally at her breasts, cupping the soft mounds with his palms and then tested the softness with his fingers as he drew his hands away from her chest until he was merely pinching the tight, rosy buds at the tips between his fingers.

Moving his hands after a moment, he settled them on her ribs just beneath her breasts and traced the shape of her to the indentation of her waist and then over the flare of her hips and down along her thighs. His mouth watered with want and he swallowed with an effort, lifting his gaze to meet hers. "You are so beautiful, Chloe," he said, finding his voice oddly hoarse.

She looked surprised and then pleased. When her lips began to curl upward in a smile and her eyes to gleam with delight and amusement, he caught her shoulders and drew her down again. Curling an arm tightly around her shoulders, he nestled those curving lips beneath his and sucked lightly at them.

Blood surged through him in a heated tide the moment her lips parted for him. He penetrated the heated cavern of her mouth with his tongue, intoxicated within moments by the heat and taste of her. He explored her mouth until impatience to explore the rest of her with his mouth surpassed the desire to linger and lifted his lips from hers and pushed lower to take a breast into his mouth. The hard little nub at the tip was perfect to curl his tongue around, made his groin tighten with pleasure as he sucked it.

It was for her, he reminded himself, to arouse her to pleasure, but he found it so enjoyable himself he lost track of everything else until her tugging reminded him that she had another that needed equal attention. By the time he'd thoroughly appreciated it and scooted downward further still to examine her soft belly he'd forgotten he was searching for the pleasure points. All of it pleasured him, every silky, yielding inch of her body, but her gasps had become groans and she was writhing beneath him and pulling at him until it pierced his mind that she wanted what he wanted.

Anticipation made his heart pound in his chest as frantically as hers was pounding as he shifted upward again and sought the sweet, hot cavern between her legs with the part of himself that fit her as if she had been made for him. He sucked in a harsh breath as he felt her flesh fist tightly around his cock, sending waves of tortuous pleasure through him.

His groin tightened threateningly the moment he burrowed deeply into her and he paused, counting in his mind to calm the threatening spasms before he began to move. Realizing after a moment that he wanted to see her face, he shifted onto his elbows, hunching his back until he could watch her each time he glided into her and then withdrew. He wanted to see her face when she found ecstasy, but he discovered that the longer he watched the more his control slipped.

He gritted his teeth, struggling to maintain the rhythm that seemed to pleasure her and retain control of his body. He'd begun to despair that he could manage it when she abruptly arched her head back, arched her entire body. He felt her muscles along her channel quake as she opened her mouth and uttered a low groan. His flesh pebbled all over. His belly clenched as if someone had punched him. When she arched again, he lost his hold on himself, yielded to the urge to pump into her until he felt his own body begin to spasm. He released a choked breath, sucked in another as one convulsion passed and another hit him. His mind seemed to fragment. He drove into her mindlessly until the convulsions finally ceased and he could drag air into his lungs again.

He felt so drained in the aftermath that it took an effort to lever himself up high enough to fall off of her, but he had nearly crushed with his weight before. He was the next thing to unconscious, but that thought filtered through his mind. Relieved when he felt the mattress beneath his shoulder and hip, he released a ragged breath and allowed himself to slip toward oblivion.

Chloe turned to him, snuggling her face against his chest. "I'm glad you aren't angry with me anymore."

Angry? He struggled with trying to figure that out for a moment and finally gave up the fight.

Chapter Eleven

"Shifting to hyper drive in sixty seconds."

Chloe jolted awake at the sudden announcement over the com and rolled off the bunk, slamming into the cold, metal plate of the deck hard enough it rattled her teeth.

"Fifty nine seconds."

Bounding to her feet in panic, Chloe glanced wildly around in search of something to put on and discovered Jared was still in her bed. "We're fixing to jump!"

He caught her around the waist as she charged toward the door naked having discarded the idea of finding clothes and still getting into harness. "There is an emergency harness on the bunk."

"My god! That thing's ancient! I've never used it and it's only for one!" Chloe gasped as he hauled her back to the bunk.

"Two will fit," he said grimly. Planting her on the bed and climbing in with her, he placed his back against the wall, grabbed the straps and dragged them over his shoulders. Chloe had managed to get up on her knees and was debating whether to make another attempt to reach the nearest jump seat or not. Grabbing her, Jared settled her astride his lap facing him, adjusted the harness around both of them and clamped it behind her back. He pulled her snugly against his chest then and tightened the harness until she almost had to breathe in sync with him to breathe at all.

"Ten seconds, nine, eight …."

Bending his knees, he braced his heels against the frame and coiled his arms tightly around her, pressing her head against his shoulder and holding it there with his hand.

Chloe felt the heaviness settle over her and increase until darkness engulfed her and she floated free. She came to as the ship completed the jump and the abrupt deceleration slammed the two of them against the harness.

Relieved that the harness had held, she slumped weakly against him.

It was more than that, though. The protectiveness of his hold felt so good she was in no hurry at all to move.

"You are alright?" he asked finally in a rumbling voice still rough with sleep.

She nodded and, to her vast disappointment, his hold eased on her.

She felt him reach for the buckle to release the harness. It occurred to her the moment he did that she'd damned near slept through the jump!

She should've been on the bridge! She'd set the computer for the jump the night before, but she should *still* have been on the bridge monitoring the ship! Galvanized by that thought, she slid off his lap as he removed the harness. "I need to get to the bridge and run a systems check!" she said, dashing to her locker to retrieve a flight suit. Shoving her legs and then her arms in, she grabbed her boots, hopping on one foot as she pulled on first one and then the other. She'd already headed toward the door, fastening the closure when it occurred to her that she hadn't even told Jared good morning.

Whirling, she raced back to him. He'd moved to the edge of the bunk, but he looked heavy-eyed—and no wonder! Catching his face between her hands, she kissed him soundly on the lips but eluded him when he made a grab for her. "Later, bud!" she threw at him over her shoulder with a quick grin as she dashed across the cabin and went out.

Jared was halfway to the showers, a bemused smile still curling his lips, when that finally sank in. His smile vanished abruptly and his dark brows descended over the bridge of his nose in a frown of confusion. By the time he'd showered he wasn't just puzzled. He was pissed.

His mood didn't improve when he reached the mess hall and discovered it vacant. He glared at the empty room for several moments before it dawned on him that everyone was supposed to report to the bay to work on the shuttles. He hesitated, but he was hungry gods damn it! Stalking across the eating area, he pushed the door to the galley open and searched the cooling unit until he found enough leftovers to appease his appetite and moved to the heating unit with it. He was gulping down a glass of fruit juice when one of Reuel's crewmen wandered in, his hair standing on end.

He sniffed. "Anything left?"

Jared shrugged. "Help yourself. I have eaten what I wanted." He paused at the door. "You may want to find a flight suit and do something with the hair before you report to the bay."

The man nearly choked on his food. "Fuck! I forgot!"

Apparently, that made five of them. He caught up with two more before he reached the bay and Reuel was already dressing down a man when they arrived. Glancing warily at one another, they split up and strode as swiftly as they could toward the workgroups without making it too obvious that they'd just arrived.

Kane greeted Jared with a scowl.

It caught Jared off guard until it dawned on him, when he discovered that all the others looked equally peeved, that he had spent the night with Chloe and they were none too happy about it.

He had mixed feelings about it himself if it came to that. What the fuck was that 'bud' shit about, gods damn it!

He had pleasured her! He knew absolutely that she had come the second time and she had told him that she had the first. Two climaxes, gods damn it! She did not call that fucking fuck droid 'bud'!

Still stewing over it, he tried to focus on what was going on around him. After watching the others removing one thing after another from the shuttle for several moments, however, he realized he *still* did not know what the fuck was going on. Following Kane as he stalked up the gang plank, he stopped and asked.

"If you had been at the gods damned meeting this morning, you would know!"

"Well, I was not at the gods damned meeting!"

"Exactly!" Kane snarled. "It was not enough to fuck once or twice? You had to fuck all night?"

"I did not fuck all night, gods damn it! I fell asleep afterwards," he muttered.

Kane sent him a disbelieving look. "And slept through the jump?"

"I did not sleep through the fucking jump! Chloe woke me when she fell off the bed!"

"You are saying that you were still asleep when the countdown started? You slept through reveille?"

Jared stared at him blankly. "When did we begin to have reveille onboard the Salvager?"

"This morning when we were to report for duty ... which you did not!"

"I am here, gods damn it! I just do not know what it is that we are supposed to do."

"*We* are removing everything from the shuttles that can be removed," Sebastian growled. "I do not know what you are doing beyond standing around with your thumb up your ass complaining!"

Still with no clearer idea of what the objective was and what, therefore, would be considered nonessential, Jared finally grabbed up a piece of equipment Sebastian had unbolted and headed down the gang plank with it. Reuel met him at the foot of the gang plank. He had just decided that he had not slipped in without notice as he had thought when Reuel summoned Kane.

Mystified, he followed Reuel across the bay. "I understand that Chloe and her father picked the two of you up on Xeno-12."

Frowning, Jared flicked a glance at Kane and nodded. "They were collecting salvage, correct?"

Jared flushed. "Correct."

"Is this some of the salvage that is still in the hold?"

Jared caught the direction of his thoughts. "It is. Most of it is useless, but there may be some weapons that can be repaired."

Reuel smiled with satisfaction. "Let us see what there is, shall we?" Turning, he summoned three of his own men and followed Kane and Jared to the hold where the salvage was stored. By the time they stopped for the midday meal, they had uncovered two photon cannons and three pulse lasers. Carrying them up to the bay where the men were still working on the shuttles, they left them and headed to the mess.

Jared had managed to, mostly, put Chloe from his mind while they were sifting through the debris from the late war, or at least his dissatisfaction with their parting that morning. The salvage brought back far too many unpleasant memories for that to remain in the forefront of his mind, but it also brought back the memory of when he had been taken aboard the Salvager, the first time that he had seen Chloe.

He had known that he was dying, that he had reached the point where even his nanos could not repair the damage because he had had no food to provide the necessary elements the nanos needed to repair him. And then he had opened his eyes and seen her staring down at him. He had not understood then what that expression on her face and in her eyes had meant. He still was not entirely sure—but pity certainly. He knew that she must also have felt revulsion, but he had not seen that, only the pity and sorrow.

And then she had realized that he was looking at her and she had sucked in her breath and jumped, falling back on her ass in the debris around them. He had expected her to scream. To leap to her feet and run. Instead, she had hesitated and then moved closer. It heartened him enough that he had thought she might help. "Water."

Her face had crumpled. She had looked like she might cry. "Wait! I'll be right back."

Her father had been with her when she had returned, but she had brought water. He could not lift his head and she could not, although she struggled trying to for a moment before she gave up. He had thought that he would not get water, but she had carefully tipped the cup until it dropped onto his lips and he had licked it off until his tongue ceased to feel swollen with dryness.

"He's a cyborg, pumpkin. Leave him alone. They're dangerous."

She glanced at her father with an expression he had not been able to interpret until she spoke—with anger. "He's hurt! I'm not going to leave him alone! He's needs help."

"He's not a pet, pumpkin! He's a soldier and he's dangerous."

"Go away if you won't help!"

"He's gonna die anyway."

"I can at least make him more comfortable if you'd help me."

"Damn it, Chloe! He's a gods damn cyborg! You can't make him comfortable. He isn't *un*comfortable!"

"He asked for water!"

Her father stared at her for a long moment. "He needs something for energy. He's starving." He looked disgusted and worried. "I'll get something to lift him."

"Kane," he had managed to say, remembering his partner. "Kane, too."

He had worried that she had not understood, but when she straightened, she began to push the debris aside. "He's here."

"Alive?"

"There's another one, Pops! His friend's over here. We need to move him, too."

"Gods damn it, Chloe!"

"Damn it, Pops! Just help me move them! Please?"

When he reached the mess hall and saw Chloe sitting at the table, absently nibbling on something, it brought another memory to the surface—Chloe sitting cross-legged between him and Kane. When he could not sit up, when he could barely chew the food she gave him, she sat for hours tearing bread into tidbits small enough to swallow, dipping them in broth, and feeding him with her fingers. He still did not understand why she had helped him and Kane, but he had long since given up trying to understand Chloe. She was as much of an enigma to him now as she had been then, even though he understood far more than he had then.

Sensing his presence, she looked up at him, met his gaze, and smiled, and he forgot that he was pissed off with her for calling him friend when he wanted her to think of him as her lover. He did not know how he was going to make her look at him as she did that fucking fuck bastard! He did not know how he would make her think of him in that way, but he would if he had to think of some way to get rid of the bastard to do it!

* * * *

Chloe thought it was a good thing, overall, that Reuel had thought to bring up the Maritime Sex Act and put it into effect. By the time she and the other women had given out recreational sex to most, if not all, of the men, it seemed to her that the entire crew had changed dramatically. There were still fights from time to time, but attitudes in general had changed, and they didn't have another all-out brawl—or hadn't so far. There didn't seem to be nearly as much tension overall.

She thought it was probably a good thing for her, too, although she was pretty exhausted. She supposed she should have realized after the night she spent with Jared that he wasn't the exception but the rule and that that was why Reuel had figured they should plan on one night per man. To the good, though, she had been too busy entertaining her crew to do anything stupid—like fall for another one. If it had been left entirely up to her, she thought she would have confined her activities to Damon, Jared, and Kane and that probably wouldn't have been good for her when she was already very attached to them. She thought she might have begun to feel too personal about it when, really, it wasn't supposed to be. In fact, that was the entire reason for the Sex Act—to prevent actual relationships from developing that might be too distracting to the crew.

The men, due to their natures, were pretty well fixated on sex, especially when there were any females around. By not allowing things to get too personal and the parties to form bonds, by insuring that no one was left out or ignored, it kept jealousy and resentment to a minimum. It prevented couples from sneaking off to a dark corner to fuck instead of attending their duties when such activities carried the potential for disaster for the entire crew. And of course, it improved overall mental health since sex was a stress reliever and it was stressful to spend too much time in space. Sex also allowed for touch, and humans, at least, seemed to have a fundamental need for it. Sensory deprivation could drive them bonky faster than just about anything else and, unfortunately, without such an act that included all crewmembers, there were always some that were shunned for one reason or another. Those people, deprived of any sort of comfort, could become a danger by themselves, were many times more likely to suddenly snap and run amuck.

There was certainly no doubt in her mind that they had all been badly in need of sexual release! Again, her ignorance and lack of experience might have led her to false conclusions if she had had her way and refused to service her fair share of the men. Jared's raw passion hadn't exactly come as a complete surprise after that kiss in the corridor. She'd thoroughly enjoyed it even though she'd found it just a little unnerving at first, but she thought she had pretty much been expecting it. The problem was, she was naïve enough that she'd thought it was just for her. By the time Sebastian, Lucien, and Thor had pounced on her with equal enthusiasm, though, she'd tumbled to the fact that it was just plain deprivation.

The poor things! They had really, really needed some relief!

Under the circumstances, though, she'd had to revise her initial impression of her night with Jared, had been forced to see that it wasn't her in particular, but need in general. It had still made her unhappy, but at least she hadn't had time to get really carried away with her imaginings. It was bad enough that she was having to deal with trying to extract her emotions over Damon and get it into her head that he wasn't anymore 'in love' with her than he had been with all of the women he'd had to service at the brothel. Their first time together wasn't special. *She* wasn't special. Even if he'd been a real man and not a cyborg that wouldn't have been the case, but it certainly was when he *was* a cyborg.

She thought she was going to be alright—eventually. She thought the sex was therapeutic for her in a very real sense, although not in the same sense as it was for the guys. She thought it was going to help her bring things into perspective. It was just way too easy for her to let her emotions rule her and to try to attach herself to anyone that was kind to her or gave her attention.

She was probably a total basket case from spending way too much time in space and away from other people and she just didn't realize it, but, to the good, she wasn't alone anymore or even restricted to just a small handful of people. With the addition of Reuel and his crew it was almost like living in a real community. It was a little disturbing that Reuel seemed to be taking over, but when all was said and done she hadn't had a choice about taking over after her father died and it hadn't been something she'd ever thought about doing or wanting to do. He still gave her the courtesy of always discussing everything and asking her opinion or permission and she felt like he really did want her to be a friend, that he wanted her to think of his people as friends. So she hadn't spent a lot of time worrying about it.

It was actually nice to see all the changes in the old ship. It looked better than it had in her lifetime and she was willing to bet, better than it had in her father's. It had already been old when he had bought it, but it had paid off and then some. The business he'd run from the ship had not only eventually paid for the ship, but it had supported them comfortably.

She was ready to retire it—or at least retire from it. She figured the cyborgs might as well get some use out of it. It wasn't as if anybody else was willing to help them—or that she was going to have a lot of need for it once she found a place to settle.

She thought she'd finally remembered enough about that long ago trip with her father to at least have a fair idea of where to start looking. As Reuel had pointed out, somewhat wryly, the quadrant she'd marked out was vast and she hadn't narrowed down the possibilities by a hell of a lot. She *had* remembered that it was a star very close to Earth's sun in size and magnitude and that the system had six planets. Those two factors narrowed it down some. She figured they could send out probes in every direction when they reached the frontier closest to the quadrant she'd marked off. She was well aware that it could take months even if they found it relatively quickly and that meant they were going to have to take on a lot of supplies.

Reuel had pointed out that they didn't want their last stop to stock the ship anywhere near where they intended to go and she could see the sense in that. If they created a pattern by hopping from system to system, it wouldn't be hard for the authorities to begin to anticipate their next jump.

She still wasn't crazy about his plan, but he was a soldier. He understood these things a lot better than she did and, as uncomfortable as she was with the idea of pirating what they needed, she also had to agree that they were due compensation for their efforts for the Confederation—which they hadn't gotten. They'd been left with no choice but to take to survive when that should never have been the case.

As her father had always said, two wrongs didn't make a right, and she knew her conscience was going to bother her for agreeing to something that was wrong. She also felt like survival trumped laws that were formulated for a society that needed boundaries and rules, however. The people of such societies were rarely subjected to the need to affect their own survival. The society that created the laws saw to their protection. Reuel and his people fell outside that protection because they'd been forced outside it, not because they had chosen that road.

* * * *

Kane grinned broadly when Chloe opened the door. "It is my night."

He looked so happy—poor man!—when he was nearly last that Chloe felt her chest tighten, but she couldn't help but chuckle at his eagerness. Catching his hand, she pulled him into the room and closed the door.

He pulled free the moment she did, bent to scoop her into his arms and carried her to her bunk. To her surprise, he merely settled her on it and then lay down on his side beside her, studying her intently. She was a little disconcerted but since he seemed more interested at the moment in examining her body than getting right to the point, she studied him.

It was odd, but it made a world of difference to look at him as a potential lover than it had before. She supposed that was because it was impolite to stare, and she hadn't really looked, certainly not at such close proximity. In any case, the few times she'd come upon Jared and Kane in the bathing facilities, she'd been so shocked to see so much naked flesh that she'd come away from the experience with little more than the impression of a wall of flesh.

For that matter, she hadn't actually gotten the chance to study any of the others, even Damon. She'd been too nervous to capture impressions with her eyes with him and with Jared and Sebastian and too swept up in the way they made her feel to come away with much more than that. She hadn't been nearly as nervous after that, but Lucien and Thor had been as near frantic to get down to business as any of the others and that had precluded much of an opportunity for familiarizing herself with their bodies.

The only significant impression that she'd gotten beyond the fact that they were dark or fair was that they were all massive, very tall and bulked with muscles—even Damon. They were not carbon copies of one another, though, she realized abruptly. They were all tall and heavily muscled, but beyond the skin tones and hair color, they were each as unique in build as anyone else. There was a difference in their proportions and even their shapes, she realized.

Damon, despite his large, well defined muscles, was of a more slender build than either Kane or Jared. Sebastian also seemed long and lanky compared to them and Lucien seemed shorter and stockier, although she doubted he could possibly be much under six feet tall if he wasn't every bit of six feet.

Kane wasn't as big as Jared, she realized, although she hadn't before. His chest wasn't as broad or deep and his hips were narrower. His skin, which she'd somehow had in her mind was sun bronzed, obviously wasn't, for she saw now that his skin tones were even all over his body.

He had bruises, she saw as she examined his belly and chest—fresh bruises—and when she lifted her gaze to his face, she saw that his nose was slightly swollen and one cheek seemed more puffy than the other. Clearly, he'd been in a fight recently because it never took long for them to heal from the sort of 'light' battering they dealt each other when they were 'sparring'.

Consternation filled her. It might not be much damage, but it had to hurt if he was bruised and swollen. "What happened?"

He looked blank for a moment, then she could see the thoughts churning in his head while he tried to decide what to say. "I tripped."

She gave him a look, lifting her hand to lightly touch the bruise on his cheek. "Who helped you?"

He looked surprised. Anger flickered in his eyes briefly, but then he shrugged. "Jared is strange lately."

Chloe felt her heart flutter a little wildly. "Really?"

He grunted. "I was working with Sebastian, Thor, and Lucien and had asked them what they did when they came to you ... because I wanted to be sure to do something different and Jared hit me with his wrench."

"In the face?" Chloe gasped, horrified.

"No. On the back of the head. When I came to, he said it slipped, but I do not believe that for a moment!" he added indignantly. "It is damned strange to me that he begins to have trouble holding on to the fucking thing the minute any one of us mentions your name! He clocked the fucking fuck droid ... uh ... Damon on the forehead with it only a week ago."

Chloe's thoughts went a little wild for a moment, but she ruthlessly reined them in. "He hit Damon, too?" she asked disapprovingly. "Why?"

"As I said." He frowned, thinking it over. "Jared said that he should be first because he was first onboard the ship and Damon said that he could *not* be first because he had been first onboard ... uh ... Actually, I do not recall exactly what the discussion was about."

Chloe looked down at his chest, struggling with an odd mixture of anger, embarrassment, hopefulness, anxiety, and amusement. She didn't like to think about them fighting over her—fighting at all—but especially over her. It wasn't as if their fighting over her was going to win them points! Or that *they* could decide who was going to have her with a battle! The hopefulness .... Jealousy because they cared? Or possessiveness because they felt like they had some kind of claim to her?

As much as she hated it, she had to conclude the latter. What else *could* it be if they were fighting over who was first as if that somehow gave them more of a claim?

"So ... what did Sebastian and the others tell you?" she asked, determined to focus on Kane and dismiss the others from her mind. It was *his* night. She wasn't going to spend it speculating over how the others felt about her. Except for Damon, he had ended up dead last on the list, and she'd had sex with Damon before the list was even made up, so he actually *was* last even though Damon had the last night on her card.

"Not to begin with the kiss," he said promptly.

She sent him a startled look, immediately disappointed and worried that she hadn't been a very good kisser. "Why not?"

"Because *they* all did and none of them could remember much that they had done afterwards. Well, I do not know about Jared. He would only scowl at us after the fight."

Chloe blinked at him. "There was a fight? I thought you said he knocked you out with the wrench?"

Kane looked uncomfortable. "Well, I was not out long. Sebastian gave me the wrench and I allowed it to slip out of my hand and into his face and then we sparred for a few minutes. But then Sebastian and Lucien and Thor stepped in and stopped it, reminding us that we would end up in the brig and I would not get to come tonight."

"Well! That was a dirty trick!"

"Yes, and that is what I told him! It is one thing to do something like that to the fucking … uh …. Never mind!"

Chloe might have followed that line of discussion. It seemed to her to be a strong indication that all of them thought it was perfectly alright to pull dirty tricks on poor Damon! Kane apparently decided he'd spent enough time talking, however, he caught her shoulder and pushed her onto her back.

"I will start here," he said decisively, staring at her breasts.

Chloe instantly felt her belly tighten even though she found it a little disconcerting to carry on a conversation that was certainly not calculated foreplay and then leap right in. Shrugging inwardly, she folded her arms behind her head and smiled faintly at him. "Why there?" she asked.

He scooted down the bed, sat up and leaned across her, propping himself up with his elbow and forearm planted along her side opposite him. "Because if I kiss your mouth I will be as mad to get inside of you as the others and I also will not remember whether I gave you pleasure or not." He lifted his free hand and cupped first one breast and then the other. "And also because I have been wanting to touch these since the first time I saw them."

Chloe was beginning to feel very warm all over. "When was that?" she asked in a suffocated whisper.

"When you leaned over me to give me water that first day," he murmured absently, watching her nipples pucker and tighten with apparent fascination as he stroked first one and then the other with his fingers. "They looked soft and just the right size for my mouth."

Chloe chuckled despite the pang it caused her to remember that day, in spite of the warmth he'd already drawn from her core. "That small?"

His lips curled up at one corner. "Jared is always saying I have a big mouth."

Chapter Twelve

"Let me be the judge of that," Chloe said huskily. "I like your mouth."

He flicked a glance at her face. For a moment, he met her gaze and then his gaze dropped to her lips. "Not yet," he murmured. "I will forget all of my programming and I am trying very hard now to remember it."

Chloe felt her throat close with a mixture of emotions she had trouble identifying. Foremost, though, was the warmth of desire and the tickle of curiosity. "What are you supposed to do with those?"

"Massage them gently because they are very sensitive and when arousal begins they will be more sensitive because plucking at them and pinching the tips lightly brings a rush of blood to them. And when the nipples are very tight and flushed then I can pull them into my mouth," he added, leaning down and pulling at the one nearest him with his lips.

Chloe's breath caught in her chest with anticipation. Her belly shimmied. She closed her eyes when he opened his mouth and she felt his heat, felt his tongue curl around the tip and then the pull of the suction of his mouth. She focused on the image that rose in her mind of his mouth at her breast for a moment and opened her eyes and watched him.

More warmth flowed through her, and yet an odd sort of tightness gathered in her chest that had nothing to do with desire. She pulled her arms from beneath her head and stroked his head and then cradled him to her. Both sensations increased but it would've been hard to say if it was only emotion that created it or a combination of that and the tease of his tongue.

In a few moments, her mind shifted to focus entirely on the feel of his mouth as the warmth became heat and the heat began a molten river flowing through her body to her sex. The muscles along her channel began to flex and relax involuntarily. She felt the warm flow of her body's natural lubricant seeping from the walls in anticipation of his possession. By the time he lifted his head and moved to her other breast, she was having trouble being still for him, trouble catching her breath. Her mouth had dried from the gasping pants she couldn't seem to control. Her mind had clouded with a dizzying influx of nature's pleasure drug.

She felt the rise of his own desire, as well, and that fed the fire his touch had begun. His breath had accelerated until he was breathing more heavily even than her. A faint quiver had begun in the hand that held her breast to his mouth. He ceased to tease with practiced flicks of his tongue and began to pull at her hungrily.

She arched her back in silent demand when he lifted his mouth from her breast, but he seemed oblivious to it, intent on exploring further. He traced a wandering path along her ribs to her belly and found places with his mouth and tongue that she'd had no idea were so sensitive that his lightest touch would make her belly quake and clench almost painfully.

She was so focused on the heated, torturous currents jolting through her, she hardly noticed, at first, when he dragged one knee up and pushed her leg to one side until he had nibbled along it from just above her knee to the top of her thigh. She jerked all over at the jolt that went through her when he sucked on that little patch of skin, trying to slam her legs back together.

He caught her other leg as she clamped his head between her thighs and pulled until she realized it was useless to try to struggle against his strength and yielded. His heated breath whispered over the lips of her sex as he turned his head and bit lightly at the opposite thigh. She gasped, and then gasped more sharply, clamping her hands on his head when he turned his head again and dragged his tongue along her nether lips, parting them with the tip and tracing a path upwards along the excruciatingly sensitive skin until he found a spot that was more sensitive than anything else.

She curled her fingers into claws as he paused to explore her clit, alternately flicking at it and sucking, too mindless within moments to decide whether she liked it or if it was too intense, if she could stand it. She decided she couldn't. She couldn't be still. She couldn't process the jolts running through her.

She discovered he was not to be discouraged. For a few moments, she tried to fight him off and then, abruptly, such a rush went through her that it took her breath. She gasped hoarsely, trying to take in air, but the spasms were so intense she couldn't seem to manage anything more than the hoarse attempts to breathe. She'd reached the point where she was nearly screaming before he finally lifted his head and allowed her body to cease convulsing in ecstasy.

Expelling a breath of relief, she went perfectly limp as all the strength left her body. When he released his grip on her legs, they fell to either side of her as limply as the rest of her body. She very quickly discovered, however, that the blood was still pounding in every pulse point.

Kane discovered them on his return path. She was so exquisitely sensitive his light kisses almost made her skin hurt, and she was thrashing almost as frantically for release by the time he reached her breasts as she had been when he'd tortured a climax out of her from pulling at her clit.

She groaned a little desperately when he began teasing her nipples, locking her arms around his head, struggling with the urge to beg him to stop. Thankfully, he moved upward after a very brief salute of each and nuzzled his face against her throat. "I pleasured you?" he asked hoarsely.

"My god, Kane!" Chloe gasped, catching his face between her hands and dragging him closer.

A shudder rippled all the way through him as he locked his mouth to hers, kissing her deeply, with desperation that told her how much it had taken for him to wait to pleasure her first. She pulled at him, urging him to penetrate her, lifting a leg to his buttocks and trying to pull his hips to her when he didn't respond quickly enough to suit her. He broke from her mouth, gasping harshly, reached shakily between them to match his body to hers, and pumped his hips to sheathe his cock inside her. She was nearly as frantic as he was by the time he'd claimed her completely, bucking and pulling at him to try to help overcome the strain of her own body to yield to his girth.

A harder shudder traveled through him as he sawed slowly in and out a few times. He paused, breathing harshly against the side of her neck. The muscles along her channel quaked plaintively around his shaft, demanding stimulation. He caught his breath, held it a long moment and began to move with smooth even strokes. She clung, squeezing her eyes tightly as she felt the gathering inside of her. It rose higher and faster than she'd felt it before. Her body stammered at the edge of the precipice, teasing her until she'd begun to despair that it would give her what she wanted and then, when she felt him begin to shake, felt the jerk of his cock inside of her, her body exploded with release. A long, animalistic groan tore its way free of her chest at the force of it.

He encircled her with his arms, rolling onto his back and taking her with him. Replete, she lay limply on his chest, trying to catch her breath. Her belly clenched in an aftershock and he shifted his hands to her hips, bearing down on them. "You will push me out," he muttered.

"You didn't come?" she murmured tiredly.

"Yes ... or you could not push me out. It is limp like the rest of me now."

He sounded disappointed. "Then it doesn't need to be in there."

"I like it in there."

She smiled against his shoulder and moved her face closer to his neck, nibbling light kisses there. "I don't know what you did, but I think I liked it."

He tensed slightly. "You do not know?"

She thought about it. "I'm not sure. You might have to do it a few more times before I'm completely sure."

He drew away to study her face and abruptly grimaced. "My cock is dead now. Your pussy choked it."

Chloe chuckled and then laughed.

"Now you have done it! You have pushed it out! Next time I will know not to make you laugh."

* * * *

Chloe hadn't actually believed Kane had clobbered Jared with the wrench until she saw him the following morning. He had a knot on his forehead the size of an egg, however. She stared at it, aghast, for several moments before she decided it might not be a good thing to draw attention to it when Reuel was sitting at the table.

There was very little that escaped Reuel's attention, though. He was studying her with a mixture of irritation and amusement when she flicked a quick look at him. "The sex act has certainly calmed things down around here," he said dryly. "Now if we can just tone down the accidents in the work place …."

"There've been accidents?" Chloe gasped, horrified.

Reuel's lips thinned. "Mostly minor," he said soothingly.

She felt her face heat as it abruptly dawned on her that he'd been referring to the 'reports' the men had invented to cover the fact that they were still fighting. Really! She just wasn't at her best that early in the damn morning, especially since she hardly ever got a decent night's sleep anymore!

She was beginning to get used to having most of her bed taken up by man meat, but if they weren't sleeping all over her, or taking up most of the bed so that she had to turn in place if she wanted to roll over, they were awake and wanted to fuck!

"I need to get a bigger bed," she muttered.

Apparently not low enough. When she glanced up as she reached for her glass of juice, she discovered all of the men were looking at her.

Reuel changed the subject abruptly. "We should settle into orbit around Climatius by 1600 Earth Standard Time today. Would you like to accompany me on a final inspection of the ships that will take part in the raid?"

Chloe tensed immediately at the reminder that they'd scheduled the raid to coincide with midnight Climatius time. They'd timed their approach to make certain that the target site would be on the dark side of the planet when they settled into orbit. Theoretically, there would be less personnel on duty and those who were would be more lax.

She didn't know if they would find that to be the actual case or not but, regardless, she didn't think the raid Reuel had planned would be a 'little' thing. She nodded, hoping it would make her feel better about the business if she could see how well planned out it was.

A flicker of surprise went through her when she glanced at the other men at the table, however. All six of them were staring at Reuel with varying degrees of distrust and anger. She frowned, uncertain of what to make of that, although she could hardly question them about it in front of Reuel if they'd decided they didn't trust him. Deciding she would find an opportunity sometime during the day before the raid was launched to discuss it with them, she finished her breakfast and returned her tray.

"Their distrust is not of a military nature," Reuel said dryly when he'd walked her out of the mess hall.

Chloe glanced at him sharply but forbore comment.

"They are concerned that I might have an interest in you," he continued pensively.

Chloe gaped at him, feeling her face heat and then frowned thoughtfully, wondering it if was true or if he was just guessing.

He uttered a derisive snort of amusement. "You disappoint me. I thought that you would ask if I did."

She threw him a startled look. "Do you? Never mind! Don't answer that!"

He frowned but after a moment his brow cleared. "You are right. It will be best not to go there. There are some boundaries it is best not to cross. I only brought it up because I could see you were wondering at the suspicious glares they bent upon me. I could be wrong, but I believe they trust me implicitly in all matters military and also trust that I always have the best interests of our people at heart. They are not quite as trusting in ... other matters more personal."

Chloe felt her heart skip a beat at the suggestion that they had a personal interest in her. She struggled with it, trying to decide whether Reuel had misunderstood or not and realized it was possible he had. She would just have to have that discussion with them, she decided. It wasn't a bad idea to be sure that it at least wasn't doubts they'd begun to have about Reuel.

"I begin to foresee problems ahead for us," he muttered. "But, one thing at the time. No doubt we will face many challenges."

That was pretty cryptic as far as Chloe was concerned, but then she was, admittedly, a little preoccupied.

The small lander that was little more than an escape pod and the shuttle that belonged to the Salvager had both been transformed. All of the seats had been removed from both except for the pilot seat and a handful of jump seats as well as everything else that wasn't absolutely essential to flight or navigation. A sniper's observation turret and a pulse laser had been added to each, both low profile in a way that would make it difficult to spot them until and unless they were needed. The lander had been designated to collect miscellaneous essential.

"This will be primarily, but not limited to, medical supplies. It will be manned by a squad that will include a medic who has been instructed to compile an essentials list," Reuel explained.

Chloe looked at him in surprise. "But … your nanos heal you, right?"

He studied her for a moment. "You do not have nanos," he finally said gently and then shrugged. "I am also disturbed by the … difficulty that Salina has had adjusting. I cannot keep her in the brig indefinitely and our medics are not certain that they can come up with a treatment to help her to adjust. I also cannot rule out the possibility of others. The medics will use her to try to develop an effective treatment, but they have expressed a … need to have some sort of drug to aid them."

Chloe felt as if the bottom had fallen out of her stomach. She nodded, trying not to think about what sort of experimentation they might be doing on the woman or the possibility that *she* might need medical help. She hadn't thought about that, at all, when she'd considered settling on the new world. "Thank you."

Reuel lifted his brows questioningly.

"For thinking about me."

He looked uncomfortable. "I would like to take full credit, but it was Jared and Kane who pointed it out to me." He shrugged. "I find myself inclined to think of you as one of us."

Chloe felt her chest swell with a heady pleasure that was probably disproportionate to the compliment and Jared's and Kane's thoughtfulness, but it made her happy and helped her to dismiss the shadows that had gathered from the somber discussion of medications and treatments. "Then thank you for that … and I'll thank Jared and Kane for thinking of me."

Nodding acknowledgement, he led her out of the lander and to the shuttle. This had been stripped down and equipped as the lander had. A steel cage had been added in the cleared area. "This detail will focus on acquiring whatever weaponry and ammunition is available."

Chloe studied the cage and finally realized it was to protect the crew from flying debris if they had to outmaneuver pursuit. Almost as if Reuel had read her thoughts, he explained that their mechanics had done what they could to boost the engines, increase maneuverability, and that the ships could also benefit in both areas from the weight they had removed.

She hadn't actually been in Reuel's ship before, but she knew they had had a med bay and that he'd arrived with nearly a troop of men so she realized immediately that it, too, had been stripped. The jump seats to carry the troops had been squeezed into a tight area on either side, leaving the center of the ship open except for the large cargo area they'd created that was surrounded by a similar cage to the one for weapons.

Reuel's ship was to load what they'd primarily come for—food. It comforted Chloe that his main concern was a focus on feeding the people on the long journey they anticipated and not on weapons. "Did you add sniper's turrets to this ship, too?"

Reuel smiled faintly. "This ship was already well armed. We modified it as a battleship as soon as we took it. There is a photon cannon front and rear and three pulse lasers on either side, front, center, and rear. This ship will lead the raid and cover the retreat of the other two since they are poorly armed and do not have the speed of my ship.

"In the event that the Salvager comes under attack, we have outfitted it with two photon cannons that we found in the hold and repaired and a pulse laser. I do not anticipate that," he added when she sent him an uneasy look. "As the leader of one of Earth's great early civilizations once said, however, 'walk softly and carry a big stick'. It is far better to be prepared for attack and not need it than to need protection and not have it. If it should become necessary, we will cover the Salvager's retreat and rendezvous at the next jump point."

He took her to tour the 'improvements' to the Salvager once they'd finished inspecting the smaller ships. "Sebastian, Lucien, and Thor will stay behind to man the guns."

Chloe frowned, not only because he had left her out of the selection process, but also because that meant that Damon, Jared, and Kane would be going with him.

"Jared suggested it," he said. "The three were part of a cavalry unit during the late war and are experienced with handling heavy artillery. He and Kane were infantry and Damon, of course, has no battle experience."

Chloe swallowed her protest with an effort. She didn't like it, at all, but if Jared thought it was for the best, she thought she should trust his judgment. They needed a ship to get back to, after all.

She decided to dispense with any attempt at subtlety in speaking with the men about her concerns. "I'd like to speak with my crewmen in my quarters before the raid," she said flatly.

Reuel nodded. "I will see to it that they report to you at 1800 EST ... before we launch our assault."

She really *wished* he hadn't put it that way! Raid sounded much better. It suggested that they would sneak in and sneak out again without detection. Assault suggested that he expected trouble.

She discovered she didn't get an opportunity to speak with them privately before that. They shared the noon meal, but everyone seemed preoccupied and untalkative—*not* that they were chatty at any time!

Their preoccupation worried her more. She supposed she should have been reassured by it. If they were that focused on the upcoming 'campaign' that was a good thing since it ruled out the possibility of them being shot because they had their mind on things they shouldn't. She didn't find that those thoughts actually did comfort her much, though, because she couldn't convince herself that they weren't worried.

It didn't occur to her until the three of them reported to her quarters as Reuel had promised that she should've demanded a private interview with each of them. It was too late for that, though. They were clearly tense and preoccupied with the need to get down to the bay and load up with everyone else.

"You have concerns?" Jared asked before she could formulate the questions she'd wanted to ask him.

"I wanted to know if any of you had concerns," Chloe asked baldly. "It seemed to me when Reuel asked me to inspect the ships that you might. I didn't want you to leave with him if you have any doubts about this ... any part of it. This is still my ship and you're still my crew and my concerns are with my crew and my ship first."

The three men glanced at one another comfortably. "You are asking if we trust Reuel?" Jared asked finally.

"Yes! That's exactly what I'm asking. Should I?"

Jared and Kane seemed to be wrestling with their answer.

"I do not especially care for his interest in you!" Damon snapped. "I could not say about anything else—I think that he is a great man and that he can be completely relied upon to do what is best for everyone ... overall. He is still a man, however."

Relief and hopefulness flooded her. "He didn't sign my dance card," she said pointedly.

"He did not sign *any* of the dance cards," Jared said. "He is the general. He does not need to."

"And the other women will be all too delighted to accommodate him," Chloe said. "As I said, my first interest and loyalty is to my own crew and their well being." Dismissing her qualms about whether she should or shouldn't behave in a personal way in a professional situation, she closed the distance between her and Jared and slipped her arms around his waist, hugging him tightly. Before she could pull away completely, he caught her and dragged her back, kissing her. It was no friendly peck, but deep penetration that was both possessive and hungry.

When he finally released her, she saw that Damon and Kane were headed out the door. "Get back here! I didn't dismiss you!"

They halted and turned to look at her in surprise. Jared, she saw, was also surprised and not especially pleased. She ignored his disapproval, hugging each one tightly and kissing them as Jared had kissed her. "We're a family," she admonished them. "Families take care of each other. Watch your backs and watch out for each other! Promise me!"

They stared at her with a good deal of bemusement but finally nodded and left.

She wanted to fling herself on her bunk and cry her eyes out when they had. Instead, she gulped back the urge and, when she thought she had herself firmly in control, she made her way to the control room that overlooked the docking bay, watching as Reuel gave the troops last minute instructions and then the men split up and headed to the gangplank. As she'd hoped, Damon, Kane, and Jared paused before they went inside and looked up.

She placed her palm on the partition glass. "Come back to me!" She knew they couldn't hear her. She doubted that they could see the movement of her lips much less read them at such a distance, but it was a prayer of sorts. The images of the ships wavered in her vision as they shot from the bay and into space. Sniffing, she scrubbed at her eyes and closed the bay door.

Sebastian, Lucien, and Thor had been standing behind her, she discovered when she turned. She couldn't tell anything about their expressions, but she thought it was probably a good bet that they'd come in when she did. Or maybe they'd already been in the control room? She'd been too distressed and focused on what was happening in the bay to really notice.

She sniffed again. "Nothing really to do now but wait," she muttered. "You guys want to play a few rounds of chess?"

* * * *

Jared was still in turmoil when he settled in his seat and pulled his harness on. He found himself wavering between his anger at being ordered to watch Damon's back when he had more than half hoped that the bastard would take a bullet in the head or catch a mortar in the chest, and confusion and hope.

"She said that we were family," Kane said, a touch of wonder in his voice. "Do you think that she meant that in the most intimate sense that humans use that term? Or do you think she was only saying that because we are crewmates?"

Damon scowled at him. "Do not be more of an idiot that you can help!" he growled. "There is no blood bond and certainly no contractual bond! She could not have meant it in any sense beyond the fact that we are crewmates!"

"Do not call my friend an idiot!" Jared snapped. "He *is* an idiot, but I will brain you with something if you call him one again!"

Kane divided a glare between the two men, trying to decide which of them had most insulted him. "You only think that you are brilliant because you know how to seduce a woman, but you know no more about courting than either of us, for that is not the same! *I* pleasured her! I have that programming as well as you, although it is not as sophisticated, and I have not had experience to learn more! So you need not feel so gods damned superior, you fucking fuck droid!

"I am sorry that I promised Chloe to watch your back! I had thought that this would be a very good time to throw you under something that would flatten you!"

"I was thinking more along the lines of blowing his head off," Jared said grimly. "Or mayhap throwing him into a recycling crusher."

"If you believe that that comes as any great surprise," Damon snapped, "then you are as much an idiot as Kane! I am not *just* a fucking fuck droid, gods damn it! I have the same programming for combat as you do. Regretfully, I cannot regress to the muscle bound ape mentality that the two of you share, but I had planned to throw the two of you into the recycling crusher when you made your move. I suppose I will not be able to now, however, when Chloe made me promise not to."

Jared decided to access his data to discover what an ape was before he brained Damon for the insult. As he had expected, he was outraged when he discovered what the creature was. Apparently, Kane had accessed it, as well. He punched Damon in the face. Damon punched him back.

"Gods damn it!" Jared yelled when Kane jolted him. "I am trying to fly here! Save it until we are on the ground!"

"If this is what the three of you consider watching one another's back," Reuel's man, Corin, snapped, "I believe that I will join one of the other squads when we are on the ground. Or better yet, I will shoot all three of you! It will make room for more at Chloe's table."

"You had better mean Chloe's table in the gods damned mess hall!" Kane growled, "because if you mean what I think you mean I will kick your ass when we land!"

"I will help him!" Damon offered. "Because I am thinking the gods damned bastard was *not* thinking about the table in the mess hall!"

"She is *our* family!" Jared growled. "And there are already five too gods damned many men in this fucking family!"

"Exactly what do you mean *five too many*?" Kane demanded. "She did not say you were her family and stop there! I know that you would like to think that you count more than anyone else only because they dragged you onto the ship first, but Chloe does not think that way and it is *her* opinion that matters!"

"He cannot be first with Chloe, gods damn it!" Damon said tightly. "*I* was first with Chloe!"

"If you keep throwing that up to me," Jared growled, "I will knock your teeth down your throat … again."

"You did not knock my teeth down my throat!" Damon snapped. "You only knocked *one* down my throat and loosened two others. And you will not catch me off guard to do so again! It takes too gods damn long to grow another!"

"He is worried that Chloe will not think him as pretty without his teeth," Kane said with a snort.

"That is a very good thought," Jared said meditatively. "It is worth a try."

"You will not be as pretty to her, either, if I knock your nose a little to the left!"

Jared thought about it for a few minutes. "Well, there are at least *three* too many, gods damn it! I am damned if I understand why Sebastian, Lucien, and Thor believe they have any claim at all!"

"If Chloe considers you knuckle-heads family," Corin growled, "then you will have plenty of opportunity to beat the shit out of one another later. Can we focus on the gods damned mission?"

Damon and Kane exchanged a look and turned almost at the same moment to slug Corin. His eyes rolled back in his head. "Now that he has decided to shut his mouth," Kane growled, "I would like to know what we are going to do about Sebastian's squad. I do not see that they have any sort of claim either and if we rid ourselves of them, then we will have twice as much time with Chloe."

Chapter Thirteen

"We can always fuck," Thor suggested hopefully. "That would be a far more pleasurable way to spend the time, and it would help to relieve stress, as well."

Chloe gaped at him for a moment and then glared. "How can you think of fucking at a time like this?" she demanded.

Thor frowned. "I have not seen that a very great deal distracts my mind from fucking, especially now that I have. Before, I had only thought that I would like to very much. Now that I have, I *know* that I like it very much. It is very odd, I suppose, that I think of it more now than I did before, but my balls did not bother me nearly as much before I had done it as they do now. I cannot tell a great deal of difference between now and before with my cock. It was always standing up at the least comfortable times, but the balls are definitely different."

Chloe stared at him in fascination for several moments and finally glanced at Sebastian and Lucien. Their hopeful expressions made it clear that, while Thor was the one who had brought it up, they certainly weren't against the suggestion. "No!"

Their faces fell. It was almost amusing. It might have been if she hadn't been so worried about Jared, Kane, and Damon. Under the circumstances, she was mildly annoyed.

"Mayhap you could play naked?" Sebastian suggested tentatively. "Then we could at least look at them."

Chloe blinked at him. It was impossible to completely ignore the warmth that flickered through her at the suggestion, but she thought it was something for another time ... when she might feel a little more inclined to play. "Them?"

"Your pretty breasts and your beautiful pussy."

Chloe bit her lip, unable to prevent a flicker of amusement despite her irritation. "My ... pussy's beautiful?" she asked tentatively. "I thought *I* was beautiful."

Sebastian elbowed Thor when he started to answer. Evidently, he had figured out it was a trick question even though Thor apparently hadn't.

"You are the most beautiful woman I have ever seen," Sebastian answered. "You have a beautiful face, a beautiful smile, beautiful eyes .... Beautiful breasts and *the* most beautiful pussy."

"Exactly how many pussies have you seen?" Chloe asked dryly.

Something flickered in his eyes. He glanced at Lucien.

"In person?" Lucien asked uneasily. "Because there are easily fifty in my memory banks."

Chloe thought that over and decided it was close enough to an actual comparison not to put them on the spot. "Well, you guys have beautiful dicks. Let's play chess."

They followed her to the bridge. "How many dicks have you seen?" Sebastian asked.

Chloe frowned. "I'm pretty sure I've seen all of them on the ship by now," she retorted dryly. "I've only played with six, though."

"You did not study them," Sebastian pointed out, frowning.

"Well, I felt them. I'll study them later."

"You may study them now if you like."

"No thanks! I'll do that another time."

"Can I study your pussy while you do that?" Thor asked.

"I thought you'd already studied it and decided it was the most beautiful pussy you'd ever seen?" Chloe said absently, pulling the chessboard out of the locker and searching for the pieces.

"I did not study it as much as I wanted to. I was trying to get my dick inside of it."

"Next time, then."

"You have seen other cocks?" Sebastian asked as she set the chessboard on the table they usually used, a faint edge to his voice.

Chloe paused, thinking about it, and shuddered. "Don't remind me! I did accidently arrive at the showers when the old crew was in there once. That was a real shock ... on so many levels! I mean, they hardly ever used the damned facilities. Pops was in there, too. Thank *god* I have amnesia over that!"

"You did not think they had beautiful dicks?" Sebastian asked suspiciously.

She shuddered again. "Didn't I just tell you not to remind me! They were gross—all of them. Well, I don't know about Pops. Like I said, I blanked that from my mind! To be perfectly honest, I'm not even sure he was facing my direction so I might not have seen it anyway. Ok. First challenger!"

Sebastian took the seat across from her. "Why do you get black?"

"Because I always get black. I'm used to it. If I switch, I'll be trying to move your pieces."

To her relief, they settled to studying the board. Honestly! She'd begun to think she wouldn't be able to divert them from fucking!

"Damon is last and you have one free day," Sebastian said as she made her first move. "Lucien, Thor, and I were wondering if you would be interested in trying two three ways or mayhap one four?"

Chloe lifted her head and stared at him, trying to decide whether she was more horrified or intrigued. A brief inventory squelched the interest. "I only have two holes," she said dryly. "And one is exit only!"

"You did not count your mouth," Thor pointed out.

She stared at him, trying to summon an image that included the four of them and finally gave up when she couldn't figure out the logistics. "I don't think I'm ready for that, guys! I'm still getting used to the regular stuff. Maybe later? I'm not at all sure about the ... uh ... backdoor thing, though. I mean, I could see where you might like it, I suppose, but I don't think I would. Sounds ... uncomfortable."

"But you are not completely against it?" Sebastian asked hopefully.

"I tell you what ... if you guys won't bug me about it anymore for a while, I'll think about it."

* * * *

Despite an earnest desire to take their disagreement to the next level, Jared tamped it when he heard ground control issue permission for them to land. As he'd been ordered, he waited until Reuel's ship had landed before he settled the lander that he was piloting. The Salvager's shuttle was the last to set down. The gangplank had already been lowered and Reuel had started down it when Jared lowered theirs. Checking to make certain Damon, Kane, and Corin had the electronic devices they were to distribute among the ships likely to give them trouble, he strolled casually to the hatch and stood at the top of the gangplank as if he was merely awaiting orders from Reuel. Behind him, Kane opened the secondary hatch and he, Damon, and Corin dropped through it and scattered, hopefully shielded from detection by the gangplank and Jared. Since there was no immediate evidence that they'd been noticed, Jared descended the gangplank as soon as the last had closed the hatch behind him.

Reuel met the senior space port authority on duty on the tarmac and presented him with the requisitions orders they had compiled and then forged into 'official' paperwork.

"Well shit!" the man said when he'd studied the list. "This is the second gods damned time we've been hit up for supplies from the fucking government in as many months!"

"You do not have what we need?" Reuel demanded sharply.

The man sent him a disgusted look. "We've got it—most of it anyway. We just got a gods damned supply ship in a week ago." He expelled an explosive breath. "Well, I'll get somebody on it. The government's credits is as good as anybody else's, I reckon, except for the fucking discount they demand. When you want it?"

"We are here now," Reuel said pointedly.

"Hey! No fucking problem. It is the middle of the fucking night, but what the fuck! You got anybody to load it? Because I don't have enough men on the nightshift to handle this."

Reuel nodded. "I brought a detachment of cyborgs."

The man looked startled. "No shit? I thought they'd all been recalled."

"These were naturally cleared before they were returned to duty. If you have any that you have taken, we are instructed to pick them up and return them to the manufacturer."

The man blew out a breath. "Man you can have them! I will be glad to get those scary mother fuckers out of here!"

"So … you do have some held here?"

"About a dozen, I guess. Let's go back to my office and do the paperwork. You can transfer the credits and we're in business."

Nodding, Reuel signaled the man stationed at the top of the gangplank of his ship and walked into the space terminal with the officer of the port authority.

Jared relaxed fractionally when that part of the plan, at least, seemed to go off without a hitch. Now, if they could just manage to get everything loaded and get off the ground without anyone noticing the transfer of funds from the government account, they would be home free!

He did not particularly like that part of the plan. Although he was in complete agreement that the government owed them for time served in the forces even if they disregarded compensation for being abandoned on that fucking planet, it seemed too risky to him to thumb their noses at the government.

On the other hand, it was not as if they had any monetary resources of their own, and Chloe had spent all of hers bribing the last port authority. They did not have a lot of options and it was certainly better to try Reuel's ruse rather than to come in with guns blazing and try to load their supplies and shoot their way out again. At least this way they had some possibility of getting what they needed without being filled full of holes.

Damon, Kane, and finally Corin returned after a time. Jared scanned the windows of the building overlooking the tarmac and finally signaled that it was safe for them to show themselves. A half a dozen men had wandered casually down the gangplank of Reuel's craft and ranged themselves around the ship.

There was nothing at all casual about it, of course, but he thought they made a good impression of men simply walking around and stretching their legs. He and the others with him crouched, or took positions leaning against the ship in an attempt to appear bored with waiting.

The truth was, the longer they waited the more tense they became, however. He'd begun to suspect they had been discovered and Reuel taken when Reuel appeared again, walking briskly toward his ship. Behind him, armed men marched a group of cyborgs, heavily manacled and chained, toward Reuel's ship.

As they neared, Jared straightened and searched the faces of the cyborgs being led out. He did not recognize any of them, however, and disappointment flickered through him. He had been certain that the other men who had formed his squad had not made it, but there had been other salvagers scanning the planet for anything that might be salvageable. He had thought there was at least a chance that some of the others had made it.

He supposed there still was. They could be anywhere, though. It had been absurd even to look.

The cyborgs had reached the gangplank and Reuel's men had emerged to take custody of them when a convoy of mover drones rounded a building in the distance and approached them. Jared tensed immediately, waiting until the drones had pulled to a stop and opened before he relaxed.

"Let us get to it," he said grimly, striding briskly toward the cargo drones to look for the weapons he and his men were to transport. It would have been far more efficient to form a line as the cyborgs unloading the food supplies had besides giving him the possibility of knocking the fuck out of Damon, but he thought it best not to make too much of a display of their strength. It tended to unnerve humans and, in any case, he could not recall whether he and his crew were supposed to be cyborgs or not. They unloaded their cases by pairs and carried them to the lander.

They had finished loading their cargo as had the squad piloting the shuttle when the moment that Jared had hoped would not arrive, did.

The officer that had arranged their pickup came running from the terminal with a half dozen men screaming 'stop them!' at the top of his lungs to the contingent of guards who had escorted the prisoners and lingered to gawk.

It was unfortunate for the guards. The soldiers who had been waiting just inside the ship instantly burst through the open hatch and opened fire, mowing them down while they were still trying to figure out what was happening. Jared leapt up the gangplank, grabbed the weapons they had left by the open hatch, and pitched them to the men on the ground before he grabbed his own.

The drone carriers parked in front of Reuel's ship shielded both the ship and the men for the most part, but it had the same benefit to the port authority on the other side. They had hit the tarmac the moment Reuel's men shot the guards and were taking potshots at the men still frantically unloading the supplies and pitching them into the ship.

Jared's squad and the squad from the Salvager's shuttle rounded the carriers and lay down fire, killing at least three of the men with the officer immediately. They picked off the others as they leapt to their feet and tried to retreat to the building.

The first Jared realized that there were men on upper floors of the building shooting at them was when a laser guided projectile slammed into his shoulder hard enough it rocked him back on his heels. Before the pain could even register, a second projectile struck him in the thigh. His knee buckled, throwing his aim off as he tossed his weapon to his other arm to fire.

Kane and Damon both leapt at him, Kane to plant himself in front of him and return fire while Damon hooked an arm beneath his and hauled him to his feet. Reuel was bellowing at the four of them as they pulled back with Kane and Corin covering their retreat. "Get in the air, gods damn it! We are done here!"

Jared nodded groggily, too focused on trying to keep both feet under him when one leg seemed completely uncooperative. Damon pitched his weapon inside the ship when they reached the gangplank, hauled Jared over his shoulder and dashed up the gangplank with him. Kane and Corin charged up behind them. Kane leapt over Damon and Jared as Damon bent down to lower Jared to the floor.

"Do not leave him on the floor!" Kane bellowed. "Strap him into a jump seat!"

Nodding, Damon hauled Jared up again and dropped him into a seat. When he had fastened his harness, he caught Jared's hands and planted one over each wound. "Hold them there until the nanos have slowed the bleeding. You are loosing too much too fast!"

Nodding drunkenly, Jared gritted his teeth and tightened his hands over the holes, counting in his head to try to keep from passing out. His stomach went weightless, alerting him to the fact that the ship had taken off. It began to buck almost immediately. "You never could fly worth a fuck, Kane," he said drunkenly.

"He is wounded also," Corin said, unfastening his harness and staggering toward the front. "Give me the controls, Kane! I am not wounded as badly as you are."

The lander pitched and dipped from side to side as the two traded places and then the craft leveled out briefly. Kane made his way to the back and settled in the jump seat beside Jared, pulling the safety harness on.

Jared managed to lift his head. "You are wounded?"

"It has stopped bleeding. Lift your hands and let me see yours."

Jared discovered he had to focus really hard to lift either hand. "The wound on your leg has stopped bleeding. Put your hand back on your shoulder."

Jared studied his hands, trying to figure out which one he'd had on his shoulder. While he was trying to figure it out, someone clamped a hand over his throbbing shoulder and he passed out.

Kane studied him, glanced at Damon, who had clamped his hand over Jared's wound and finally settled back. "Good! He will rest a bit and he will be a little better when he awakens. Were you wounded?"

"Nothing significant," Damon said tightly.

"Chloe would say that anything was significant," Kane said with a touch of amusement, then added a little hopefully. "You did not mar that lovely face? Or catch shrapnel in your dick?"

Damon made an obscene gesture at him. "It pains me to disappoint you, but no. I caught one in the arm and another in my side. They have stopped bleeding. I believe the projectiles passed through."

"It is a very good thing that I was there to catch those that missed you," Kane said wryly.

* * * *

Chloe jumped so violently when the com-link suddenly burst to life that she scattered chess pieces everywhere. "Salvager! This is Reuel. We are coming home with company! Salvager acknowledge!"

"Battle stations!" Chloe bellowed, leaping to her feet and charging toward the console. "This is the Salvager. Acknowledge receipt of transmission. Preparing a welcome!"

"Prepare to jump. ETA your pups, in twenty. We will rendezvous!"

"Acknowledged!"

"Computer. Prepare the Salvager for the jump ordered for 1900 EST."

"Checking systems. Initiating drives. Calculating required speed."

"Give it a kick in the ass, computer! We'll need to jump in … estimate thirty minutes."

"Mark."

Discovering when she turned that she had the bridge to herself, Chloe glanced at the game board and the pieces all over the floor. She turned to the console again and depressed the inner ship com-link. "Sound off when you reach your stations."

"Sebastian, on station, Captain!"

She chewed a fingernail, waiting.

"Lucien, on station, Captain!"

"Thor present, Captain. How many bogies?"

"Unknown. Our pups are leading the pack. Watch out for them.

Reuel estimates …," she paused to check the time. It seemed impossible that ten minutes had already passed, "ten."

"Affirmative. I have a visual on the runt now."

Chloe felt her heart slam into her ribs painfully. Her guys were on the lander, 'the runt'. Struggling not to race down to the bay, she checked the data scrolling across her console. Systems check was good—no failures. "ETA on the jump, computer."

"Estimate the Salvager will be prepared to jump in fifteen minutes thirty seconds EST."

Chloe chewed her lip, trying to decide if that would give the men time to bail out and get into jump harnesses. It might, but the shuttle was trailing them and it didn't have jump capabilities either. "Prepare to place a hold on the jump!"

"Affirmative, Captain. I can only hold five minutes to begin a new count."

"Acknowledged," Chloe responded, whirling and racing to the door of the bridge.

Maybe they didn't need her down there, but she couldn't stand on the bridge wondering if everyone was safely aboard. She had to see it with her own eyes.

The bay doors were opening as she reached the control room. Her heart in her throat, she rushed to the viewing window as the ship slipped through the opening and skidded across the bay. It hadn't even come to a complete halt when the shuttle slid in behind it.

"Salvager! Change of plan! We are coming with!"

Chloe raced to the com unit. "Make it quick! We're on count down now."

"We will unload after the jump. We are right on you, Salvager."

Chloe whipped a look around and spied the ship. It looked like it was coming in way too fast to her. She felt her belly clench as it skimmed through the closing bay doors close enough she heard the scrape of metal. Fortunately, it wasn't enough of a jolt to the doors to make them halt and open again. They continued their slow advance, narrowly missing the tail of the craft as it slipped through.

"Five minutes," the computer announced.

Reuel's ship slid to a halt with a grind of metal that made her wince.

"Do not delay! Repeat, do not delay! Initiate!" she shouted, racing to reach the jump harness in the corner of the control room and get into it, praying the bay doors would close before they made the jump.

She had no idea what might happen if the doors didn't, but it occurred to her that the entire bay might empty.

She felt the pull before she'd finished buckling her harness. Gritting her teeth, she managed to bring the two halves of the clasp together. It locked with a click a split second before something hit the hull hard enough to shake the entire ship. Her last thought before blackout was that they'd been hit.

The warning alarm was blaring deafeningly when she roused again. It connected instantly in her mind with the jolt she'd felt just before blackout. Scrambling out of her harness, she moved to the com-link. "Status?" she shouted over the alarms.

"Hull breach in sector six B deck, locked down. Breach in sector seven B deck, locked down."

Her mind went blank. She couldn't remember where her men were. "Sound off! Sebastian! Lucien! Thor!"

Relief flooded her when she heard them. "Turn off the damned alarms, computer! You guys get over to B deck and check those breaches."

"I am on B deck," Sebastian responded.

"My god! Are you alright?"

"Minimal damage," he responded.

"What the fuck is minimal damage? Are you talking about yourself? Or the ship?" Chloe exclaimed. "Damn it! I'm coming up."

She crossed to the observation window to check on the crews in the ships in the bay and halted in horror. There were men limping from all three, but she instantly saw that Damon and another man were carrying a third.

Wrenching the door open, she raced across the bay to meet them, skidding to a halt when she saw that it was Jared they carrying. She clapped a hand over her mouth when she saw the blood. "Is he ...?"

"He is only unconscious," Kane said, his voice strained.

Dragging her gaze from Jared, she looked at him and saw that he wasn't in much better shape that Jared. He was bloody all over and there were blackened holes burned in his flight suit to dispel any hope that it was Jared's blood and not his. Damon, she saw, was also wounded, his face pale. She moved away when she realized they were near to dropping themselves and that she'd held them up.

She glanced around a little frantically. "Medic! We need a couple of medics over here!"

Damon and the other man—she didn't know his name—settled Jared on the deck a little roughly and dropped to the deck themselves. She rushed to help Kane when she saw that he was trying to sit down.

"Get away, Chloe!" he growled. "I will fall on you and hurt you."

Her chin wobbled, but she backed off, struggling to keep from crying as she watched him drop to his knees and then fall clumsily onto his side.

Two men approached them that she assumed were medics. One

moved to Jared and the other to Kane.

After examining them briefly, they got up and left again. Chloe watched them as they headed into the shuttle. Reuel, she saw, was examining his men's wounds. Almost as if he felt her attention, though, he lifted his head and glanced toward her. He studied her for a long moment and strode toward her, moving past her to study her men before he returned. "They will recover."

Blinding anger boiled up the instant he said that. Balling her hand into a fist, Chloe punched him in the belly. She thought for a few moments she might have broken her hand, but she wasn't about to let on that it had hurt her far worse than it had him! "You bastard! They're shot all to hell and gone!"

He caught her wrists before she could injure herself more. "They are cyborgs, Chloe!" he said tightly. "It would take far more damage than they have sustained to destroy them. They will live."

Chloe felt her throat close with hope. She turned to look at Jared and Kane again. "They aren't going to die?"

"No. The medics will extract the projectiles that are preventing the wounds from closing properly and then their nanos will repair them."

She swallowed convulsively. "But they're hurt."

"They are damaged, yes, but they will recover."

Her lips tightened. "But they're in pain, right? They feel pain?"

Something flickered in his eyes. "We feel everything that you would feel."

"Well that isn't alright!" she screamed at him. "It isn't alright with me for them to be hurt, damn it! It isn't OK just because they're going to live!"

His lips flattened with anger for a moment. "It is not alright with me either, Chloe. We did what we had to to survive."

It took all she could do to keep from bursting into tears. Her shoulders slumped as the fight went out of her. Reuel released his grip on her wrists, studied her for a long moment, and finally pulled her close and held her. "They will be alright, I promise you. I regret that they were injured in the raid, but, the gods willing, they will not have to take part in another."

Chloe nodded, comforted by his embrace and his words. "Could you get someone to move them to their bunks, please? The floor's cold. I don't like for them to be cold, not after ... Xeno-12."

Chapter Fourteen

Chloe discovered when Reuel pulled away to look for someone to move them that all the cyborgs were staring at her. Feeling her face heat with discomfort, she turned away, moving back to crouch beside Jared.

She'd never felt more separated and different before, she realized, and yet she didn't feel distanced from her own men. Somehow, when she looked at Damon, Jared, and Kane, she felt far closer than she ever had before.

Those thoughts, naturally enough, led her to the rest of her crew and dismay jolted through her. Sebastian had been hurt, too, and she had no idea how badly.

He'd been able to respond, she told herself, watching anxiously as the medics returned and removed the slugs from Jared and Kane. Blood welled again when they had, but when they had applied pressure for a few minutes, she saw to her relief that the bleeding had stopped.

The men Reuel had summoned came to carry Jared and Kane, and to help Damon to their bunks. She followed them until they reached B deck, where all the crew quarters were and then, after searching her mind to recall where the gun turret was located, jogged down the corridor to find Sebastian. Lucien and Thor were already with him. Touching Lucien's shoulder, she crouched down to look at Sebastian.

There were jagged cuts all over him from flying shrapnel. He was conscious, but barely. "Get him up and to his bunk," she said straightening.

Bending, Lucien and Thor grasped him and hauled him to his feet. Chloe stopped by the med bay to collect bandages, antiseptic, a bowl for water and some sterile cloths.

Lucien and Thor gaped at her when she told them to help her get his flight suit off and then settled on the bunk beside him and carefully cleaned the cuts and bandaged them.

"His nanos will close those," Lucien said after a moment.

"Will it interfere if I go ahead and close them?" Chloe asked.

He blinked at her. "I do not know. I do not suppose so."

"Then I'm going to go ahead and do that. It seems to me that it would lessen the pain if the nerves aren't exposed to the air. I know it lessens the pain when I bandage my own cuts. Anyway, I want to make sure there isn't anything in the wounds that would slow the healing or create an infection."

"The nanos would kill the infection."

Chloe let out a huff. "I'm doing this because it will make me feel better to think I've made him feel better, ok?"

"It is alright with me," Sebastian said in a slightly slurred voice.

Delighted, Chloe surged toward him, clasped his face in her hands and kissed him lightly on the lips. "I'm so sorry I didn't get there sooner, sweety! Jared and Kane were hurt pretty badly and I stopped to check on them and Damon—although I don't think Damon was hurt as badly as they were." She frowned. "I haven't had the chance to check on him. I need to." She glanced toward the other two men. "Can you keep an eye on him and get him whatever he needs while I go check on the others?"

They looked disconcerted, but they nodded.

Leaning down, she kissed Sebastian again and rose, hurrying away.

Lucien glanced around for a place to sit and finally moved to the foot of the bunk. Shoving Sebastian's legs out of the way, he sat down and settled his back against the wall. Sebastian sucked in a hiss of a breath when he pushed his legs out of the way. "What the fuck?"

"Chloe said watch you. I do not know why, but I do not feel like sitting on the floor to do it."

"Why does she want me to be watched?" Sebastian asked irritably. "I am not going anywhere."

Thor grunted. "Well I am hungry. I believe that I will go to the mess hall and see if I can find something."

"I will go with you," Lucien volunteered, scooting off of the bunk and jarring Sebastian again in the process.

"I would not mind food myself," Sebastian called out when he'd recovered.

"Why do you not just wait until you are feeling better and get it yourself?" Lucien asked irritably.

"Because I am hungry now, gods damn it!"

"Fine! We will bring you something."

* * * *

As badly as she wanted to hover over the invalids, Chloe finally left them to rest and went to the bridge. She was listening to the status report when Reuel joined her a little later.

She studied him uncomfortably for a moment after he'd settled in the seat across from her. "I apologize for hitting you and for behaving so badly. There's no excuse for it, I know, but I *am* sorry for what it's worth."

"Is your wrist alright?"

She blushed. "A little sore. I'll live."

He frowned. "I was angry that you challenged my authority, especially in front of the troops, but I realized that you were right. You are the captain of this ship and those are your men. You had every right to ... reproach me for their injuries. They were on loan to me and it was my responsibility to return them to you unharmed." He shrugged. "I would have succeeded if they had not charged into the fray when the port authority was trying to pin us down. My own men, unfortunately, were prevented from effectively returning fire by the barricade the transports had created between them and the attackers. It was your squad and the squad in the shuttle that made it possible for us to finish loading the supplies. Their actions were necessary to the successful conclusion of the mission and they acted just as they should have."

She felt her blush grow hotter. "I think I made more of a fool out of myself than I damaged your reputation," she said uncomfortably. "But I'll make a public apology if you want me to."

He shook his head. "That is unnecessary. The troops felt that we were both right ... and they did not think that you made a fool out of yourself. They were impressed that you had the nerve to assault me. They are certain that you were just a little ...."

"Nuts?"

He smiled faintly. "Emotional or you would not have, but I am fairly certain they admired your spunk, regardless, especially in defense of your men. I appreciate that myself."

She shook her head. "I lost it. There's just no getting around that. In all honesty, I think I was a little nuts. I just ... I guess I'd convinced myself that they wouldn't be hurt and I was just so afraid when I saw they had been that they ...." She halted, swallowing with an effort. "I know they're cyborgs, alright? I also know that they aren't invincible. Close, maybe, but not indestructible. Jared and Kane nearly died on Xeno-12. They came so close I can't bear to think about it. I just don't want anything else bad to happen to them."

Reuel studied her thoughtfully and finally shrugged. "We are at war, Chloe," he said gently. "I hope to avoid the worst of it, but there can be no true peace for us so long as we are hunted. Your men know this, too. The difference now is that we are fighting for ourselves, not for the Confederation. We are fighting for the right to live. We pulled a dozen more cyborgs from the space port when we were there. My people are scattered, defenseless because they are outnumbered and being systematically hunted down and killed. I can not turn my back on them ... any of them.

"But for now, we will search for a place to live. We did manage to get away with the supplies, though there was some damage due to the hail of gunfire when we loaded the last of it."

"The ship was damaged, too. I guess some of your company managed a hit, either that or Sebastian hit it and it was the flying debris that breached the hull. Either way, we're going to have to do some repairs before we can make another jump."

Reuel frowned. "Not good. I will get men on it right away. As I said, we brought more with us. They will have the locators ... although I sent them directly to the med-bay to have them removed and destroyed. Regardless, it cannot be done quickly enough, I fear, to prevent the hunters from getting a fix on us. We will need to initiate the evasive maneuvers we had planned as quickly as possible."

He rose. "You should try to get some rest."

Chloe hadn't realized until he suggested it just how exhausted she was. Instructing the computer to scan for other crafts and alert her immediately if it picked anything up, she headed down to check on the men and then showered and collapsed on her bunk.

She felt so refreshed when she woke, she decided she'd slept far longer than she should have. She knew positively that she had when she stepped out of the shower and heard the computer announce that they were preparing for a jump. Grabbing her clothes, she dashed back to her cabin, nearly skidding past the door since she hadn't had time to dry off. She managed to get the bottom half of her suit on, but the damned thing was so clingy because of her wet skin, she gave up and climbed into her harness. She debated, briefly, whether to unbuckle the harness and finish dressing when they emerged from the jump. They had settled on a series of jumps, however—two hops, a skip, and a jump.

Settling back, she waited for the next hop.

The ship shuddered when it emerged the second time and that wasn't a good thing. Unfastening the harness, she finished dressing and went to check on the guys. All of them were up and about—moving stiffly and with obvious pain, but up—with the exception of Jared and Kane. She was heartened, though, by the fact that they'd improved enough to be grouchy and complain about having to lie on the bunk. "If you'll stay put, I'll go get your breakfast and feed it to you myself. If you don't, I'll have the guys strap you to the bunks and then I'll let them feed you."

She had a sudden thought that cheered her even more while she was scrounging in the galley for something to feed herself and the invalids.

It was her time of the month! Ordinarily, that wouldn't have been cause for celebration, but it occurred to her fairly quickly that the timing couldn't have been better. She was out of commission. The guys were out of commission. By the time she was over the hump, they'd be ready to hump again!

"Good deal!" she murmured to herself with a chuckle, double checking the calendar she kept just to be sure.

Damon had missed his night. He wasn't going to be happy about that!

He was, in point of fact, royally pissed off.

"You're hurt. You shouldn't even be thinking about sex!" Chloe said testily when she stopped to check on him and he reminded her that it was his night.

"Well, I am not hurt that much and I am thinking about it," he said a little sullenly.

"Let me see."

He studied her through narrowed eyes but finally peeled his suit down to his waist to let her look. "As you see."

"Yes, I do see and it's just as I thought. You should wait."

"I have already waited," he said pointedly.

She released a huff. "Alright! If you're still feeling like it tonight, come to my cabin. Last night was supposed to be your night, but you obviously weren't in any shape for it so I'll just figure that as my free night."

Sebastian was outraged that she'd switched her free night for Damon. "Last night was his night! If he missed it, then he missed it!"

"He was wounded! It isn't like he just forgot."

"Nevertheless!"

"Even so!" Chloe shot back at him. "If he feels up to it, it's his night. I didn't promise you I'd try that weird thing you wanted to do, you know. I said I'd think about it, but things changed and I can't. I wouldn't be surprised if I started tonight and I had to put Damon off."

"Started what?" he asked blankly.

"My cycle? Or, I guess, ended it. Anyway, pussy can't play right now, so you'll just have to deal with it."

He looked more confused instead of less.

Chloe sought patience. "My time of the month? The fertility cycle," she said tartly. "It's a monthly thing—28 Earth days, roughly."

He frowned thoughtfully. She patted him on the cheek. "Check your data banks. I'm going to be off limits for about a week and it's just as well because none of you are really in any shape to be looking for recreation."

He looked so disappointed she felt her resolution falter. She sighed in defeat. "Ok. Next time I have a free day, I promise—to give it a try. I'm not going to promise to do it, because I'm not at all sure about this wild orgy you have in mind, but we'll try a couple of positions and if it isn't too scary, we'll go with it. Alright?"

He brightened so quickly she couldn't help but think she'd been manipulated, but she let it go. Truthfully, she was intrigued by the idea. It just made her a little nervous.

When she finally tracked Reuel down, it was to discover that he was overseeing more repairs to the Salvager. She hadn't just imagined that shudder when the ship emerged. Some of the repair welds, so hastily performed, hadn't held. They devoted a full day to reinforcing the hull where the explosion had weakened it before they took the 'skip', a longer jump than the first two and entirely in a different direction. The 'skip' landed them on the frontier, but several quadrants from their ultimate goal. They waited several days to see if they had anyone trailing them before they took the final jump.

Before them lay an almost endless blackness. It gave Chloe the creeps just looking at it, but it also brought back far stronger memories. She'd stood on the bridge with her father, she knew, many years ago, staring at the vast darkness of deep space, fearful that her father would decide to explore the smattering of stars they could see in the distance.

She thought he would have except that the crew was more vocal about their own fears than she was, and angry. They demanded that he turn around.

"This is the place," Chloe whispered. "I remember."

Reuel stood staring out for a very long time and finally addressed the computer. "Run calculations on the distances of the stars to our position." He glanced at Chloe. "You were somewhere around here when you made the jump?"

She shook her head. "I don't know. But I remember staring out at this."

"You do not remember what the destination was that your father chose when the jump failed? Or what the last star system you visited was before you reached this point?"

She frowned. "I've tried."

"We'll send out the probes once the computer has calculated the distances for us and the probability of planets of a size that we would be looking for."

"I'll study the charts again. Maybe something will come back to me."

* * * *

Chloe had so lost track of time that when she answered the knock on her door and discovered Sebastian, Lucien, and Thor on the other side she merely gaped at them blankly wondering what all three were doing visiting her at the same time.

"It is your free night," Sebastian prompted.

Chloe blinked at him. Slowly, a frown formed on her brow. "Well, if it's my free night, what are you doing here?"

Sebastian's face fell. "You said that we would try that position?"

It still took a few minutes for that to sink in. "Oh. Oh shit! It slipped my mind!" She studied the three of them, feeling her belly go weightless. It wasn't altogether nerves, however, although there was a healthy dose of uneasiness threading the sense of anticipation. Truthfully, she'd figured all the time on convincing them to do something a little less ... fraught with potential for injury that would be just as fun. She supposed that was why she'd dismissed it from her mind. "I did promise," she muttered. "I must have been out of my mind at the time."

Stepping back as it occurred to her that she didn't really want them all standing in the corridor—at her door—she gestured for them to enter and poked her head out to look up and down the corridor to see if anyone had seen them.

As luck would have it, Salina was propped against the door of the shower room, looking straight at her. Chloe's face went slack with surprise and dismay when she spotted the woman, and she quickly ducked back into her cabin and closed the door.

She frowned, suspicious immediately that 'luck' good or bad didn't have anything to do with it. It seemed to her that Salina was always somewhere around since she'd finally been released. Granted, they had a fairly small community, but she sure as hell didn't bump into other members as often as she did Salina.

Which suggested psycho bitch was stalking her.

It gave her the creeps, but she discovered when she turned around that Sebastian, Lucien, and Thor had already stripped naked and that effectively distracted her from her anxiety about the woman and redirected her anxiety to a more immediate problem. "Ok. I'm tense."

"I will give foreplay," Sebastian volunteered immediately, surging toward her and sweeping her up.

"I do not know why you should give foreplay," Lucien complained, glaring at Sebastian as he carried Chloe to the bed.

"I am squad leader," Sebastian said pointedly when he had set Chloe down and commenced to stripping her flight suit off.

"Yes, but this is not a military operation," Thor said tightly. "I think we should all give foreplay. I am willing to take turns according to squad position, but I do not see why I should be left out!"

This was starting to sound better and better, Chloe decided. Plus, there was always the chance that, once they got worked up and got her worked up, they'd forget all about trying to stick something in every hole! Not that that didn't sound interesting, and she certainly enjoyed having their tongues in her mouth, but she still didn't see how it was supposed to be that much fun for her. "Maybe we should try to figure out how all of you are going to manage the ... uh ... penetration at the same time before we go any further?"

"We have already worked that out," Sebastian informed her, pushing her down onto the bunk and sprawling half on top of her. "It is in our programming. Well, three way. We have modified for four."

"Yes, but I haven't been modified for four."

"We will pyramid," Sebastian said, preventing any further argument by clamping his mouth over hers. She was still tense when he began to kiss her, but she had to say one thing for Sebastian, he had become very proficient in a very short length of time. Warmth was already flushing the anxious tension from her and replacing it with anticipation by the time he'd thoroughly explored her mouth and moved lower to stimulate her other pulse points. By the time he'd gnawed his way all the way down her body and back again, her skin had begun to feel as if it might catch fire.

"It is my turn," Lucien said challengingly when Sebastian broke the second kiss. Sebastian lifted his head to glare at him for a moment, but finally rolled off of her. By the time Lucien had thoroughly familiarized himself with her body, she was certain she was going to catch fire if someone didn't do something to put her out.

She groaned a little piteously when Thor demanded his turn. "I'm relaxed," she said through gritted teeth when he began tugging at her nipples. She wasn't. She was so anxious to be mounted she began to think she was going to come just from all the foreplay and she was nearly mindless by the time he decided she'd had enough stimulation.

Alright, she *was* mindless! She was ready to claw something. She was so drunk and weak she felt like a rag doll and when Lucien took Thor's place, she groaned in misery, too confused to figure out what they were doing or understand the instructions they were trying to give her.

Fortunately, they didn't actually need her cooperation at that point. Lucien assumed the position, caught her around the waist and lifted her onto his lap ... backwards. That confused her even more until she felt him probing her rectum—with his finger. Whatever it was he used to lubricate her was icy cold. Her nipples, already hard, tighten to rock and goosebumps rushed frantically all over her in every direction as he replaced his finger with his cock. Discomfort wafted through her, but just as she reached the point where she was seesawing between discomfort and actual pain, the pain stopped and the discomfort began to dissipate.

She panted from the sense of fullness and the confusion of pleasurable and uncomfortable quakes rippling through her and colliding. Pushing her legs off of his until they were dangling on either side of him, he spread his legs wide, spreading hers as he did. He lifted his hands to her breasts, cupping them and teasing her painfully erect nipples for a moment and then pulled her slowly back until she was resting lightly against his chest. Sebastian, she discovered was waiting, his expression so taut with his need that she felt her kegels clap together in anticipation even as he leaned over her and probed the mouth of her sex with the head of his cock.

She squeezed her eyes closed as she felt him driving slowly but surely inside of her, felt herself stretched to the edge of pain. Holding her between them, they began to move slowly in and out of her the moment Sebastian had fully penetrated her. The sensation was incredible. She wasn't certain for a few moments if it was incredibly wonderful or just incredibly tight, but her body was in no doubt. It began to flutter and quake almost immediately, threatening release.

She'd completely forgotten Thor until she felt a cock bump against her lips. Actually, she was too mindless by that time to even figure out who was demanding oral stimulation. The moment she felt it, though, a hunger seized her to have it in her mouth. Her body screamed that it was all she needed to take her the rest of the way. She grabbed it with both hands, opened her mouth and began to suck at him frantically while Lucien and Sebastian drove into her at an ever increasing pace. She came almost instantly, her body spasming so hard, her mind clouded with the explosion of ecstasy. Instead of reaching a crescendo and dropping her, however, her body quaked wonderfully and then seemed to climb to another peak. It seized again, harder than before, longer and then began to climb again until dread began to war with anticipation.

And yet, when she felt the men begin to shudder and jerk as they reached their own crises, she struggled greedily to capture that third promised climax. She'd almost begun to despair that she could grasp it before they'd finished, and then it hit her so explosively that when she hit the high note and began to drift down again, she hit oblivion.

She aroused to a chorus of hoarse, panting breaths, one of which was hers. Twin puffs were hitting the back of her neck and her face and a third was off to her left somewhere. It was the opening of her cabin door that really aroused her, however. Sebastian rolled to glance behind him at the intrusion and she popped her own head up to see who it was.

Her eyes widened when she saw Jared, Kane, and Damon in the door. For a handful of seconds, everyone was frozen, their faces blank with shock. Then Jared's, Kane's, and Damon's faces contorted with pure fury. The three uttered a roar that galvanized the four on the bed. Thor and Sebastian leapt up to meet the three charging them. Lucien dismounted her, plunked her on the bed, and leapt up to counter the challenge roared by the other three men and in a few moments the entire cabin had erupted into bedlam.

Chloe was too stunned and too weak from her climaxes to do more than gape for several moments. When Jared and Sebastian landed on her bunk beside her, however, she uttered a shriek and leapt from the bed. After glancing wildly around for a place of safety and discovering that the other four men were waltzing back and forth between her and the door, she dropped to her belly and slithered under the bunk.

It was too much to hope that the brawl would go unnoticed. With six cyborgs pounding at each other and slinging one another against the walls, the floor, and every stick of furniture she had in the room, there was a crowd outside her door within a very few minutes.

Salina, a 'cat that ate the canary' look on her face, was in the forefront. Chloe peered at the woman in disbelief from beneath her bunk for several moments before it hit her that there was absolutely no surprise in her expression, nothing but gloating satisfaction. The fucking bitch, she thought! She'd rounded Jared, Kane, and Damon up and set up the entire thing!

Reuel plowed his way past the gawkers at the door, surveying the brawl in progress. Finally his gaze settled on her beneath the bunk. "Enough!" he bellowed. "Take these men into custody and escort them to the brig!"

None of the men brawling had even acknowledged Reuel's presence let alone given any indication that they heard the order. The fight was halted by sheer weight of numbers as Reuel's men rushed in to break it up and wrestled the fighters away from each other. Jared, Kane, and Damon were still bellowing threats at the top of their lungs as they were hauled away. Sebastian's group was a little more subdued, but not by much. The men who'd taken them into custody paused long enough to collect their clothing and shove it at them before they hauled them out.

Reuel crouched and looked at Chloe questioningly. Her lips tight with anger, her face scarlet with embarrassment, Chloe climbed out from beneath the bunk with as much dignity as she could master and looked around for her own clothes.

Reuel straightened, turned, and scattered the lingerers with a scowl. "Just what the hell was going on here?" he asked mildly when Chloe had managed to get her flight suit on and sat down to pull on her boots.

"You should ask that *bitch* Salina!" Chloe snapped. "She orchestrated the entire disaster!"

Reuel's eyes narrowed. "How does she figure into this ... debacle?"

Chloe shook her head. "I don't know. She was standing in the shower room when the guys came."

Amusement flickered in Reuel's eyes. "Which time?"

Chapter Fifteen

Chloe stared at Reuel blankly for several moments before it dawned on her that he was referring to the orgy. A flicker of amusement went through her, as well. She would've been more amused, however, if her men weren't headed for the brig. She cleared her throat. "It's my day off," she said pointedly, more than a little stiffly. "Sebastian had asked if he and his guys could … ah … visit and .. uh …. Well, never mind. That's beside the point."

"You are right. It is. The point is that your cabin has been destroyed. You could have been seriously injured at the very least and we have six men in the brig when they could be put to better use in overhauling the Salvager and repairing the damage to the ships that took part in the raid. I think that we are reasonably safe here, but I do not like the idea of getting caught with my pants down." He paused, amusement flickering in his eyes again. "No pun intended."

Chloe sent him a look and marched past him, headed for the brig, which she knew Reuel had set up somewhere in the hold of the ship.

Reuel fell into step beside her and they made the trip in grim silence. Chloe's belly clenched when they reached the brig and she surveyed the cells. Sebastian, Lucien, and Thor were together in one, Jared, Kane, and Damien in the other and both groups were pacing the small space like angry lions and glaring threateningly and each other.

Some of the tension went out of the six when they saw Chloe and Reuel. More accurately, it appeared that they forced down some of the tension. The two groups separated, assuming more causal and less aggressive stances.

Chloe didn't believe it for a moment and she doubted Reuel did either. "I want to know why you burst into my cabin and started a fight," Chloe demanded.

Jared narrowed his eyes at her, his jaw tightening until a muscle began to jump there, as if he was grinding his teeth. After studying him a moment, she glanced at Kane and Damon. They looked just as furious. Her heart thudded dully with dismay as it became clear that they were as angry with her as they were the three men they'd tried to beat the shit out of. "Salina said something to you, didn't she?"

Something flickered in Jared's eyes.

"At least tell me what she said."

"She told them that you had called a meeting in your cabin with the three of us and she wondered why they had not also been summoned," Sebastian growled angrily.

Chloe turned triumphantly to Reuel. "You see! I *told* you it was that bitch! She started the whole thing!"

Reuel's face hardened with anger. "That might well be true, and I will certainly discuss the matter with her, but she did not finish. If it is true, she merely brought the two groups together and they took it from there. Your men have been a discipline problem for some time, although I have tried to overlook it. I believed, eventually, that they would recall that they are a team and that they should work together as such. I have not seen that this is the case, however. In point of fact, that debacle in your cabin seems a stronger indication that they will become worse not better."

Chloe swallowed uneasily. "Well! They did trash the cabin. I say they should cool their heels here in the brig for a few days ... maybe a week and then they'll have to put it back together."

Reuel narrowed his eyes at her thoughtfully. "I believe you are as much a part of the problem as Salina is in your own way."

Chloe gaped at him indignantly.

"I believe that I should remove them from your dance card and assign a different group to you. They will be rotated to some of the other women."

Outrage instantly overcame Chloe's speechless indignation. "Woah! No fucking way are you sending *my* men to fuck those other women! And I'm not taking 'replacements' damn it! They are *my* men! I'm not assigning any-damned-body else to take care of their recreation."

Reuel stared at her in surprise. "You agreed that it was necessary to the morale of the crew to offer recreational sex."

"I still do, but *they* are my crew. I don't see any reason at all to switch things around when I'm perfectly capable of taking care of them myself. Your crew can mix it up as much as they want to. There's plenty of women. In fact, they don't have as many men to entertain as I do ... and I'm handling it just fine!"

"If you were handling it fine, they would not be fighting one another," Reuel said pointedly. "And I might add, that my crew is now larger by a dozen more—males. There were no females among those we took."

It was impossible not to feel hurt at that comment. She lifted her head and glanced at her crewmen, but she discovered she couldn't meet their gazes. She swallowed a couple of time convulsively and finally nodded. "Whatever you think is best." She cleared her throat. "You should probably just exclude me. I'm not a cyborg and ,,, well, that's probably the problem."

Pushing past Reuel, she left the hold at a brisk walk, trying not to give the appearance of fleeing the scene.

She should've known that fucking cunt, Salina would be laying in wait to enjoy the fruits of her labor! She smiled gloatingly when Chloe passed through the crew quarters and it was all Chloe could do to ignore the provocation. The reflection that the bitch would probably break her in half was certainly a factor in trying to ignore her, but she thought it was her wounded pride and her hurt that was mostly responsible. She couldn't think beyond the absolute necessity of convincing anyone that happened to look her way that she was completely unaffected.

It was only recreational sex anyway, she reminded herself—supposed to be therapeutic in relieving stress more than anything else. And clearly Reuel was right if it was true that her guys had still been fighting among themselves.

Well, she knew it was true. She'd been working hard to pretend she hadn't noticed they almost always looked like they'd traded punches with someone even when they weren't battered enough to look like they'd been beaten half to death.

She desperately wanted to retreat to her cabin and cry her eyes out, but it was a disaster area and besides, she had her pride, damn it! She wasn't going to let the damned cyborgs know she didn't have any spine! She did stop to survey the damage for a few moments, trying to decide what she was going to do about a place to sleep until her cabin was put back to rights. As she stood staring glumly at the mess, though, some of Reuel's crewmen arrived and began to sort through the rubble.

Heaving a shaky breath, she left and headed to the bridge. She didn't especially want or need to go to the bridge. It was pretty much the only place on the ship that she still had, mostly, to herself, though. For a while she simply sat glumly in the captain's chair, staring at nothing in particular and struggling with her thoughts. They rambled from one thing to another—mostly things that only depressed her more—but she found herself re-evaluating her decision to settle on this new planet they were looking for.

What was the point, really? She didn't have to go to such lengths to avoid the law. She wasn't a cyborg. She didn't doubt that they were after her, but it always came down to fines more than anything else. That was mostly what the laws were about—getting more money.

Actually, even if she spent a little time in jail, just how different was that going to be from living on the damned ship? Her cabin probably wasn't much bigger than a jail cell.

She hadn't actually viewed the Salvager as a prison before, but that was what it was, she thought abruptly. She was secluded from life by the metal hull of the ship just as surely as she would've been if she'd spent most of her life in prison—and it *was* most of her life, she realized, well over half of it now.

What would she do with herself on the planet even saying they found it? She hadn't ever done anything but ramble around space collecting junk to sell to people that sorted the junk and resold it for something else.

She frowned. She'd pretty much agreed to turn the ship over to Reuel to collect the cyborgs that were scattered all over everywhere. It occurred to her that that would be a worthwhile job. There would be a living in it—of sorts. She didn't see why it wouldn't work if she kept up her salvage operation, for that matter. It would be a good cover for Reuel, a good reason to go from one planet to another.

It wouldn't be that big of a change from what she'd been doing already and, really, she was pretty much a creature of habit. She'd never been like her father. She didn't especially enjoy wandering just for the sake of seeing different things. The only reason she'd ever been comfortable was because they had their own little world and nothing changed that much—until they took Jared and Kane onboard.

She didn't want to think about them, though. Shrugging her thoughts off, she went back to the task of studying star charts. Something flickered in her mind when she looked at one star system and she frowned, trying to decide whether it was familiar because she'd looked at it so many times or if it was a memory. As she stared at the name of the primary colony world, a faint memory did surface—of Billy and Bud arguing with her father about stopping there.

Her father had pointed out that they didn't *need* supplies and they'd pointed it out that it wasn't *supplies* they were after.

Was that memory from then, though? Or had she been struggling so hard to dredge something up from her mind that her mind had finally supplied her with something?

She glanced up absently at Reuel when he came in and settled across from her.

"Are you alright?"

She stared at him blankly for a moment. "You know, I think this place right here rings a bell. I keep getting these vibes about it and it seems to me that I remember Pops arguing with our crewmen about stopping there. The guys were horny and wanted to stop at one of the brothels and Pops said it was a little too wild there to suit him ... a pirate den or maybe he just said a den of thieves. Anyway, they argued a while and Pops finally said they'd head for ... Arturious if they were hell bent and determined they couldn't wait a while to get their pipes cleaned."

Reuel had tensed during the course of that dialogue and sat forward to study the charts. "Are you certain?"

Chloe thought about it. "No. It could be a memory from another time. Or, it could be that I've just stared at these damned things so much that my mind is playing tricks on me and none of it ever happened. I think I remember it, though. And if I'm right, then we would've been right about there when we made that jump," she said pointing.

"Then let us feed this information into the computer and let it run some simulations to see if we can arrive at the best possibility, shall we?"

"It's worth a try," Chloe said a little doubtfully.

They focused on that for a time, feeding in not only that information, but the data they'd gotten so far from the probes they'd sent out. Reuel turned to study her speculatively when they sat back to wait for the computer to run its simulations.

"I did not mean those things I said to you ... not in the way that you took it, at any rate."

Chloe felt a blush climb into her cheeks. It made it pretty damned impossible to pretend she had no idea what he was talking about. She considered trying to pretend anyway and finally discarded that notion. "That's alright. I really don't want to talk about it."

"It will make things more difficult if you refuse to take part," he said tentatively.

She shrugged. "I'd thought about that, but really—that's ridiculous. They're cyborg women. And three of them were pleasure droids anyway. They would be used to handling a lot of customers, I imagine. They can just step things up a bit and still take care of it. Plus Salina isn't in the brig anymore so she can help out."

"You think I should assign your crewmen to her?"

Anger flickered to life. Chloe wrestled with it a few moments and finally mastered it. Her throat felt clogged with the emotions roiling through her, though, and she found that no amount of swallowing could rid her of it. "I sort of figured you were going to do the dance cards and let the guys chose, but ... whatever. Like I said, I'm going to let you handle that.

"I was starting to feel pretty worn out anyway, if you want the truth of it. I just don't have the stamina you cyborgs do! Never thought I'd say it, but it would sure come in handy to be a cyborg right about now! Anyway, I'm not, and I shouldn't have gotten involved in it to start with ... being an outsider and all. You guys need to handle your own issues. You've had enough interference, I imagine, from humans.

"Speaking of which," she added before he could bring the subject back to sex—Really! They were so fixated on it! "I've been giving some thought to my situation. I don't see why you and I couldn't partner up and sort of have a dual operation with the Salvager. I mean, it would be perfect cover if you think about it. I would have a good reason to stop at all sorts of places to sell salvage. And you could send a squad out everywhere we stopped to look for them."

Reuel frowned. "I had thought that you wanted to settle when we found the planet," he said slowly.

She shrugged. "Well, what can I say? I guess I'm more like Pops than I realized. I was daydreaming, I guess. Practically speaking ... well, it's totally impractical. I wouldn't have a thing to offer, you know. I've never done anything but the salvage business and there wouldn't be much call for that!"

"I think you would enrich our lives far more than you think you would."

Chloe managed a chuckle. "Aw! That's sweet! I really don't think settling in one place is for me, though." She dragged in a shaky breath, pasted a smile on her lips and looked around the bridge. "I don't even hardly remember living on a planet anymore. This place is home. Not that I think I could contribute that much to your operation, but I'm a pretty decent pilot and, like I said, I could handle salvage and dealing with the salvagers on the planets while you and your guys did your thing and I'll bet we could round everybody up before you know it!"

Reuel studied her speculatively for several moments and finally shrugged. "It is early days to worry about that now."

"You're probably right," Chloe said wryly, "but just think about it, alright? I mean, I'm not going back on my word. I *want* you to have the ship to help the others out, but I do know this ship better than anybody ... alive. And I know the salvage business. I can spot good stuff and shit without the probes and know right off whether its worth going any closer for a look."

"As you did when you found Jared and Kane?"

Chloe thought for a moment that she was going to loose it, but she managed to beat her emotions back. "Exactly!" she managed. "They were *so* worth saving! And even Pops couldn't see it at the time. They're great soldiers. I know it. I think they're probably just a little out of the habit, you know—no discipline here! My fault, I'm sure, because I always acted like they were my buddies when I'm sure I should've kept it professional, them being crewmembers."

* * * *

"*Now* look what you have done!" Kane growled furiously when Reuel and Chloe had left.

"*We?*" Sebastian demanded, outraged. "You are the ones who started the fight!"

"Like hell!" Jared snarled. "What the fuck were the three of you doing in Chloe's gods damned cabin when it was her day off? That is what I would like to know! Sneaking behind our backs! That is what you were doing, you fucking assholes!"

"We did not sneak!" Lucien snapped. "And if you have figured it out, then I do not see why you are even asking!"

"Because we have not figured it out!" Damon ground out. "The three of you were all over her when we came in, gods damn it! What the fuck made you think that it would be alright to fuck her all the at same time?"

"She agreed to it!" Sebastian said stiffly. "And what is more, she enjoyed it! She came three times … and then she passed out."

"How would you know if she fainted from passion or because you suffocated her?" Damon snarled.

Sebastian, Lucien, and Thor glanced at one another uneasily. "She had my cock in her mouth, so she was either groaning in ecstasy or humming, gods damn it! I felt the vibration. That is why I came! If she had wanted to scream, she would have taken it out of her mouth!"

Jared, Kane, and Damon glared at them with a mixture of uncertainty, resentment, and envy. "I still do not know what put you in mind of it, and what is more, I am not sure that I believe Chloe agreed!" Jared said finally.

"It is in the handbook, gods damn it!" Sebastian said. "Under decadence and kink."

"*That* is not in my gods damned programming!" Jared snarled.

Sebastian shrugged uncomfortably. "We modified it … but only a little. I will not say that Chloe was particularly enthusiastic … when I asked her, but she said that she was willing to try it."

"Well! You should not have asked her, gods damn it! You know that she can be talked into almost anything—whether it is good for her or not!"

Sebastian looked uncomfortable. "You cannot say it was not far more efficient, at least! Even I could see that she was tired from having someone different each night!"

"So you very thoughtfully came up with this brilliant plan to fuck her all at once on her free night … when she should have been resting, because, gods damn it, tomorrow was supposed to be my gods damned night!"

"Yes, and now no one will get to fuck her at all because of your stupid idea!" Kane said angrily.

Sebastian, Lucien, and Thor exchanged a look and moved to settle on the single bunk their cell boasted. "It would not have come to this," Sebastian said after a while, "if the three of you had not decided to kick our asses when it was not your business to begin with!"

Jared surged toward the bars that separated them from the other cell. "If it concerns Chloe, it *is* our business, gods damn it! And I am going to choke the life out of all three of you when they let me out of here!"

"*That* will get her back," Kane said irritably, heading to the bunk and sprawling on it.

Jared turned to stare at Kane angrily for several moments as it slowly settled inside him that Kane was right. They had lost her. The concept was incomprehensible, but he felt his belly twist nauseatingly. "We have not lost her," he muttered.

"Are you deaf as well as blind?" Damon demanded angrily. "You did not see the way she looked when she left? You did not hear her say that she would have nothing else to do with it—us?"

Jared swallowed convulsively several times. "She did not mean it," he said a little doubtfully. "She said that we were her crewmen and she would entertain us and that she would not allow any of the other females to. She said that."

"We are her crewmen, too!" Lucien said angrily.

Jared, Kane, and Damon all whipped a look at him. "Shut the fuck up!" they snarled almost in unison.

"You are only … strays that she picked up only because you were there!" Kane added angrily.

"And you are not *strays* that she also collected?" Sebastian shot back at him.

Kane and Jared exchanged an uncomfortable look. Jared made an obscene gesture at the party in the other cage and joined Kane on the bunk.

"If you ask me, you are all right and you are all a bunch of fucking idiots," the guard outside said grimly. "She is a human! Granted, she is a pretty one and she is very sweet even if she is also weak, emotional, and clumsy as bedamned, besides not being able to take care of herself! She has gathered you all up like pets and that is the only way that she thinks of any of you … as pets! Because you are cyborgs and you are not the same as she is. You will be better off to take a good cyborg woman!"

"Prick!" Kane snarled.

"No one asked for your fucking opinion!" Jared snapped. "If I wanted it, I would choke it out of you!"

"I am more in favor of just beating the shit out of the son-of-a-bitch myself," Damon said. "Did you hear what that bastard said about our Chloe?"

"I heard. I think I will give him some good cyborg foot up his fucking ass when I get out!" Sebastian said angrily. "She is not clumsy, gods damn it!"

"He is just jealous because she has no interest in anyone but us!" Lucien said coldly.

"Well, it did not sound to me as if she had any interest in any of you when she left!" the guard said tightly.

All six men scowled at him, but since they couldn't think of a retort to that, they decided to ignore the bastard.

* * * *

"Oh my god! Reuel! This is it! I think this is really it!" Chloe exclaimed, bouncing up and down in her excitement.

She discovered when she turned to look at him that he seemed to be singularly unenthusiastic. In point of fact, his expression was down right sardonic. "You said the same thing the last three times," he retorted.

Chloe gaped at him and then frowned. "Ok, so I was wrong a couple of times. I really do think this is it, though."

"I hope so," Reuel drawled. "We are getting low on supplies. We will not be able to spend six months out here searching without having to plan another raid."

Irritation flickered through Chloe. "We've only checked out a handful of star systems. We can't be getting low on supplies, yet."

"We are not … yet. But we have checked a *dozen* star systems, Chloe and, even jumping, we do not have time to check them all. We will not *live* long enough to check them all!"

Chloe frowned. "Just how are the supplies holding up?"

Reuel shrugged. "We have only been looking for a couple of weeks. We have plenty to hold us a while, but we will need several months in supplies after we reach the planet. That is my main concern. Hopefully, we will be able to begin to supplement food stores right away, but we cannot count on that. I did not lay in so much because I expected to be in space so long but rather to begin the settlement."

She studied him in dismay. She hadn't thought about that. Then again, that was why Reuel was running the show—because he thought of everything. "I really do think this is it," she said a little doubtfully.

Nodding, Reuel got up decisively. "We will leave the Salvager here and take my craft to check out the system. It is faster and we might as well leave the Salvager where it will be conveniently located for another jump ... if necessary."

Depression settled over Chloe in spite of all she could do as she headed to the bay with Reuel. It wasn't enough that she felt her inadequacy in everything else she tried to do? She couldn't even find a damned planet!

She managed to throw off much of her depression once she'd settled in the co-pilot's seat and Reuel had glanced at her. She was actually starting to be really good at it, she thought, pretending she wasn't completely miserable.

She didn't know what she was going to do when Reuel finally let the guys out of the brig, though. She was pretty sure the only reason she'd managed to get a grip on her wayward emotions at all was because she hadn't had to meet up with any of them. She'd been trying really hard to brace herself for that eventuality, but she couldn't convince herself that she was going to handle it well at all.

She was *sure* she wasn't going to be able to handle it when they finally did get out and Reuel put them on someone else's dance card. It made her feel like crying every time she thought about it—which was most of the time and the reason she had to work so hard to keep everybody from knowing how miserable she was.

"Fasten your safety harness," Reuel said.

"Oh! Forgot!" Chloe grabbed the harness, glad for something to distract her.

Reuel glanced at her several times, but thankfully forbore comment. "Ready?"

She finally managed to untangle the harness and fasten it. "Yep!"

She discovered she actually wasn't. When Reuel's ship shot from the hanger, the G's the damned thing pulled plastered her against her seat so tightly she could hardly breathe for several minutes. She'd begun to see dancing spots when the pull finally decreased. "Boy this thing sure can go!" she said shakily, focusing on her fingers and trying to pry them loose from the armrests.

Reuel grunted. "It seemed like a good idea to make sure it could outrun most other crafts."

"I see your point. I doubt there are many that can move nearly as fast."

"There are some advantages to being a cyborg," he said dryly.

"A lot actually," Chloe retorted. "I've never felt so inadequate in my life! I didn't even know how many things I was bad at until I got around you guys!"

"You are best at teaching men who were born machines to understand the half of themselves that is human," Reuel said gently. "You have all of their very best qualities."

"Now you're going to make me cry!"

"Please do not!" Reuel said, chuckling. "I find it … disturbs me a very great deal."

Chloe smiled at him with an effort. "Still, it's nice to think there's something I'm good at. But I actually think all of you have the best qualities. It isn't that we don't aspire for greatness or that we don't have lofty ideals. It's just that we can never seem to … achieve that sort of graciousness for ourselves. I think that's why they're afraid of you. They made you what they wanted to be and they know they can never be as great as their creations."

"You are a true and loyal friend to those fortunate enough to earn your … trust."

It wasn't a good thing that that instantly brought Jared and Kane to her mind. A knot the size of a golf ball formed in her throat. She swallowed against it a couple of times, trying to dislodge it and finally cleared her throat. "Hopefully, I can prove I can also find the right planet so you won't decide your trust in me was misplaced," she managed to say finally.

Reuel was studying his computer readout. "Well, the star appears to be consistent with what you recalled and the computer has detected six planets."

Hopefulness surged in her. She sat up straighter, pushing her unhappiness to the back of her mind. "It would have to be roughly the same distance from the star as Earth," she said.

They'd been traveling a while before the computer confirmed that there was a planet in orbit around the star that fell within the 'comfort' range necessary to human life. Excitement began to thread Chloe's veins. She could see from the tension in Reuel that he'd begun to think they'd found the planet she'd told them about, too.

Nearly an hour passed before he pointed to a tiny speck in the distance. "That is our target."

Chloe felt her heart contract almost painfully in her chest when she stared at the spot. It *was* the planet! She knew it was! She remembered when her father had pointed it out. Even from this distance she could see the blue.

She tamped the urge to tell Reuel, however. There was still just enough doubt in her mind that she thought she preferred to err on the side of caution—especially when she'd already been wrong so many times.

Two hours later, however, the almost microscopic dot had become a big blue ball against the velvety black backdrop of space. Reuel focused the ship's sensors on the planet they were approaching, studying the readouts with frowning intensity. He looked up at her finally. "I believe you have found our planet," he said, his lips slowly curling into a smile.

Chloe chuckled excitedly. "I was sure it was it! I was just scared to say so after I was wrong before!"

He chuckled. "*I* am sure of it! If I did not know that your men would tear my head off and castrate me, I would kiss you Chloe Armstein!"

Chloe gaped at him, but he had turned his attention to the com-link. She listened as he instructed the crew to bring the Salvager in. She could hear excited voices in the background on the other end.

"We will celebrate tonight on land!" Reuel said, his voice deep with excitement.

Uneasiness flickered through Chloe at that. "Don't forget the creepy natives."

He shook his head, his attitude swiftly changing to grim determination. "I have not forgotten. I am certain they will not want to share, but we have not come so far, or fought so hard, that I will accept that. They will have to learn to share this world with us."

Chloe felt her belly clench at the ruthlessness she saw in him. The natives would learn to share, she realized, or they would die.

Chapter Sixteen

Not surprisingly, Reuel didn't wait for the Salvager to arrive. Giddy wasn't a word that Chloe would ever even think to use to describe Reuel. He was far too reserved for that, but she sensed his excitement in his quick movements, his focus, the tension in him, even the taut set of his face.

Chloe felt her own excitement rise as the great blue orb filled the forward view. The rattle and buck of the ship as it dipped into the atmosphere and was pelted by air currents only seemed to accentuate the fluttery feeling in her stomach, her breathlessness, the awe that filled her as she caught her first glimpse of the beautiful blue sea she remembered.

For a while, that was all they saw, and Chloe was beginning to feel anxiety filtering through her excitement, beginning to wonder if she'd been wrong after all, when they reached the dark side of the planet just as the sun crested the horizon. Before them lay the planet's emerald jewel. It seemed to stretch from pole to pole and far into the distant horizon, just as the sea had.

One enormous land mass, she wondered? Or had they simply missed other, smaller masses?

Reuel took the craft down, skimming along the coast for some time, low enough Chloe could see the surf breaking against the pale sand of the beach, before he turned inland. The plant life grew so thick it was almost impossible to catch more than a quick glimpse of the ground every once in a great while.

Eventually, they saw a rise in the land in the distance and outcroppings of yellowish-brown stone and the thick jungle gave way to a squat mountain. Reuel circled it slowly and finally landed. He gave away his excitement in the speed he threw off his harness and got up.

Smiling faintly, Chloe followed him as quickly as she could and he'd still descended the gangplank and strode to stare out over the jungle before she even reached the gangplank.

"We will need to survey the planet carefully," he said when he heard her approach, "but I am thinking that this would be a very promising spot to build our first city."

Chloe was impressed. "A city?"

He grinned abruptly. "A city. A very great city. I have lain out the plans already and designed the buildings we will need." He turned to survey the plateau and frowned. "I may need to throw them away and begin again. I do not want to make the same mistake that our creators did, not when it is known, now, that it is important to protect the world that is your home and not rape it of all that it has to give and give nothing back."

"I know it'll be beautiful," Chloe said, smiling. She dragged in a deep breath and released it slowly, wrinkling her nose. "The air will take a little getting used to, I suppose."

Reuel mimicked her and sent her a quizzical look. "It is good air! Fresh, filled with the scent of life."

"Ah! I wondered what that smell was!" Chloe said chuckling. "Dirt? Plants?"

He grinned at her. "You are too accustomed to breathing the recycled air of a ship!"

"Hey! I have my greenhouse!"

He snorted. "I have seen your greenhouse. There are not more than a handful of scraggly plants in it. It is a wonder there is enough air in that ship to breathe."

Chloe shrugged. "I supplement it with bottled air. I never was very good with plants."

"Because they must have water," Reuel said dryly.

Chloe blinked at him. "Was that the problem? I thought there was an automatic watering system."

"There was at one time, but it has not been maintained."

She shook her head. "Well, Billy and Bud were lazy sots. They never did more than the bare minimum to get by. I wasn't sorry to see them go." She swallowed uncomfortably. "Jared and Kane were worlds better, but I figured the garden was a lost cause." She frowned, glancing around. "Do you think this will be a good place to grow things? There doesn't seem to be much growing here now."

"Buildings will grow here."

"Yes, but … never mind. I guess you'll grow the food in the valley below?" She moved to the edge to look out over the jungle. "It doesn't look like there'll be a problem growing anything there. It's going to take a lot of clearing to make fields."

"It will take a great deal of work to make everything that must be made, but we are cyborgs. We were built to work hard."

There was bitterness in his voice. She couldn't blame him. It was actually sad, now she thought about it, that he—none of them—hadn't gotten the chance to be children. Not that that wasn't hell at times, but she'd had her mother, even if it hadn't been for very long, and they hadn't had one at all.

"When do you think everybody else will get here?"

He lifted his head to look upward even though she knew he couldn't have seen the ship if it had made orbit. Maybe at night, but not during the day.

"It will be hours yet before the Salvager makes orbit. Shall we go up again so that I can get started on the surveys?"

She smiled faintly. "Bor-ring! I think I'll take a nap while you survey."

"You will find a hard bed," he said wryly, "with the ship still gutted from our raid."

"I'll find a spot."

She didn't find a particularly comfortable spot, but she didn't really need much comfort. She hadn't slept well in weeks and she stayed tired. If it hadn't been for the fact that she knew she wasn't sleeping well, she might've thought she had a problem, but that *was* the case. At first, she couldn't sleep because the guys wanted to fuck half the night and then crowded her afterward. Then she got used to having them in her bed and discovered when they weren't there she couldn't sleep and, of course, no one had been in her bed in weeks and now she was horny because she was used to having sex.

The good thing, she told herself, was that she could get *un*used to those changes just as easily and go back to being comfortable sleeping alone and not having sex. It seemed to be taking longer than she thought it should, but then she'd been pretty depressed about the whole business and that sure as hell wasn't helping her sleep, or rest, anyway.

She didn't actually sleep when she finally found a spot to lie down. She dozed off and on, but it seemed to her that she felt every bump of the air currents. She knew when Reuel descended for a closer look at something and when he went up again. Hunger finally drove her from her efforts to nap and she got up and went to ask Reuel if he'd brought food onboard.

He stared at her blankly for so long that she knew his mind was somewhere far, far away. "I did not think to bring food," he finally said.

She wasn't surprised since she knew he hadn't expected to find the planet. He'd thought they would fly close enough in to survey, see it wasn't livable, and return to the Salvager.

"We will go back. I have surveyed a good bit. I should study the data anyway, and I am starving. I had not realized that was why I had begun to feel … empty."

They discovered their timing was good. The Salvager came into view almost as soon as they broke through the atmosphere and they rendezvoused with the mother ship just as it began to pull into an orbital position.

"Will you join us in the mess tonight to celebrate?" Reuel asked as they descended the gangplank and crossed the docking bay.

Chloe considered it and discarded the idea. "I appreciate it, but I think I'll just have something in my cabin. I don't know why, but ... well, I feel a little ill smelling all the food."

Reuel sent her a disbelieving look, but he didn't argue and they parted company as soon as they reached B deck. She was a little irritated by that look. Maybe it was a slight exaggeration, but it wasn't a lie. She did feel a little ill thinking about eating in the mess hall and at least some of the smells did bother her.

Not that it was any of his business!

She decided, since she could hear activity in the mess hall as she passed it and knew everyone was in there, that she'd stop by the facilities and take a bath before she headed to her cabin. She peered in cautiously when she reached it, just to be sure, and finally went in when she saw it really was empty.

She thought she was more tired from trying to nap than she would've been if she hadn't. Or maybe she was just tired from flying most of the day? That was fatiguing in itself when it was so restrictive of movement.

Or maybe she was tired because she hadn't eaten since breakfast and she hadn't eaten much of that?

She was tempted to join them in the mess hall after all once she realized that, but the moment she thought about having to walk across the hall in full view of everyone, she lost interest in it. She didn't know that they would stare at her. The chances were they probably wouldn't notice her at all, but it made her uncomfortable even thinking they might notice.

She was being hypersensitive about it, she knew, but she hadn't mastered it yet. Every time she was around any of them, she was reminded of the brawl in her cabin and the gawkers that had come to watch. She supposed she couldn't blame them. There wasn't a lot that happened on the ship to entertain. She would probably have been one of the gawkers if it had happened to anyone else.

The fact remained that she was embarrassed, though, and beyond that, she wasn't ready to face the guys. Reuel had told her he had let them out several days earlier and she had lived in terror ever since that she might run in to one of them.

Not that she was *afraid* of them! But she was a total coward about dealing with her feelings. God! If *thinking* about them was enough to make her feel like squalling, she knew it would be unpleasant for all concerned if she tried to talk to them!

No, it was way better to get a little distance and perspective and gain control of her emotions. Then, maybe, she could carry it off without being awkward and making them feel ill at ease.

The shower, as she'd hoped, left her feeling pleasantly relaxed, enough that she decided as she headed to her cabin that she might just try to take a nap instead of eating first and then look for something later.

* * * *

Jared stared at Chloe's empty chair and glanced questioningly at his fellow crewmembers. They merely shrugged, obviously as confused as he was. "Chloe is not eating?" he asked Reuel pointedly.

It seemed to take a moment for the question to register. He glanced at her empty seat. "She said that she would eat in her room. She does that now."

"She does not eat in the mess with everyone else anymore?" Kane asked tightly.

"She has not since …." Reuel shrugged. "I think she is ill at ease. She does not say so. She says that she is not hungry or she will eat later or she feels sick. Tonight, she is sick."

Jared frowned. "She is ill?"

Reuel shrugged but then frowned. "I do not think so. She has not visited the medics. She knows that I brought medicines for her in case of need when we raided."

He got up and left the table before they could ask more, stopping to speak with one of his men before he returned. Jared watched through narrowed eyes as the man rose and left.

Instead taking his seat again once he returned he addressed the crewmen in the hall. "As you will have heard, Chloe has led us to the planet she spoke of and I have been there. It is a beautiful planet, full of life, and ours to claim!"

There was a collective hoorah in response and Reuel smiled faintly. "I began surveying immediately. I have not completed a survey of the entire continent, but I see no reason to delay colonization when I have found a site that seems ideal for our first home!

"I suggest that everyone retire early and get as much rest as possible. Tomorrow, we will begin ferrying everyone to the surface so that we may begin to build! There is a very great deal that must be done, but the planet is ripe with bounty for us to build with!"

Jared found that he could not summon a great deal of enthusiasm.

He was pleased that Chloe had found it and that Reuel had given her credit for having led them to a new home as she promised, but he felt ... uneasy in his mind.

What he did not understand was why Chloe was not with them to celebrate! If she was not ill, why was she not here, with them?

"Mayhap she is still angry with us?" Kane muttered as if his thoughts had traveled the same path.

Jared frowned. "She is never angry longer than a minute. I do not believe that."

"She did not *seem* angry then," Sebastian said uneasily. "What do you suppose Reuel meant when he said that she was ill at ease?"

They pondered it for a while.

"Mayhap she is ill at ease because she told Reuel that she would not take part in the recreational sex anymore?" Lucien offered. "Mayhap she feels that they will disapprove of her now because of that?"

"She did not have to take part to begin with!" Jared said angrily. "She is the captain of the Salvager. It was gracious that she agreed at all and they must know that! I am going to speak with her," he ended decisively.

The others got up and followed him. It irritated the fuck out of him, but not nearly as much as the discovery that Reuel had posted a guard to prevent them from reaching Chloe's cabin.

He had thought it suspicious that Reuel had sent the man out! Fucking bastard!

"Reuel has ordered that she not be disturbed," the guard said tightly.

"We are her crewmen. We will not disturb her. We are only going to speak to her," Kane said reasonably.

"No."

"There are six of us," Jared growled. "Stand aside!"

"No."

Jared had already grabbed the man by the throat when Kane caught his attention by punching him on the side of his head. "They will throw us in the brig again, gods damn it! And I am tired of sleeping on the fucking floor! And I am more tired of not seeing Chloe!"

Jared released the man. After staring at Chloe's door for several moments, he turned and headed to his own quarters. He had already flung himself on his bunk when Kane followed him inside and directly behind him, Damon, Sebastian, Lucien, and Thor. They looked around the tiny cabin and finally simply leaned against the wall.

"I do not like this worth a fuck!" Kane said tightly.

"I do not like this worth a fuck either," Jared growled. "I came to *my* quarters because I did not want company! It is not enough that we have shared the same fucking cell for two fucking weeks?"

Kane ignored his outburst. "Why would he set a guard to prevent us from speaking to Chloe?"

"Because he wants her for himself!" Sebastian said abruptly. "I have seen the way he looks at her and he has made a great effort to be very friendly, gods damn it!"

"That is gods damned underhanded!" Lucien snapped. "You mean to say the bastard has been romancing *our* woman while he had us locked up?"

"When the fuck did she become *your* woman?" Jared growled. "That is what I would like to know!"

"I said ours!" Lucien said indignantly. "We are all her crewmen and she said that we were family!"

"Yes, but … Never mind! I think I will go and speak to Reuel!" Jared said, getting up from his bunk.

The others turned to the door even as he got up, however, and he discovered that he had to wait until they had filed out before he could leave. Thor, who had been closest to the door, led the way until they reached Reuel's quarters and then stopped and turned to look at Jared expectantly.

"Why are you looking at me? You led us here!" Jared growled.

"It was your idea."

Rolling his eyes, Jared stalked past the other men and rapped on Reuel's door.

Reuel opened it more swiftly than he had expected. He would not have admitted it under torture, but he found that singularly unnerving. It was almost as if Reuel had been expecting them.

He glanced around the edge of the door, surveyed the men lined up along the wall, and nodded. "I have been expecting you. Come in."

Frowning, Jared glanced at the others, but he followed Reuel inside.

"You are wondering why I placed the guard in the corridor, I do not doubt."

"We were wondering *exactly* that!" Jared informed him. "Sir."

Reuel gestured for them to sit although where the fuck he expected them to sit when there was only one chair besides the one he took himself was beyond Jared. Everyone glanced at the chair and then folded their arms and planted their backs against the wall instead since he had indicated that they were guests.

"I do not claim a vast understanding of the humans in general and the women—well, their own men do not understand them—I have been trying to understand Chloe, however. It seemed completely illogical to me that she would insist that she be solely responsible for the …

welfare of her crew one moment and then dismiss it in the next ... even for a human.

"She will not speak to me about it either and the only thing that I have been able to grasp is that she is deeply wounded and she desires privacy to heal."

Jared felt his belly clench sickeningly. "Why is she wounded?"

"How is she wounded?" Kane demanded.

"Who hurt her?" Damon ground out.

Reuel held up his hand. "I do not think that anyone wounded her, but if you are suggesting that it was I ... Well, mayhap I was careless in speaking. There was no intention to wound her. I was only speaking the truth as I saw it."

"Begging your pardon, sir," Jared said tightly. "But I do not understand a gods damned thing that you just said!"

Reuel's lips tightened. "She is human. I believe that she has begun to realize that she has no place living among cyborgs and that is why she is unhappy and also why she has avoided being around any of us."

The men exchanged looks of angry confusion. "Why has she no place living among cyborgs?" Jared growled. "You said that she was welcome to settle among us when we found this gods damned place!"

"She is *still* welcome," Reuel snapped. "She no longer feels welcome, however, and she has decided that she will not settle with us."

"Why does she not feel welcome?" Sebastian demanded.

"I can not explain that when I do not perfectly understand it myself. But it is true."

"It is *not* true, gods damn it!" Jared snarled. "She has lived among us for months!"

Reuel studied him for a long moment. "And *twice* the six of you have battled over her head as if it has not *once* occurred to any of you that she is as frail as ... a flower! That you could crush her fragile little body only by *falling* upon her! *She* is not a cyborg. She does not have nanos to heal her. She does not have an alloy chassis that would take a direct mortar hit to damage. She is flesh and bone.

"Beyond that, you are not human and you cannot give her what a male of her own kind could. You cannot give her your child. You cannot *be* a family when there will be no off-spring. We have the chance to live here on this world in peace, to build something, to enjoy life, but that is all that we will have.

"I believe that I understand what your instincts are driving you to do. You want to breed a child on her, but it is not something that we are capable of ... not now. Mayhap, in time, we will have this, as well, but there is no guarantee of it.

"I believe that she does care for you, but I also believe that she has come to understand that it was not meant to be and she is trying to stop. This is the wound that she needs peace to heal."

Jared felt so dizzy and weak, he decided to take the chair after all. Leaning forward, he settled his elbows on his knees to support his head.

"Well! I do not want her to stop caring, gods damn it!" Kane said.

"We will not fight anymore," Sebastian said and then glanced at the others. "Around her. And it is not true that we did not give it a thought, gods damn it! Lucien, Thor, and I were trying to remove her to safety that first time!"

Damon glared at him. "I was trying to remove her to safety! I *did* remove her to safety!"

Kane scowled at him. "You removed her to the safety of her cabin to fuck her! That does not count!"

Reuel released an irritated breath. "You cannot even discuss her without fighting! How do you think that you can form a family when you cannot get along at all?"

"We are a family already!" Kane said tightly. "Chloe said so. And I do not believe that she wants to stop caring about us, gods damn it!"

Reuel stood abruptly. "Take your argument elsewhere—just do not take it to Chloe's door!"

Saluting him stiffly, they turned and stalked toward the door. It took Jared a few moments to push himself from the chair.

"It would be kinder to her to leave her alone," Reuel said. "As I said, we are not the same."

"I do not care and I do not think it matters to Chloe. She has always treated me as a man. She has always looked upon me as a man. I cannot leave her alone. She is afraid to be alone. And ... I love her."

Reuel studied him critically for a moment. "Then you must try to court her and convince her that you can offer her more than a man of her own kind."

Jared frowned. "I do not think I know how to do that."

Reuel thought it over. "I do not know either. Mayhap you should try what the beasts do when they want a mate? Build her a nest. You cannot fill it, or her, with off-spring, but I think there are enough of you to keep her busy and keep her mind off of that," he finished dryly.

Chapter Seventeen

Jared was not pleased when he had made his way back to his cabin to discover that the others had beat him there and made themselves at home. "Get off my gods damned bunk!" he snarled when he entered.

They scowled at him but got up.

"What did Reuel say when we left?"

Jared stretched out tiredly on his bunk, staring at the ceiling. "He said that we should court her if we do not want to lose her."

The other men looked at each other. "But we have *been* courting her, have we not?" Kane demanded.

"Fucking does not count as courting!" Damon said dryly.

"I do not know why not!" Kane said indignantly. "In fact, I am certain that it is part of it and it is my favorite part, gods damn it!"

"The objective of courtship is to convince the one you adore that you cherish them!" Damon said tightly.

"I have cherished every inch of her … several times!" Sebastian said tightly. "And I would have more than that if I had gotten the gods damned chance!"

"What I would like to know," Kane snarled, "is what a fucking fuck droid would know about courting! That is not in *my* programming!"

"It is *because* I am a fucking fuck droid!" Damon growled. "Do you think the women only came to fuck? They came to complain, gods damn it! Sometimes they complained *while* I fucked them! I am as certain as I can be that I know all of the *wrong* ways for a man to court a woman! And even appearing to *want* to fuck when they want courtship is the wrong way to go about it! You must convince them that you cherish them for other things."

Sebastian frowned at him in confusion. "*What* other things?"

Damon sighed irritably. "They never got around to explaining that … or if they did, I was not listening by that time. They do not want to be wanted for sex, however, and they were equally incensed if a man mentioned that he needed a woman to keep house, or mother his children if he had them by another woman, anything to do with domestic chores. I did not understand that, especially when they would say they needed to be needed in almost the same breath. That is completely illogical."

Jared frowned. "Reuel suggested that we build her a nest."

Kane gaped at him. "What the fuck would she do with a gods damned nest? She is not a bird! Unless he thinks that we could catch a bird for her like that and that she would like to have a bird? But I certainly do not recall that she ever mentioned that she likes birds."

Jared gave him a sardonic look, his lips tightening.

"I think he meant a house," Lucien said helpfully.

"Well if he meant house, why did he not say house, gods damn it! It sounds to me as if he is *trying* to confuse us, not be helpful!"

"The beasts!" Jared snapped. "He was referring to the courtship of the beasts!"

"*I* am not a beast!" Kane said indignantly.

"We are all beasts," Thor said. "Or at least, I do not suppose we are more than half since we are only part human, but *they* are beasts. They are civilized beasts, but they are still animals—because they are not plants."

Kane frowned at him. "I do not see that that is at all helpful!"

"The males try to attract the females by showing them that they are a good mate. They can provide for them and their off-spring," Jared said. "Except that we cannot give her off-spring."

"We do not know that we cannot," Kane said. "Six months ago, I could not make up my own mind and now I can, except that I am not certain any longer what it is that I want to do—much of the time."

Sebastian stared at him. "That does not make any fucking sense!"

"Of course it does. Six months ago, I ate when I was hungry and it did not matter what I ate so long as it had the correct balance of nutrients and there was enough. Now I know what it tastes like and I like some things better than others!"

"Well, we cannot worry about that now!" Jared said irritably. "It is not as if Chloe does not know what we are. I think that we should build her a beautiful nest and show her that we can provide for her."

Kane studied him unhappily. "Can we not also show her how much we want to mate with her?"

"Not if you mean fuck her!" Damon snapped. "Did I not just *say* that they do not want to be wanted for that?"

Kane stared him sullenly. "She enjoyed it, gods damn it! I do not see why she would not *still* enjoy it!"

"I do not think she would mind kisses," Damon said thoughtfully.

"Where can we kiss her?" Kane asked with renewed interest.

Damon gave him a look. "Where do you think?"

Kane heaved an irritated breath. "Well, I cannot kiss her and *not* want to fuck her!"

"And you do not feel the same way when you are kissing her breasts? Or her pussy?"

Kane thought it over. "I suppose I should just not kiss her."

"I do not think we will have a problem with that if she is going to avoid us altogether," Jared said glumly.

"I do not especially like the idea of making a nest for her when we have no idea what she likes or where she would like it," Damon said. "If she does not, we will have to start over!"

Jared frowned. "She said that her father had promised to build her a castle of sand on the beach."

The others stared at him with varying degrees of disbelief. "We cannot make it out of sand! It will blow away!" Thor snapped.

"Or the tide will wash it away," Kane said, nodding.

Jared rolled his eyes. "I am only saying that she seemed to like the idea of the beach and castles."

"I am not at all certain that I can wait that long," Kane said after a prolonged silence. "My balls hurt now, gods damn it! It could take … months to build a castle at the very least!"

* * * *

"Well, it was a thought," Sebastian said as they stood on the edge of the plateau Reuel had chosen for their first city.

"I can not even see the beach from here," Kane said in disgust.

Jared's expression was angry and disgusted. He pulled his gaze from the view after a few moments and turned to look for Chloe. He had not managed to catch more than a glimpse of her and it seemed that she was always heading away from him when he did. He did not entirely understand the misery that seemed to have become his constant companion, but he had no trouble understanding that it was directly connected to Chloe. When he saw her, gladness would fill him for a handful of moments, his heart would lose all rhythm, and his chest would tighten and when she walked away, his chest would tighten more and he would feel only misery.

He did not think that he could endure much more of it and the only ray of promise that he had been able to think of was the suggestion that Reuel had made. He feared it would not be as simple as that, but he could not think of anything else to try.

And now it seemed that he could not even try that. He supposed she might be satisfied with something else, but he did not know what that might be. He had never heard her speak of anything else.

It would be far easier if he could speak to her and ask her to tell him what she wanted so that he could get it for her, but Damon had said that that was not as gratifying to a woman as 'surprising' her. He certainly wanted to get the most benefit from the gift, but it had occurred to him that surprise was not always a good thing. Sometimes surprise was a very bad thing and not what one wanted at all.

As he stood watching her work with the others, though, he saw Reuel approach her. Resentment flooded him the moment she stopped to speak to him and before he entirely knew what he was doing, he found himself striding briskly toward the two of them. Without a great deal of surprise, he discovered the other five had fallen into step around him. Annoyance went through him, but then an idea formed.

Battle formation! She could not retreat if they cut off her retreat!

It worked very well indeed. He might have congratulated himself on it if he had not suddenly discovered that there was a fist in his throat that made it nigh impossible to swallow or speak and his mind had gone perfectly blank. Worse, a look of panic crossed her features when she discovered that they had completely surrounded her.

To his surprise, Reuel came to his aid. "Have you men decided upon a site where you will build the home that you spoke to me about for your family?"

He swallowed convulsively a couple of times, his gaze still on Chloe, but overall that was not a bad thing. She had sent Reuel a startled look when he spoke and then sent him a wide-eyed look that made him hopeful. "My woman …."

Kane punched him in the side hard enough to jolt him.

He turned and glared at him. "*Our* woman said that she liked the beach, but we are too far away to build a home for her that looks out over the beach. This stone, I believe would work for the castle she wanted, because it looks like sand, but it is much better for building—but we cannot find a place where she would be able to see the beach. I do not know where we should build."

Reuel nodded. "The site will be important. We are building the barracks here for now for those who have no family to claim. The city will be there," he said, gesturing, and then turned to Chloe. "Mayhap you will help us for a little while? They can spare you from the clearing."

Chloe gaped at him blankly when he held out his portable computer terminal. "The city plans that I have worked out are on here. If you will carry this and give us the distances, we will make a rough marking of the placement of the heart of the city and location of buildings of importance. Then we will have a better idea of where the personal residences would be located and, of course, the limits of the city if you … they are more interested in a rural setting."

Chloe's emotions had erupted into complete turmoil the moment she'd discovered her guys had surrounded her and she didn't have a route of escape. She hadn't managed to fully assimilate much of anything about the conversation but the little that she did grasp only added to her state of confusion. Hope and misery warred within her.

It wasn't hard to find the source of the misery at all. She hadn't felt anything else since she'd realized how totally impossible and ridiculous her dreams of settling in the colony with her guys was. On top of that was the fear that they didn't know that she'd decided to go with Reuel and not stay—not surprising since she hadn't had the nerve to tell them herself. Coward that she was, she'd hoped that Reuel might mention it, though, and she wouldn't have to.

The hope was a little harder to pinpoint, but she finally realized that it hinged on the totally false assumption that they knew she'd decided not to stay and were trying to tell her that they wanted her to. She didn't think she should feel any sort of hopefulness at all if it was only that they assumed she would because they didn't know she'd changed her plans.

For a time, the war had her hovering on the brink of bursting into tears, but she was able to regain a modicum of composure as she walked around with them and Reuel, and he pointed out where the city's marketing center would be, the med center, the judicial center and municipal auditorium for town meetings. To save her life, she couldn't behave 'normally' around them. She was afraid to meet their gazes for fear it might encourage them to ask her questions she didn't think she could answer without squalling.

"Now," Reuel said several hours later, "as you can see, the city proper will take up much of the plateau with private residences spiraling out around the work center. I am certain most of our men will choose to remain soldiers—and we will certainly need a standing army when there is always the threat of our colony being found and coming under attack. There are the natives to consider, as well. We do not yet have their measure, but I anticipate hostility and territorialism so we will need to guard against attack from that direction, as well, although I believe they are primitive enough they will not be a great threat to us. The city will have patrols to keep the peace, also.

"I am thinking, though, that *family* men will wish to take up other occupations, however—possibly as planters since that is an occupation of importance to a colony like ours. Keeping in mind that all men will be expected to take up arms when necessary to defend the colony—would you men be considering something like that?"

Chloe looked at the men. Jared, Kane, Damon, Sebastian, Lucien, and Thor all exchanged perplexed looks and looked at Reuel again. He nodded. Kane blinked at him, but caught the prompt. "I have been thinking along those lines," he said. "I would want to stay close and guard my ... our woman so that she would feel safe."

He beamed at Chloe when she glanced at him. She looked away almost at once, but she smiled.

The others, he discovered, were glaring at him.

"I was thinking that a salvage operation would not be a bad idea since the colony will have need of things that may not be readily available here," Jared volunteered. "That would require a good bit of space and *also* allow me to stay close to guard our woman most of the time."

"I will also be a planter," Damon offered.

The other three looked uncomfortable and vaguely angry.

"Well! There is plenty of time for everyone to find their niche within the colony!" Reuel said bracingly. "If we are talking planting and salvaging, this suggests a rural setting." He fixed Chloe with a questioning look. She gulped, glanced around uneasily, and finally met Reuel's gaze again. "Something not too far out in case ... the natives?"

Reuel nodded. "Good thinking. Fortunately, we are wide open. Let us examine the view and terrain. I am thinking a castle perched upon the side of the hill—close in to the city for safety and yet apart for privacy and then the working part of the plantation could fall below and away.

Chloe had become so tired by the time they had traveled a third of the distance that she'd lost most of her nervousness. She didn't complain. She wasn't comfortable enough to want to draw attention to the fact that she was human and tired far more quickly than they did. She had reason to be glad she hadn't begged off. They finally reached a point where the view was so beautiful that she stopped abruptly and stared at it with a sense of awe. It seemed to be an older section of forest, for the trees that grew there were much taller and thicker around the trunks. The fall was gentle and more rolling and she could see a narrow ribbon of a stream flowing across it. "This is so pretty!"

The men looked it over with interest.

Reuel, Jared saw when he glanced at him, looked triumphant. "The only questions to be settled now are the design of the structure and the plot size to be allotted to each settler. I think we can safely agree that the plantations must be large enough to allow each grower room to supply a healthy percentage of the food to be produced. In any case, there is no reason to delay clearing and beginning the structure. You did mention that you were interested in a design that would be 'castle-like'. How many will there be in the family?"

"Seven," Jared said promptly.

He frowned at the look Reuel gave him, trying to figure out what he seemed to be trying to convey and abruptly remembered that Reuel had said Chloe would expect off-spring. He did not know *how* he was to provide that, gods damn it, if Reuel said that they were not capable of it, but he thought that was what Reuel was trying to suggest. "For now," he added uneasily.

Reuel smiled.

Jared frowned, looking away, but he saw something in Chloe's expression that gave him pause. Her cheeks were pink, but she looked … happy, not uncomfortable, and he was glad he had added that last.

He *still* did not know how he was to manage it, but he decided he would think of something.

"Good!" Reuel said. "My suggestion would be to examine all of the data available to you—from the castles of the ancients to the most modern structures that utilize all known conservations, consider the needs of the family—for instance, you may want a very large hall in which to gather—and then you can begin to work on the design. Feel free to consult with me if you like. I have done a good deal of research on the subject already. In the meanwhile, you are excused from working on the barracks since you will have need to construct your personal abode."

Jared was more than a little disappointed when Chloe excused herself and left with him, but since she asked Reuel if she could return to the ship to rest, he thought it was not altogether to avoid them.

Feeling a little less miserable, in fact, more than a little cheered that they had made some progress, he turned to survey the site Chloe had picked out and felt an even greater lift in his spirits. She was right. It was a very nice site.

"We should get tools to work with."

"I think that we should go down and study the area very carefully before we begin," Sebastian said.

"She said here," Jared said tightly.

"But she did not point to a specific site," Damon seconded Sebastian.

Jared frowned but realized they were right. "It will need to be a place where she would see this from the windows," he pointed out, gesturing at the view.

"We may need to remove a great many trees," Kane said thoughtfully.

"It is the trees she was looking at!" Lucien snapped.

"How do you know what she was looking at, gods damn it!"

"There is nothing here to see but the trees!"

"He has a point, but I can also see a stream and the sky," Damon said.

"Well, if she only wanted to see the gods damned sky, she could see that from anywhere!"

"So it can only be the trees and the stream," Jared said decisively. "We will find a place where we will not have to cut many trees down where she will also be able to look at the water."

"Mayhap we should go down to the stream and look up to see where it is most open?" Thor suggested.

"But *this* is the view!" Kane said testily. "If we are down there, how are we to know what she would see from up here?"

"I am going to survey the area," Jared said tightly. "If it is the trees she likes, we will not be able to cut them down and make fields there or clear a place for salvage. I think we must decide where those must be put before we decide where the castle must stand."

"She did not say that she wanted a castle. I noticed that," Sebastian said.

"She did not say that she did not want one either!" Jared retorted impatiently.

"What did you mean by that comment 'seven for now'?" Kane demanded abruptly. "Because if you are thinking that we might add others, I am certain I do not care for that! Chloe said that her woman's cycle was 28 days EST and that she could not have sex for five of those day because of her period—whatever that is. That only leaves 3.8 days for each of us as it is! *Less* if she also has rest days! Although I suppose we might as well consider the .8 as her rest times, otherwise we will be fighting over them. Because I do *not* think that it would be fair for some to have four when the rest have only three!"

"Off-spring," Jared said tightly.

Lucien and Kane gaped at him. "But you said that we could not *have* off-spring! Reuel said it! How are we going to manage that?"

"We will have to think of something."

"Well! If fucking will not do it I do not know what 'something' we will think of!"

* * * *

Despite his weariness from laboring all day, Jared found that he could not sleep. He *needed* to talk to Chloe. It had reassured him for a time when she had seemed to accept that they were building for her, but it ate at him that she still avoided them and she had not actually given any of them a promise.

If he could only get her to promise that she would give them time to prove to her that they would and could take care of her, he would be able to sleep at night, he thought. And he knew that if she gave her word that he could count on it.

He was just sorry, now, that he had not realized before that the things she had said were not a promise that he could count on.

His anxiety over it was not the only reason he could not sleep. His need for sexual relief was reaching a point of true suffering. He had *thought* it was bad when he had been in the brig. It was far worse now. He did not *want* anyone but Chloe. Beyond that, he did not want to make her angry when she had made it clear that the thought of him fucking anyone else made her very angry. It was getting harder and harder to remember that, though, when he knew that all of the other men—Reuel's crew—could go to their women for relief and did. He could not keep those thoughts from running through his mind no matter how hard he tried and he was afraid that he would do something stupid if he did not find relief soon.

He had begun to actually *fear* that every decision that he made would turn out to be the wrong one and he would lose Chloe.

It did not make him feel better that the others were in nearly as bad a state as he was, mayhap worse, because they were as fearful as he was and were constantly badgering him for reassurances that he could not give them. He would not have felt any hesitancy if he was on familiar ground. When he had been a soldier, he had been completely confident that he had weighed all possibilities against probabilities in anything to do with military strategy and arrived at the right decision, but he had not experienced anything like this before and, moreover, he had not cared nearly as much whether he would be successful or not.

He thought that it was a very bad idea to approach Chloe when he was not certain of what to say and not certain that he could convince her that it was not just fucking that he wanted of her. In fact, he was fairly certain if she gave him any opening at all that he was not going to be able to control himself.

The need to get a promise from her had begun to outweigh his fears of self-control, however. He had not been able to corner her, but he had known that she ate and bathed. It had not taken much effort to discover when and that had made it harder to contain himself even though he knew he would be better off if he did not get her alone.

He lay staring at the timepiece in his cabin for a time, watching the count of seconds, minutes, and hours and finally sat up. She would be in the shower room. He would wait until she had had time to dry off and dress and then he would trap her there and speak to her, he decided.

He would still have to fight temptation, but it would be easier if she was dressed. He thought he would be able to get his mind off of his dick long enough to talk.

He could hear that the shower was still running when he reached the door to the shower room and he stopped abruptly, struggling with the instant urge that washed over him to at least step into the doorway and watch her. After debating for several moments, he lost the battle and moved to the opening.

His heart nearly stopped in his chest when he discovered that he was not the only one who had discovered when Chloe went to bathe alone.

Chapter Eighteen

Jared could tell, instantly, from her stance that Salina was only waiting for Chloe to notice her to attack. Her stance was aggressive and every muscle tensed to spring upon her.

Coldness washed over him when he had managed to analyze the situation and realized that Salina had taken the possibility of interruption into account. She had placed herself within easy reach of her target. If he moved or spoke, she would be upon Chloe in an instant and there would be nothing he could do to save her ... nothing. It would not take her more than two seconds to break Chloe's neck ... if that much.

He swallowed convulsively, knowing Chloe would turn any moment and he would lose any advantage he had, any possibility. Summoning to his mind every possibility that occurred to him and then discarding it, he struggled with despair and finally seized upon the only one he thought had any chance of working as he saw Chloe reach for the lever to shut off the water.

Crouching, he calculated the trajectory and force he would need, and then bellowed loudly enough his voice echoed around the chamber, making it difficult to pinpoint his position and distracting Salina at the same time. "Get away from her!" he shouted. Launching himself into the air even as the words left his mouth, he soared over Salina's head, executing an airborne somersault and landing on his feet between her and Chloe.

Fortunately, Chloe's reaction was to jump back. Unfortunately, Salina had almost instantly realized his plan of attack. She had whipped around when he bellowed, but she had turned again almost before he touched down. Uttering a feral scream, she launched herself at him. Her attack altered his trajectory. She slammed into him full force, driving him into the wall behind him and then drove her fists into his midsection several times before he could recover enough to try to block her. He spared a quick glance to see where Chloe was even as he made a grab for Salina's arms. Relief flooded him when he saw that she had crouched in a tight ball in the corner, but it was momentary.

While his strategy had placed him in a position to shield Chloe, it had also placed him in a near indefensible situation, limiting his ability to strike both by the confines of the shower walls and Chloe's presence.

He managed to grasp one of Salina's arms. She slung the other out in an attempt to reach Chloe, striking the wall just above her head with her fist and leaving a dent in it roughly the size of Chloe's head.

Chloe sucked in a gasp of fright and cowered lower even as Jared jerked on the arm he held, pulling Salina back. His second attempt to catch her arm failed when she brought back the arm she'd tried to strike Chloe with, clobbering him hard enough on his temple to make his head ring. He'd braced himself and the blow still whipped his body sideways enough to throw his own attempted punch off. He struck her a glancing blow to the chin that still managed to rock her backwards on her heels.

Catching her upper arm, he threw his weight against her and managed to push her back far enough that the parallel walls of the shower offered Chloe some protection. She very nearly outmaneuvered him by dropping to her back and using his weight to throw him over her. She might have except that when she threw herself back to pull him, Kane and Sebastian caught her from both directions. Sebastian slammed his arms down upon hers, breaking her hold even as Kane slugged her in the jaw. It threw her into a tumbling roll, but she caught herself on the third and used her momentum to come up to one knee and plant her other foot solidly enough to launch another attack. Damon caught her by her flying hair. If she had been human, the jolt when her body continued to fly and her head stopped, would very likely have separated her spinal column at the neck.

Salina merely screamed in frustrated rage as gravity slammed her into the deck. Kane and Sebastian pounced on her the moment she landed, pinning her to the floor, but she wasn't stunned enough by the fall to give up the fight. She screamed again, trying to reach them with her nails to claw them or bite them, drumming her feet and legs against the floor in an effort to kick them.

Two medics surged forward as soon as Kane and Sebastian had managed to pin her and injected her with something potent enough to take the fight out of her.

Vaguely dizzy from the blows to his head, Jared flicked a glance at the crowd Salina had drawn with her screams and turned to check on Chloe. Her eyes were as wide as saucers and her face pale, but she'd already begun trying to get to her feet when he reached for her.

Blood ran through his hair and down his face to drip on her as he bent over and for a split second he thought it was her blood.

"Oh my god, Jared! You're bleeding."

"You are not hurt?"

She shook her head, surging forward and wrapping an arm around him. He stared down at the top of her head dubiously for a moment when it dawned on him that she thought she was offering support. He was on the point of informing her that he was not that fucking injured and that she certainly could not keep him on his feet if he was when it dawned on him that he had had a stroke of luck. Instead of pushing her gently away to make certain he did not bleed on her, he lifted an arm to her shoulders.

The rest of their men looked at him askance as he 'staggered' out with Chloe's help, but he waggled his eyebrows at them in a silent message that none of them appeared to catch. They scowled at him.

"I need to have a look at that cut," Chloe said anxiously. "Do you think you need a medic?"

Since he'd been in the process of trying to get his message across when Chloe looked up, he lifted the hand he'd been waving at the men to his head. "I do not think so. I cannot tell."

"I'll look at it when I've washed the blood off. Scalp wounds always bleed a lot, so maybe it isn't as bad as it seems."

Reuel's crewmembers, who'd been aroused by the commotion, looked even more disbelieving than his own, but Chloe was preoccupied with helping him and he managed to get her out of the chamber before she noticed.

"You are taking me to your cabin?" Jared asked.

Chloe threw him a suspicious look and frowned. "I guess I should. You had to have hit your head hard to split the scalp. You should probably be watched for any sign of a concussion."

Jared almost smiled before he thought better of it. It was sheer torture for all of that.   They moved so slowly down the corridor that his wound closed and the bleeding stopped long before they reached her cabin door. When he had sat down on the edge of her bunk, she darted off again to get water to wash his wound before he could grab her and he had to wait another five minutes for her to come back again.

Grinding his teeth with impatience, he dug at the wound until he managed to open it and bleed a little more before she returned the second time.

She'd dressed, he discovered with a good deal of disappointment, more regretful that he had not grabbed her before she had had a chance to dress.

She climbed onto the bed on her knees beside him, very carefully parting his hair to search for the wound. He took the opportunity to curl his arms around her to steady her and burrow his face against her breasts, breathing deeply and ecstatically of her scent.

She pulled on a lock of hair matted to his head with blood. He ground his teeth against the sharp pain that shot through and then thought better of it. "Ow!"

"Oh! I'm so sorry, baby!"

He frowned. *Baby?* He was not at all sure he fucking liked that, but she had not objected to his face in her breasts. He was struggling with the urge to move his face to the right or the left and capture a nipple when she abruptly pulled away.

"It's closed. Thank god! I think it'll be alright." She placed her fingers under his chin and tipped his head up, wiping at the drying blood on his face. "I can't believe that crazy fucking bitch! What the hell was she thinking?"

The question effectively dampened Jared's rising ardor. He tightened his arms around her waist reflexively. He knew what the crazy fucking bitch had been thinking—that she could kill Chloe while she was unguarded. He had no idea why she would want to, but he did not doubt for a moment that she had intended to. She would not have flown into such a rage if she had not felt thwarted. He had not attacked her. She had launched the first attack.

He swallowed with an effort. "I do not know. I am only glad that she did not succeed." Turning, he lay back against her bunk, taking her with him. She braced herself on her elbows, staring down at him questioningly.

He felt his gut clench now that he had finally gotten the opportunity to speak to her that he had been trying for. "How ...? What must I do to have your promise that you will not leave?"

Her face crumpled. He thought for several horrifying moments that she would begin to cry and tried to think of some way to head her off. "I promised that I would never leave you—Kane and I—promised. I did not think that you would consider leaving us. Tell me. We will do it."

She swallowed audibly. "You only have to ask."

Jared frowned. "That is all?" he asked, baffled and vaguely indignant that he had suffered so long, worried so much and that was all he would have had to do.

She chuckled huskily and leaned down to rest her forehead against his. "I just need to know that you want me to stay. I need for you to say it."

He caught her head between his hands, guiding her to his lips. "I want ... I *need* you to stay, Chloe," he murmured, sucking light kisses along her lips.

She turned her face, rubbing her cheek along his. "If I say yes, can we fuck?"

He pushed her away abruptly to stare at her. Slowly a frown creased his brows as it occurred to him that it might be a test of some kind. Damon had said there were always tests and a man could never tell how to pass the gods damned test. He swallowed with an effort, tried to put his raging needs from his mind. "If I say yes, will you believe I do not love you?" he asked cautiously.

Her breath caught in her throat. A look of wonder flickered over her face. "Say that again."

He frowned, more uneasy. "If I say …."

"Not that part. The last part."

"Will you believe I do not love you if I want to fuck?"

She covered his lips with her hand. "I love you, Chloe."

Relief hit him when he finally realized what she wanted. He turned, dumping her onto the bed beside him and pulled her fingers from his lips. "You did not answer my question, woman," he said gruffly.

"You aren't going to say it, are you?"

"Not when you are prompting me as if I cannot say it on my own!" he said irritably.

"Then make love to me and I'll settle for what I did get," she whispered, moving closer to match her lips to his.

He sealed his lips to hers, kissing her deeply, with a hunger that pushed everything from her mind except the longing she'd felt to feel his touch again. Anticipation soared through her like a flash fire. She found the opening of his suit, tearing at it to open it and trying to peel it from his shoulders. He was as anxious as she was, or he was in complete agreement that it was better to get the clothes out of the way as quickly as possible. He broke the kiss long enough to strip her suit off and his own and dragged her beneath him again for another kiss.

He broke the second heated kiss after only a moment, pushing himself downward to drive her into a state of frenzy by tugging at her breasts. They were both gasping and gulping air when he came up and settled his hips in the cradle of her thighs. He paused when he had breached her opening, grinding his teeth.

"Do not be angry with me if I come at once," he gasped. "I have wanted you so long I had begun to think that I would come if I sneezed hard."

Chloe chuckled and pulled him closer. "I'll catch up the second time around if you beat me to the finish line."

He smiled against her mouth. "That was not a joke."

"I know. That was what made it funny—and wonderful. You didn't go to anyone else."

He drew back and frowned at her. "I could not do that. I wanted you

… and you said that you would be angry if I did."

"Damned straight!"

He studied her face as he sawed shallowly in and out of her and finally drove deeply. He paused again, panting for breath. "It is heaven being inside you, Chloe," he said huskily. She felt a heady rush go through her, felt the muscles along her channel ripple in response.

He shuddered and began a driving pace that took her where she wanted to go—to heaven with him and when they floated downward into the valley of blissful peace, he gathered her against his length and nuzzled his face against hers.

Uttering a contented sigh as he drifted toward slumber, he muttered, "I love you, Chloe."

Chloe felt a thrill of happiness rush through her. More content than she could recall, she closed her eyes, a smile still curling her lips.

The door to her cabin opened. She turned to discover that Kane had poked his head through the opening. Behind him, Sebastian had stretched to look over his shoulder.

After studying her a moment, Kane entered, shoved Jared out of the way, scooped her up, and headed for the door. Chloe looked at him with a mixture of amusement, confusion, and a tad of irritation when they reached the corridor. "What are you doing?"

"It is my turn to talk," Kane said decisively.

Chloe looped her arms around his neck. "Somehow I don't think you've got talking in mind."

"It is not his turn anyway!" Damon snapped.

"Well, it is certainly not your turn!" Sebastian and Lucien growled almost at the same moment.

"It is my turn," Thor said tightly.

"How do you figure that?" Kane demanded.

"I am after Jared."

The men halted in the corridor and considered it. "Jared has fucked up the order entirely! It was not *his* turn, gods damn it!"

"Hey!" Chloe exclaimed enthusiastically. "I've got an idea! Let's play for it! That could be fun! You know, roll the dice?"

They all looked at her speculatively for a few moments and finally shrugged. Ten minutes later, when they'd crowded into Kane's cabin and taken turns rolling the dice, Chloe understood *why* they weren't concerned about it. They could *make* the dice hit the same number every time. "Ok! This isn't going to work. I don't *have* that many damned holes!"

The End.

Read an excerpt from Reuel's story, available through NCP.

ABIOGENESIS

by

Kaitlyn O'Connor

Chapter One

Dalia VH570 stared at the bright, white light above her, watching it flicker as she felt her thoughts dissolve into the same nothingness as the whiteness that surrounded her. She had always hated physical examinations. She just wasn't certain why.

The prick of something sharp jolted Dalia into sudden, crystal clear alertness and the absolute certainty of danger. Opening her eyes, she surveyed her surroundings, searching for the threat she sensed.

She was still in the examination room, but she was bound to the table now. Turning her head, she looked at the man who'd just stabbed a syringe into her arm.

Her movement brought his gaze to hers, and she saw his eyes dilate instantly with fear, guilt, and the certainty that he was looking into the face of death. His reaction forced a healthy shot of adrenaline through her body and her heart leapt into overtime, pumping it through her. Gritting her teeth, she concentrated, tensing every muscle and sinew in her body, and heaved upward, breaking the restraints. The technician was still staring at her stupidly when she gripped his hand. Snatching the syringe from her arm, she drove it into his carotid artery, depressing the plunger.

His eyes rolled back into his head. The saliva in his mouth boiled, foaming, spilling between his gasping lips. She sat up, grasping his throat, half lifting him from the floor. "You tried to kill me. Why?"

His mouth worked. He gagged, coughed up spittle and blood. "Help me," he pleaded.

Dalia shook him. "First tell me why."

"Gestating... you're gestating. Never supposed to be able...."

She stared at him blankly, trying to understand the word, trying to figure out what it had to do with his attempt to kill her. "What is this word?"

"Reproduction. To bear young," he gasped, clawing at her hand frantically.

She dropped him, staring down at him as he sprawled on the floor beside the gurney she sat on. Tossing the sterile sheet off that had covered her, she slipped to the floor. "A child? A baby? You tried to kill me because I'm ... breeding? It's only a fifty thousand credit fine!"

He shook his head frantically. "Not human. Not human."

She stared at him uncomprehendingly for several moments but finally lifted her head, realizing at last that the alert was sounding, had been since she'd broken her restraints. She blinked, calculating the time. Anywhere from three to five minutes had passed. The exits would be blocked by now and guarded. A contingent of guards would be racing toward this room.

She glanced down at the technician, but he'd stopped gurgling. His eyes were wide and staring now.

A wave of nausea washed over her. That should have been her. It would have been if she hadn't awakened when he'd speared her with the needle. She'd never killed another human being before, though, and she couldn't decide whether she was more horrified at having a hand in his death, revolted by what a human being looked like in their death throes, or because she'd been a hair's breadth from experiencing rather than witnessing. She didn't have time to analyze her distress, however. Shelving it for the moment, she glanced around the examination room, but no windows magically appeared. There was still only the one door.

She checked the walls, the floor, the ceiling.

Why had she allowed them to take her into a room with only one exit? Her training had taught her better. It was stupid to have relaxed her guard only because the med lab belonged to the company, the company she killed for.

She'd never trusted the damned company.

Leaping up onto the examination table, she reached up toward the ceiling and realized she was still too short. She could just touch the tiles above her with her fingertips. She went up on her tiptoes, bounced. Finally, she managed to dislodge the panel above her. It was a suspended ceiling, she saw, held aloft by thin wires. She seriously doubted it would hold her weight, but she was out of options.

Leaping up again, she caught the frame that had held the tile. As she'd more than half expected, it buckled, bringing down a rain of tiles around her.

The sound of running feet, many feet, came to her. It must be a full squad.

Good, she decided. The noise they were making would help to cover the noise she made. Leaping down from the examination table, she raced across the room, bent her knees and leapt upward, her arms extended. She crashed through the tile. It hit the floor around her. The wall, she saw went all the way up, approximately ten feet. Metal girders supported the floor above her.

It was the girders or nothing.

Whirling, she raced back toward the examination table, hit it flat footed and leapt upward, catching the bottom of a girder. With an effort, she pulled herself up, but she saw the space was too small for her to walk her way across hanging by her hands. Supporting most of her weight from her arms, she pulled her legs up and swung until she could hook her heels along the girder, as well.

It was dark above the ceiling, particularly since she had only just come from a room blindingly white, but she had excellent night vision. She focused her eyes and looked around. As far as she could see, there was nothing but girders, pipe, electrical wires and ductwork. The ductwork was too small to crawl through, and too light to support her weight.

She closed her eyes, mentally tracing her path through the building and into the examination room. Only a corridor separated her from the closest outer wall of the building, but the guards were racing down that path. She took the opposite direction. It was a good deal further from the outer wall, but it was also less likely that guards would be stationed there.

Moving swiftly now, she crawled, spider like beneath the beam until she'd reached the wall she'd seen on the other side. She turned then, following it until she found an opening. A catwalk ran through it and she dropped down onto it. Looking in first one direction and then the other, she finally decided to continue as she'd begun and crawled through the opening. She'd only just cleared it when she heard the guards pounding on the examination room door. Crouching low, she ran as fast as she could.

It wouldn't take them long to figure out she was in the overhead ceiling and probably not much more than that to realize that the only way she could traverse it was along the catwalk.

She heard them behind her before she reached the outer wall.

Dropping to her stomach, she reached for the closest ceiling tile and lifted it up just enough to study the room beneath her.

It was occupied. A woman was lying on an examination table, just as Dalia had been only minutes before.

She didn't have time to be picky.

Rolling off the catwalk, she dropped through the ceiling, landing in a half crouch on the floor. Startled, the woman sat up, opening her mouth to scream. Dalia leapt at her, covering the woman's mouth with one hand and pinching the woman's carotid artery with the other. The moment the woman's eyes rolled back in her head, Dalia released her and looked around, absently checking the woman's pulse to make certain she hadn't killed her.

This room had both a window and a door. She moved to the window first, pulled the window covering aside and looked out. She was on the sixtieth floor, about half way up the building, more or less. The outside of the building was as smooth as glass. Windows broke the monotony every ten feet or so, but most likely every one was fixed just as this one was and could not be opened and were probably nearly as impossible to break.

She couldn't fly, so that was out.

There was no point in trying to go down. They would be waiting for her. Up would only work if there were crafts on the roof.

It was a med lad. There were probably a half a dozen or more on the roof at any time.

There was one slight problem.

She didn't have a stitch of clothing on and that was bound to draw attention. Shrugging, she helped herself to the tunic and trousers the woman had been wearing. They were too big, but it wouldn't be nearly as noticeable as being naked. The woman's shoes were too big, too. It was too risky to wear them, she decided. They would slow her down at the very least. At worst, the shoes could trip her if she needed to run. She slipped the stockings on to cover her bare feet and make them less noticeable, then moved to the door, opening it a crack.

No one seemed terribly excited. She saw a couple of techs strolling along one end of the corridor, notepads in hand. There was a knot of them at one end of the corridor, waiting, she realized, for an elevator or having just gotten off one.

Obviously, security still thought they had the 'danger' contained on the other side of the firewall that ran down the building.

Stepping from the room, she walked casually toward the row of elevators and punched the button that would summon one going up. As she stood waiting, several more people joined her, staring up at the display panel above the doors. Turning her head just enough she could examine each of them in her peripheral vision, she relaxed fractionally. There was no sign of security guards ... yet.

Impatience began to gnaw at her. She'd just decided to find the stairs and take them up several flights when the bells on three of the elevators dinged, announcing the arrival of the cubicles. Having already turned away and taken a step down the corridor toward the sign marked 'exit', she glanced inside the elevator she'd been standing in front of as the doors slowly began to open.

It was packed with guards ...and the one in front was holding a tracker. He glanced up as she strode away, his eyes locking on her for about two seconds. Shoving anyone aside who lay in her path, she broke into a run as she heard the guards launch themselves against the opening doors, trying to squeeze through all at once and succeeding only in bottlenecking the exit.

The doors on the fourth elevator had already begun to close as she reached it. She leapt through the rapidly narrowing opening. The timing was perfect. She'd barely landed inside when the doors slammed closed. Her last view of the corridor, however, had been of the guards charging the elevator.

They'd spotted her. They would reroute it, she knew.

Ignoring the gasps and protests of the four people already in the elevator when she'd jumped in, she moved to the control panel, studied it a moment and finally speared her fingers through the holes drilled for the buttons, grasped the panel firmly and pulled it out of the wall, exposing the circuits. Almost simultaneously, the elevator lights blinked and the cubicle ground to a halt.

They'd already tied in.

Glancing over the circuits, she saw immediately that there was no way to rewire it. She grasped the panel and wrenched it out, tossing it to one side and evoking a round of screams from the women in the group. Grasping the main feed, she pulled on the wire until she had enough to reach, then stripped the insulation from the end, felt behind her head until she found the jack and plugged directly into the computer.

It took thirty seconds to override their override, and another five to lock them out. As the elevator jolted into motion again, Dalia examined the database and found that there were four crafts on the roof, fueled and prepped to go. One of the elevators was already on the roof. The other two were on the ground level and the tenth floor.

She was about to log out when it occurred to her that now was her opportunity to discover what the computer knew about her situation. The CPU inside her brain began displaying images before her eyes almost instantly.

Gestation was an archaic form of reproduction that had been practiced by the human race until the last century. The fertilized ovum attached itself inside the female's body, within a cavity known as the womb, and lived off of the female's body until it reached a state of maturity that would allow it to survive on its own.

Dalia frowned. *How is the parasite introduced into the host to begin with?*

Male and female each carried an element, the female an egg or ovum, which contained the DNA of the female host. The male donor provided sperm, which contained the male's DNA and would activate the egg and set off a chain reaction. The male would deliver his DNA via sexual intercourse.

Dalia mulled that over for a moment. She hadn't engaged in sex, at all. It was prohibited by the company to anyone in her position, an infraction punishable by termination. She'd always assumed they meant termination of employment, however. *In the event that the female did not have sexual intercourse with a male, was there another method of delivery? Or was it possible for the female to manipulate the ovum herself and induce it to begin to replicate cells?*

This method of reproduction was imprecise. Often the female would become impregnated when reproduction was infeasible or undesirable due to economic, health or social conditions. Occasionally, the male or female who wished to reproduce would be found to be infertile. If the male was infertile, and unable to provide his DNA, a donor would be found who was a desirable substitute and his DNA would be introduced into the female via medical procedure.

It still didn't make any sense to her. They'd impregnated her and now had decided to terminate both her and the pregnancy? She shook it off. She didn't have time to study it now. *Status?*

Passing the 100th floor.

Locate the guards for me.

Ten in elevator number one, passing the 15th floor. Five in elevator number three, passing the 40th floor. Five on elevator number two, egressing onto the roof now. Thirty on the ground floor level.

Chapter Two

Dalia removed the jack and turned to study the other passengers. They were huddled into one corner, staring at her as if she was some sort of monster. She supposed she could see their point, but it irritated the hell out of her anyway.

She had maybe five minutes before they reached the roof. That meant they had five minutes to deploy and be waiting for her. She could stop the elevator and take the stairs, but she wasn't certain that would give her any advantage. Even though she'd locked them out of the computer system, they would probably be expecting the possibility and have that exit covered too.

There was no cover for them on the roof beyond the craft moored there, but then they must know she was unarmed. There wasn't any reason for them to take cover except as a precaution in case she'd somehow located a weapon.

She finally decided they would probably assume assault positions anyway. The only thing you could count on about militia was that they always went by the book, and they always followed orders. Obviously, they didn't want or need to take her alive. They wanted her dead. That meant they would be stationed and ready to catch her in a crossfire.

She glanced at the other passengers speculatively, but she knew they were as expendable as she was. The objective wasn't to slaughter them, but the security guards weren't likely to quibble about having to go through them to get her, so using them as a shield was out.

Besides, she didn't want to be responsible for their deaths.

"They're waiting for me on the roof. If you don't want to die today, lie down on the floor as flat as you can and clasp your hands on top of your heads. With any luck, the fire will miss you." They gaped at her uncomprehendingly for several moments, then scrambled to comply, fighting briefly over who would have the position closest to the door. As she felt the elevator decelerating, Dalia jumped up onto the handrail that ran around the cubicle, bracing her hands above her head to balance herself.

The moment the door began to open, laser fire pelted the interior of the cubicle, covering almost every square inch of the walls from about one foot up to the ceiling. The side of the elevator protected Dalia as she'd hoped it would. She held her breath, waiting until she heard some call a cease fire, allowing the seconds to tick off as she envisioned them slowly stepping from their cover, advancing far enough to look into the elevator to see if they'd gotten her.

The bodies on the floor would confuse them, hopefully, for critical moments.

The trick was to time it precisely, move before they realized she wasn't one of the bodies lying on the floor of the elevator.

She held her breath, focusing on listening and interpreting the sounds she heard since she couldn't see; cautious, carefully placed footsteps--three pair. Two were still under cover.

Abruptly, she swung into action, landing on the floor of the elevator and bursting through the doors as they began to close once more. As she'd hoped, she caught them completely off guard. The three closest to the elevator opened their eyes and mouths wide in surprise. She hit the first one full tilt, bowling him over. She clotheslined the second with an extended arm, grabbing his weapon from his slackened grip even as he executed a flip. The third man, she took out with the butt of the weapon she'd grabbed. She whirled in a circle then, laying out random fire and catching the remaining two guards even as they finally managed to begin firing on her.

Within moments, five dead or groaning men lay on the flight deck. Gasping for breath, she surveyed them, her hands on her hips. "Never send a man to do a cyborg's job," she muttered in satisfaction, but then mentally shrugged. She was a rogue hunter, trained and bio-technologically enhanced to bring down rogue cyborgs, and she would've still had her hands full if they had sent even two. It was fortunate for her that they'd made an error in judgment and sent men instead.

She frowned. They either hadn't anticipated having any problem terminating her--which seemed unlikely given her training, or the decision to terminate her was of short standing.

Shaking off her questions and the weariness and apathy in the aftermath of battle, Dalia moved over them, quickly collecting their weapons and then headed for the nearest craft. Tossing the weapons into the patient bay of the ambulance craft, she scrambled into the cockpit, examined the layout to identify the craft and began flipping switches to activate the engines. Even as the craft began to lift off, the doors of one of the other elevators opened and men began to pour out, firing at her.

She punched the craft into hyper acceleration and it shot upwards and away in a sharp slingshot like motion--not, unfortunately, before it caught a dozen hits. The craft almost immediately became unstable and she knew they'd managed to hit something critical. Struggling to keep it level, she allowed it to drop toward the upper level traffic airway forty floors below her.

Bright dots lit up her radar screen both above and below her, looking like a swarm of insects. She glanced up through the viewing bubble and counted two crafts descending fast. They were ambulances like the one she'd taken, and the craft itself had no firepower. As long as she didn't let them get close enough to catch her in the sights of their handheld weapons, the risk of taking another hit was slim.

She wasn't certain if the craft needed another hit to bring it down, however. It began bucking and jolting as she hit the airway. The computer failed to adjust to oncoming traffic and she slammed into the protective force field of another craft, bounced off of it and ping ponged against three more before she dropped beneath the airway in a forward gliding descent.

In truth, it wasn't much of a glide. The craft continued to bounce and drop erratically in a controlled crash, as if it were striking solid objects instead of air currents. She managed to drop through the mid-level airway without incident, mostly because the heavy traffic was on the third level she'd already passed. A layer of greenish-yellow smog lay below her, obscuring her view of the lower airway. She landed on the roof of a passing craft when she reached the lowest level, was repelled by the protective field that surrounded it and nose dived through the airway, free falling for some twenty feet before she managed to kick the ambulance craft in the ass and get it going again.

Androids, cyborgs and pedestrians thronged the walks below her. When they looked up and saw her craft falling toward them, they scattered like fall leaves caught in a strong cross wind--in every direction. Despite that, she managed to set the craft down on the walk without smearing anyone. It's forward momentum responded sluggishly to her attempts to brake, however, and the craft slid along the walk for nearly a hundred yards before coming to rest against the base of one of the buildings that surrounded the walks like mountains, blocking so much of the light that the ground level lay in perpetual night except for artificial lighting.

The moment the craft finally stopped, Dalia threw off her restraints and struggled to stand. As far as she could tell she had suffered no more than bruises and a few minor cuts, but she knew adrenaline was pushing her now. She could be hurt much worse and not know it right away.

Regardless, she had to put as much distance between herself and the craft as possible before the guards caught up with her. Sorting through the weapons, she grabbed the two that had the fullest charges, slung one on each shoulder and scrambled out of the craft. Gawkers had already begun to converge on the downed craft when she emerged. Ignoring them, she strode purposefully toward the group milling about and pushed through. They parted before her, as if they feared she might be contaminated with something.

When she'd cleared the crowd, she broke into a jog and finally a run, glancing to her left and right each time she passed a narrow alley in search of one that was unoccupied. She'd begun to despair that there was even so much as a square inch of ground level space not inhabited when she raced past a vacant throughway. Stopping abruptly, she reversed directions and raced down it till she came to the first intersection. She began to weave her way back and forth through the narrow alleys until she came at last to the slum area of the city.

It, too, was occupied, but by the denizens of the dark--the 'subhuman' culture the upstanding citizens of the city were prone to consider did not exist. Unless the company was offering a reward for her, it was unlikely anyone would be interested enough in her to give the guards searching for her any tips.

Of course, they wouldn't need any information if she couldn't get rid of the locator surgically implanted in her hip, but she couldn't get rid of it until she could shake her pursuit long enough to stop.

Added to that little problem was the fact that she'd had to leave without her uniform--which held a med kit.

Tired now, she slowed to a brisk walk, stopping each time she found a derelict sprawled drunkenly on the walk and checking him for a knife. She found a razor on the second man she checked and studied it doubtfully. It was rusted, and she wasn't certain it could cut deeply enough, but beggars couldn't be choosers.

Straightening, she looked around for a lighted area and moved toward it. She didn't like the idea of standing in the light, but she didn't want to butcher her hip either. She needed the light to see what she was doing. After scanning the immediate area for threat and deciding it was minimal, she set her weapons down, shucked the trousers and probed the flesh of her hip until she found the locator.

Without giving herself time to think it over, she sliced the flesh as deeply as the razor would cut. Seconds passed before the pain caught up with her brain. She'd already dug her fingers into the cut, grasped the locator and yanked it free of the bone before fire poured through her. Gasping at the wave of dizziness that washed over her, she dropped the locator to the pavement, picked up one of the weapons and smashed it with the butt.

Blood was gushing from the cut. She studied it for several moments, but she knew there were no major veins in that area. Regardless, she couldn't allow it to continue to bleed. They'd be able to follow the blood trail almost as easily as the locator. Then, too, she might run out of fluids before she managed to get hold of a medical kit.

She didn't like it, but she didn't have any options. Lifting the weapon, she set it on its lowest setting and carefully sited it along the cut, firing off one quick burst.

The pain didn't take nearly as much time to reach her brain that time. She staggered back and fell to her knees, fighting the blackness that threatened to overwhelm her.

Dimly, she saw she'd attracted some attention from the local lowlifes. Lifting the weapon with an effort, she fired off several warning shots. When they scattered, she grabbed her trousers and the other weapon and began moving again. She wanted nothing so much as to crash somewhere, if only for fifteen or twenty minutes, but she couldn't afford the luxury until she'd put a lot of distance between herself and the locator she'd just destroyed. Her pursuit would almost certainly have triangulated on that position by now.

The faintness didn't recede. She had to fight it every step of the way. Finally, she managed to put at least a mile between her and the locator, before she reached a point where she knew she couldn't go another step without falling on her face.

Pausing, she leaned back against the wall of a building and searched the area. She hadn't seen anyone in a while, but that didn't mean they weren't there, watching, waiting for her to let her guard down so that they could steal anything she had of value and probably kill her in the process.

The building she was leaning against was ancient, deserted, crumbling. She climbed through the nearest opening and studied it, moving slowly through, her weapon at the ready. Skittering noises filtered to her from time to time, but she thought it must be some sort of animals. They didn't make enough noise to be human.

She came upon a partial stair leading upward and debated briefly whether it would be better to find a hiding place on one of the other floors or on the ground floor. Finally, she decided to try the second floor. It would give her a little lead time if she heard anyone coming. She could, if she had to, jump from the second floor without doing too much damage to herself ... as long as she was careful to land correctly.

Shouldering her weapon, she placed her back against the wall and moved carefully from step to step until she reached a gap. Checking the strength of the handrail to see if it would support her if the stair collapsed, she leapt the distance, coming down on her wounded hip. Her knee buckled, but she managed to catch herself with the railing.

When she'd reached the top, she turned to study the stairs and finally pulled one of the weapons from her shoulder and cut a larger section out. It would be far easier, she knew, for her to leap the hole downward than for anyone to leap it coming up. She found another set of stairs near the rear of the building, or rather a stairwell. Those stairs were completely gone.

The place reeked of death. As tempted as she was to just find a corner and collapse, she knew she couldn't rest until she'd assured herself she had the place to herself. The building had looked like it had at least six floors, even as ancient as it was, but there were only two floors accessible from the floor she was on. The upper floors had begun to slowly collapse down upon each other.

She found a badly decomposed body two floors up, which explained the god-awful smell and the lack of other occupants.

Relieved, she made her way down again, found a comfortable corner that was relatively free of debris, and collapsed. She'd hardly even settled when blackness closed in around her. She was disoriented for several moments when she woke. Sluggishly, her mind kicked in and memory flooded back to her. She had no idea how long she'd slept-- there wasn't enough sunlight filtering so far beneath the city to judge from the sun's movement. She could've been out mere minutes, or hours, or even days--but she struggled to her feet and checked her perimeter.

Satisfied that they hadn't discovered her and surrounded the building while she rested, she found a corner to relieve herself and then returned to her corner and sat down to figure out what options she might have.

There weren't a lot. She didn't know why they wanted her dead, but they seemed pretty damned set on seeing it done.

The tech had seemed to indicate that it was because she was gestating, but that was nearly as inconceivable as the fact that she was gestating at all. No one *bore* young anymore. It was too unpredictable and too inconvenient. If they happened to want one, they bought a permit and ordered one from the med lab. They hadn't practiced the 'natural' way of doing it in nearly a century. As far as she knew, though, there was no law against it, certainly not a death sentence, anyway.

She wouldn't have been surprised if they'd arrested her for breeding without a permit. She would've expected something like that, if she'd been engaging in sexual activity and stupid enough to do it without protection. But that would've been followed by a brief trial, maybe, and then release as soon as she coughed up the fine and bought a permit.

Maybe it was a law that was still on the books, but hadn't been used in so long that nobody, except the lawmakers and the law enforcers, even knew it was there anymore?

It seemed possible. The morons never got rid of laws. They just made more when the need arose. There were laws still on the books, she knew, from centuries before, laws that people didn't even understand anymore because nothing they pertained to even existed now.

Briefly, she wondered if there was any way to remove the parasite, but it occurred to her fairly quickly that that wasn't going to help. If there'd been a way, or if that would've made a difference, they would have done that instead of deciding to kill her. She hadn't come cheap. The company had spent a lot of money training her to be a rogue hunter, and even more bioengineering her for strength, stamina, high pain tolerance, computer assisted mental capabilities, and a broader hearing and sight range.

Anyway, she felt strangely possessive about it. She didn't know why, and she didn't really want to examine it at the moment. But she did know she didn't want to make any kind of decision about, possibly, removing it until she'd had time to think it through and consider every possibility.

Besides, the tech had been dying. How much faith could she place in anything he'd told her? The company's reasons for trying to terminate her could be something else entirely.

Unfortunately, no amount of carefully reconstructing her actions over the past month, or the month before that, produced any possibilities. She hadn't failed her last mission and, even if she had, punishment for failure was only a death sentence if the rogue dealt it out. The company was content to fine her all her pay and half her previous paycheck.

Shaking her head, Dalia finally decided she couldn't waste time trying to figure it out. It was enough to know she was dead if ... when they caught her. The only chance that she could see of turning the 'when' to 'if' was if she managed to get off world. Sooner or later, if she stayed, they were going to catch her, with or without the locator.

She could die a slow death here without food or water, or risk getting caught going for supplies. One retina scan and she was done for. Besides, she wouldn't be able to buy anything without having her barcode scanned, even in the black market, and once they had that, they'd have a bead on her location.

They would be expecting her to try to get off planet, though.

Her only chance, as far as she could see, was to locate a smuggler and either take the ship, or bargain a ride, and that meant she was going to have to figure out a way out of the dome.

Chapter Three

It took her almost a week to locate a man who claimed he not only knew a way out of the dome undetected, but also knew where the smugglers usually landed. It stood to reason that he would since there wouldn't be any other reason for leaving the protection of the dome.

The problem was, Dalia had nothing to bargain with. She finally convinced him to take her, however, by telling him if he did she wouldn't blow his head off. He wasn't terribly thrilled with the bargain, but he led her through the tunnels that eventually carried them beyond the city without detection.

By that time she had no problem blending with the natives. She'd had very little to eat, very little sleep, no access to bathing facilities and, since the clothes she was standing in were all she had, she looked as ragged and unkempt as everyone else. She didn't like it, but she was inclined to see it as an advantage.

The quality of the air inside the dome wasn't that great in the lower regions, but the air beyond the dome was the next thing to unbreathable. She still had her weapons, but the lack of a mask put her at a distinct disadvantage when the smugglers had more manpower and firepower at their disposal than she did.

The moment they reached the landing area, she saw immediately that simply blending wasn't going to be enough. There was no way she was going to get close enough to either overpower the smugglers and steal a ship, or slip on board. Releasing her 'guide', she watched until she was certain he was headed back the way they'd come and wouldn't alert the smugglers, and then settled down to study them and watch for an opportunity.

She'd been fully aware that smuggling was rife, but she hadn't realized that trafficking in stolen and/or illegal merchandise was done on quite as grand a scale as this. When she arrived, a large ship was already at the rendezvous point. More than a dozen smugglers had piled off of it. A third were busy unloading, a third loading new merchandise and the rest pacing restlessly about the activities with some fairly intimidating firepower.

Before they had even completed their business, a second craft nearly as large set down at a little distance and proceeded pretty much as the first had, off loading on one side and on loading on the other.

With decent air, or a mask, she might have been able to take four or five men. She wasn't stupid enough, or desperate enough to consider taking on crews as large as this, particularly when she was fairly certain that it would take no more than a hint of threat for them to combine forces.

She had very little food, however, and not a great deal of time. After a little while, she decided to change positions and see if another position would provide her with a better opportunity.

To her surprise, it did, but it had nothing to do with either of the two large ships she'd been watching. As she made her way around the perimeter, a relatively small, very sleek, racer settled into the rubble-strewn field at a little distance from the other two ships.

This might be doable.

The craft was designed for short, very fast hops, from planet to planet--and required no more than a pilot as crew or perhaps a pilot and copilot. There was no way it was being employed to haul cargo. It was too small to carry much and too short-range to go far--unless the pilot was insane enough to use the wormholes--which, upon reflection, she supposed he must.

If the pilot was smuggling anything, it was human cargo--escaped slaves or criminals fleeing justice--or possibly rogue cyborgs. He would want privacy to load his cargo. The fact that he'd landed so far from the other two ships seemed to bear up her theory.

She settled down to wait. It wasn't until the first of the two larger ships had lifted off that the gangplank was finally let down. Minutes passed. Finally, a man appeared at the top of the gangplank, stood looking out for several moments, and finally sauntered almost casually down the gangplank and stepped off of it.

The only weapons he had on him were strapped to his waist, a pistol holstered on one side and a three-foot blade on the other.

She stared at the blade. It indicated a strong familiarity with some primitive culture somewhere in the universe, but she couldn't see it well enough from this distance to place it. Not that it mattered. In the first place, she didn't particularly care where she went so long as she could elude the company for long enough to figure out what was going on and how it had come about that she'd suddenly become high on their list of public enemies. In the second, it supported the theory of rogues.

In general, cyborgs were at least half human, or half biological materials anyway, and all of that on the exterior, but anyone familiar with cyborgs could spot them within minutes. The were just ... not quite human, regardless of their appearance. It was often hard to put your finger on just what it was, but there was always something that gave them away, even to people not particularly looking or not particularly interested. The only way they could truly disappear was to find a culture too primitive to know what a cyborg was.

The question was, was he doing it for the money? For the adventure? Or because he was one of those fanatical assholes always trying to change the universe?

The latter made her want to puke. She despised fanatics, whatever their particular brand of insanity was, because they were not only incredibly boring and annoying, but they were also dangerous. They, almost inevitably, managed to convince huge numbers of 'followers' to believe them and usually managed to get them killed.

At this particular moment, however, it could prove useful.

Money was a problem. She had plenty of credits saved up, but she wasn't certain it was enough to tempt a smuggler of this caliber. If it wasn't, and he scanned her barcode for the money, she would be located in short order.

Finally, she decided to move a little closer and get a better look at him.

She managed to get several yards closer before she ran out of cover. She discovered it didn't particularly help her, however. Naturally enough, it was dark. Smugglers didn't land in the daylight, and it was smoggy as bedamned, as well. The poor visibility wasn't as much a problem, however, as the fact that her feminine side took that inopportune moment to kick in and completely distracted her.

He was, quite possibly, the finest specimen of a male she'd ever set eyes on. Even her male counterparts weren't generally so beautifully enhanced. Her first good look at him impacted on her as physically as if she'd been hit by a grenade concussion. She felt as if she'd been body slammed, too stunned to think for several moments. Finally, her training kicked in and she settled behind the pile of rubble and frowned, wondering what had just happened.

Not only was she certain she'd never had a reaction like that to a male before, she couldn't even remember experiencing anything even close. Her training had been thorough and nothing had been left to chance, certainly not something as predictable and inevitable as sexual attraction. Very little ever managed to break through her conditioning as a soldier and throw her off kilter. Some sort of chemical imbalance related to the gestation, she wondered?

The sounds of the second craft lifting off jogged her from her abstraction and into action.

She peered at the pilot, saw that he'd been distracted, as well, and began to move quickly around the ship while he stood watching the ship's ascent. Coming upon him from behind, she placed the barrel of her weapon against the center of his back, directly over his heart. "I need passage off of this rock, and I don't particularly care who I have to kill to get it. Take me, and I'll pay you for your trouble and you can get on with your life. Give me any trouble and I'll kill you."

The moment the barrel of her weapon dug into his back, he went perfectly still. As she finished her little speech, however, he moved, so fast her jaw didn't have time to drop in surprise, snatching her weapon from her hands so hard and fast she was surprised he didn't take her fingers with it.

"I only take rogues," he said coolly, taking the weapon in both hands and bending it into a bow, as if it had been made of putty instead of titanium alloy.

Dalia glanced from the bent weapon into the face that had launched a million flyers. It was Reuel CO469, the first of his kind, the first cyborg rogue, the leader of all who'd come after him, and the only rogue nobody had even come close to catching in all the time she'd worked for the company.

"Oh fuck!"

A smile curled that devastating mouth. Stepping toward her, he grasped her arms, thrusting them behind her back and bringing her up hard against his massive chest. "We could. On the other hand I'm waiting for someone and I really don't like being interrupted when I'm pleasuring a beautiful woman."

"That wasn't an invitation," Dalia snapped.

His dark brows rose. "No?" He shook his head and finally shrugged. "Machines! They can never quite grasp the subtleties of human interaction, can they? That's what always gives us away."

She didn't believe for one moment that he'd interpreted her comment literally. He was, she realized with a touch of stunned amazement, amusing himself. "Let go of me," she said through gritted teeth.

His smile vanished. "I'm not even slightly tempted ... rogue hunter."

For the first time in her memory, Dalia felt real, unmitigated fear. "I wouldn't be fleeing the city if I were."

"The question is, *are* you fleeing the city? Or was this merely a clever ruse?"

She gave him a look. "I had my weapon on your back. I could've killed you then and there would've been no point in subterfuge."

"Except that that wouldn't have gotten you into the rebel camp, would it, Dalia?"

Dalia stared at him in dismay. She licked suddenly dry lips. "My name's Kaya."

"Your name is Dalia VH570 ... and you are a rogue hunter ... gone rogue."

Of all the things he might have said, nothing could have stunned her more, or more surely inspired her to throw caution to the wind. "I'm no rogue," she spat in disgust before she thought better of it. "I'm human."

His mouth tightened until his lips were no more than a thin line. His nostrils flared as he dragged in a deep breath to calm his temper. "You have enough contempt to be a rogue hunter, whatever you want to call yourself."

Dalia twisted, testing his hold of her, but she was not the least surprised when he held her without any sign of difficulty. She supposed she should have simply accepted the fact that she was dead except for the dying part. He knew she was a rogue hunter. He wasn't going to simply let her go, and he wasn't going to take her with him.

Somehow, though, she found she simply could not give up or accept that she wasn't going to be able to find a way out of this. "If you know about me, then you know I'm on the run. I'm no threat to you."

"Not presently. But, then, you're assuming I believe any propaganda the company chooses to put out. I don't." He leaned close, placing his mouth near her ear. "They lie," he whispered.

Her body obviously didn't know or care that he was a cyborg. The heat of his breath on her ear and his scent in her nostrils combined, sending a rush of heat and weakness through her that couldn't be interpreted as anything but desire.

An unaccustomed spurt of panic followed that confusing reaction. Dalia struggled to free her hands again. She was too much shorter than him, and too close, for a head butt to have any effect on him. More likely, she'd end up knocking herself out. Finding after only a few moments that she was having no appreciable effect, she desisted again, panting with effort. "What are you going to do with me?"

His arms tightened. Slowly, he lowered his head until his mouth was near her ear again. "Don't allow your prejudice to mislead you, little flower. I am not a machine. This flesh feels. This body desires. This mind wants. So, unless you want to discover what its like to spread your legs for a cyborg, I'd advise you to stop rubbing your very tantalizing little body against mine. I might decide to fuck you until no human *man* will ever do for you again."

Two completely polar sensations went through Dalia at once; outrage that he would even consider treating her--a trained warrior and rogue hunter--as if she was nothing more than a pleasure slave, and pretty much the same jolt of stunned attraction that had hit her the moment she saw him--except that this time it was accompanied by a rush of heat and a deluge of adrenaline.

She went perfectly still, more from shocked surprise than because he had commanded it, or because she feared he might keep his word, hardly daring even to breathe. As she stared up at him, however, it occurred to her that he had offered her a bargaining chip she hadn't even realized she possessed. "I would...." She licked her dried lips and tried again. "I will barter the use of my body for transport."

He frowned. "I would sooner leave you here. I'm sure it will surprise you, but I've no taste for killing ... and not much for humans, even to slake my needs."

Dalia felt blood flood her cheeks, only to wash away so rapidly she felt slightly dizzy. "But ... you said...."

"I lied."

She blinked at him, stunned once more, not because he admitted it, or even because he had the ability, but because he'd done it so convincingly that she'd believed him. It was no wonder the company had ceased production of this particular cyborg. It was no wonder he had never been caught. He was as human as any human spawned, but capable of far more than any human being, whether enhanced or not, and therefore far more dangerous.

"If you leave me here, you leave me to die," she said finally, trying to keep the desperation from her voice.

"Why?"

"Why what?"

"Assuming you're not lying and the company is hunting you, but not because you've gone rogue, then why?"

"I don't know."

He eyed her skeptically.

"I don't! I went in for my physical examination. When I woke, the tech was stabbing me with a needle."

He studied her for several moments and finally, slowly, released her. "You didn't question him?"

Dalia shrugged. "I snatched the needle out of my arm and drove it into his throat. It wasn't pretty, but it was fast. I didn't manage to get much out of him ... except...."

"Except?"

She shook her head. "Nothing that made any sense." She studied him for several moments and finally tried again. "Look, I know you've no reason to trust me, but it's only a matter of time before they catch up to me. I got rid of the locator--that's the only thing that's given me any time, but it won't last. Take me anywhere. As long as there's breathable air and half a chance for survival, I don't care. I'll give you everything I've got," she said, shoving the sleeve of her tunic up and extending her arm to show him her barcode.

He studied it, surprise flickering briefly across his features. He was frowning thoughtfully as he looked at her again. "You're coded."

"Everybody is coded at birth."

"Except cyborgs."

She studied him. "Cyborgs aren't born. They're created ... in a lab."

"Humans are created in labs," he countered, his lips tightening.

She thought about what the tech had told her and what she'd learned from the computer. "But not necessarily, and there's the difference. They have the ability to create life inside their own bodies. The tech ... before he died, he said that I was gestating. I have ... life, here," she finished, laying a hand over her lower belly.

He stared down at her hand for many moments before he looked up at her again. She had the sense that it was because he was so jolted by the admission that it took him far longer to assimilate the information than one would have expected. Shock was the human inability to accept what they had seen or heard, not something that should ever trouble a cyborg, a creation more machine than biological entity, regardless of their appearance or their artificial intelligence.

And still she had the feeling that he'd been as shocked as she had been at the news. He glanced away from her, turning his head to study something outside her range of vision. "They're coming."

Catching her arm just above the elbow, he led her up the gangplank and into the ship. They traversed a narrow corridor and finally arrived at the captain's cabin, which lay at the prow and encompassed the entire width of the ship. Pushing her inside, he studied her for several moments in silence. "You will stay here."

10438209R0

Made in the USA
Lexington, KY
24 July 2011